WARRIORS

THE RISE OF
SCOURGE

WARRIORS
THE RISE OF SCOURGE

CREATED BY
ERIN HUNTER

WRITTEN BY
DAN JOLLEY

ART BY
BETTINA M. KURKOSKI

HAMBURG // LONDON // LOS ANGELES // TOKYO

HarperCollins*Publishers*

Warriors: The Rise of Scourge

Created by Erin Hunter

Written by Dan Jolley

Art by Bettina M. Kurkoski

Lettering - Lucas Rivera
Cover Design - Anne Marie Horne

Editor - Lillian Diaz-Przybyl
Digital Imaging Manager - Chris Buford
Pre-Production Supervisor - Erika Terriquez
Production Manager - Elisabeth Brizzi
Managing Editor - Vy Nguyen
Creative Director - Anne Marie Horne
Editor-in-Chief - Rob Tokar
Publisher - Mike Kiley
President and C.O.O. - John Parker
C.E.O. and Chief Creative Officer - Stu Levy

A TOKYOPOP Manga

TOKYOPOP and are trademarks or registered trademarks of TOKYOPOP Inc.

TOKYOPOP Inc.
5900 Wilshire Blvd. Suite 2000
Los Angeles, CA 90036

E-mail: info@TOKYOPOP.com
Come visit us online at www.TOKYOPOP.com

Text copyright © 2008 by Working Partners Limited
Art copyright © 2008 by TOKYOPOP Inc. and HarperCollins Publishers
All rights reserved. Printed in the United States of America. No part of this book may be used or reproduced in any mar
whatsoever without written permission except in the case of brief quotations embodied in critical articles and reviews.
manga is a work of fiction. Any resemblance to actual events or locales or persons, living or dead, is entirely coincider
For information address HarperCollins Children's Books, a division of HarperCollins Publishers, 195 Broadway,
New York, NY 10007.
www.harpercollinschildrens.com

ISBN 978-0-06-147867-3
Library of Congress catalog card number: 2007935239

18 19 20 PC/BVG 20 19 18

❖

First Edition

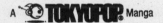

Dear readers,

Scourge, leader of BloodClan, is the closest thing to evil we will ever encounter in the forest.

When I first created him, I must confess I didn't think about his past. I just needed a truly terrifying cat—one who didn't seem physically threatening at first, but who had a hunger for violence and bloodshed that far exceeded anything the Clan cats had seen before. If ever a character were purely bad, Scourge is it. He certainly made a powerful enemy for Firestar, leader of ThunderClan, when Scourge challenged all four Clans to fight for control of the forest.

But when I stopped to consider what might have shaped his character, I realized that this was a story that could be very interesting to explore. A manga novel seemed like the perfect opportunity to go back to Scourge's origins and track his path from cute fluffy kit (because ALL kits are cute and fluffy, right?) to evil tyrant. I didn't want to make excuses for his behavior because no amount of misfortune or bullying could justify that sort of savagery; instead, I was curious to see how another smart, ambitious, and courageous young cat (is anyone else thinking FIRESTAR?) could end up following a much darker, blood-soaked path.

So walk in Scourge's pawsteps—if you dare—and see if you still judge him as harshly by the end. Every cat deserves to have his story told, and this is Scourge's hour.

Best wishes always,
Erin Hunter

WARRIORS

THE RISE OF SCOURGE

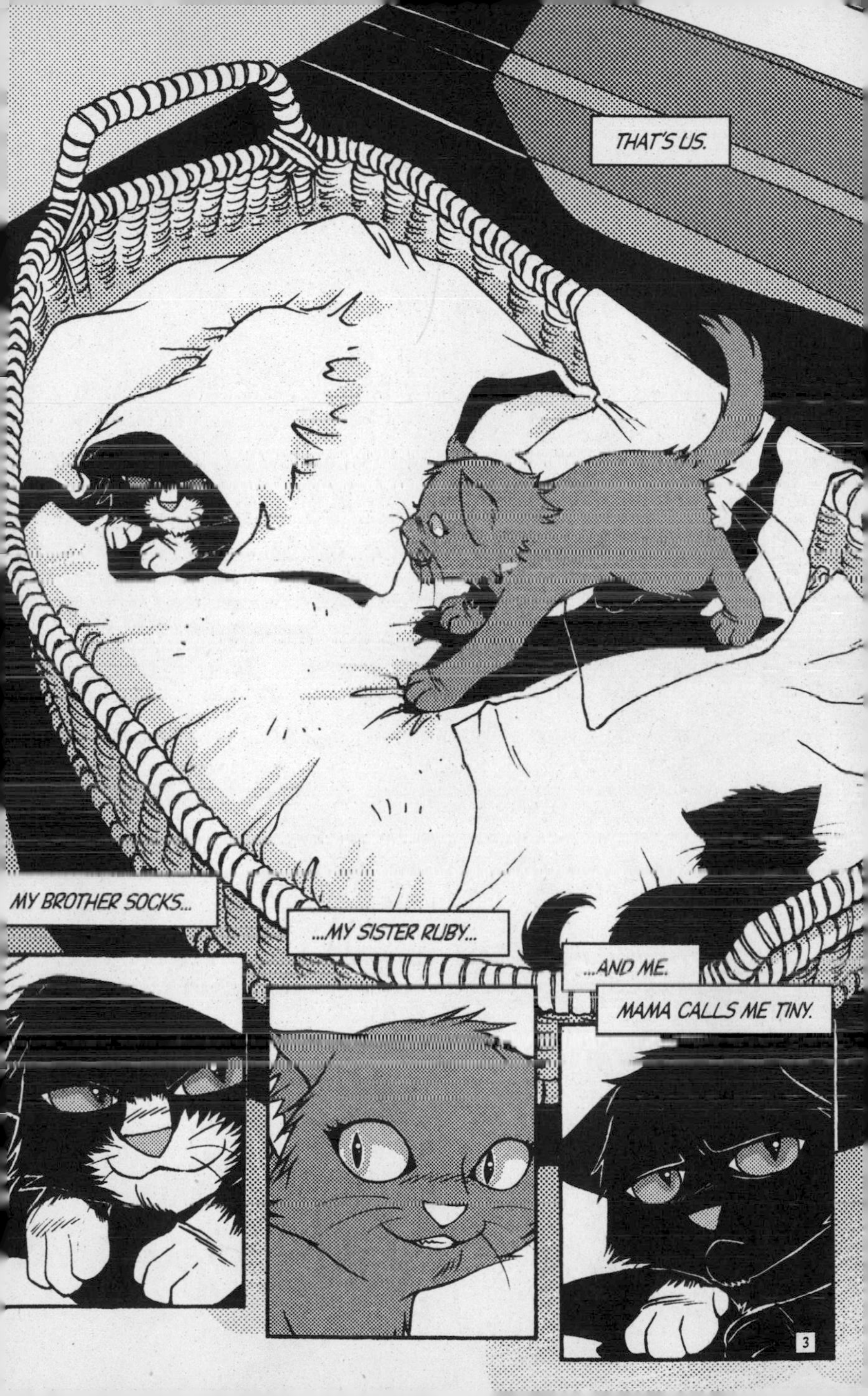
THAT'S US.
MY BROTHER SOCKS...
...MY SISTER RUBY...
...AND ME.
MAMA CALLS ME TINY.

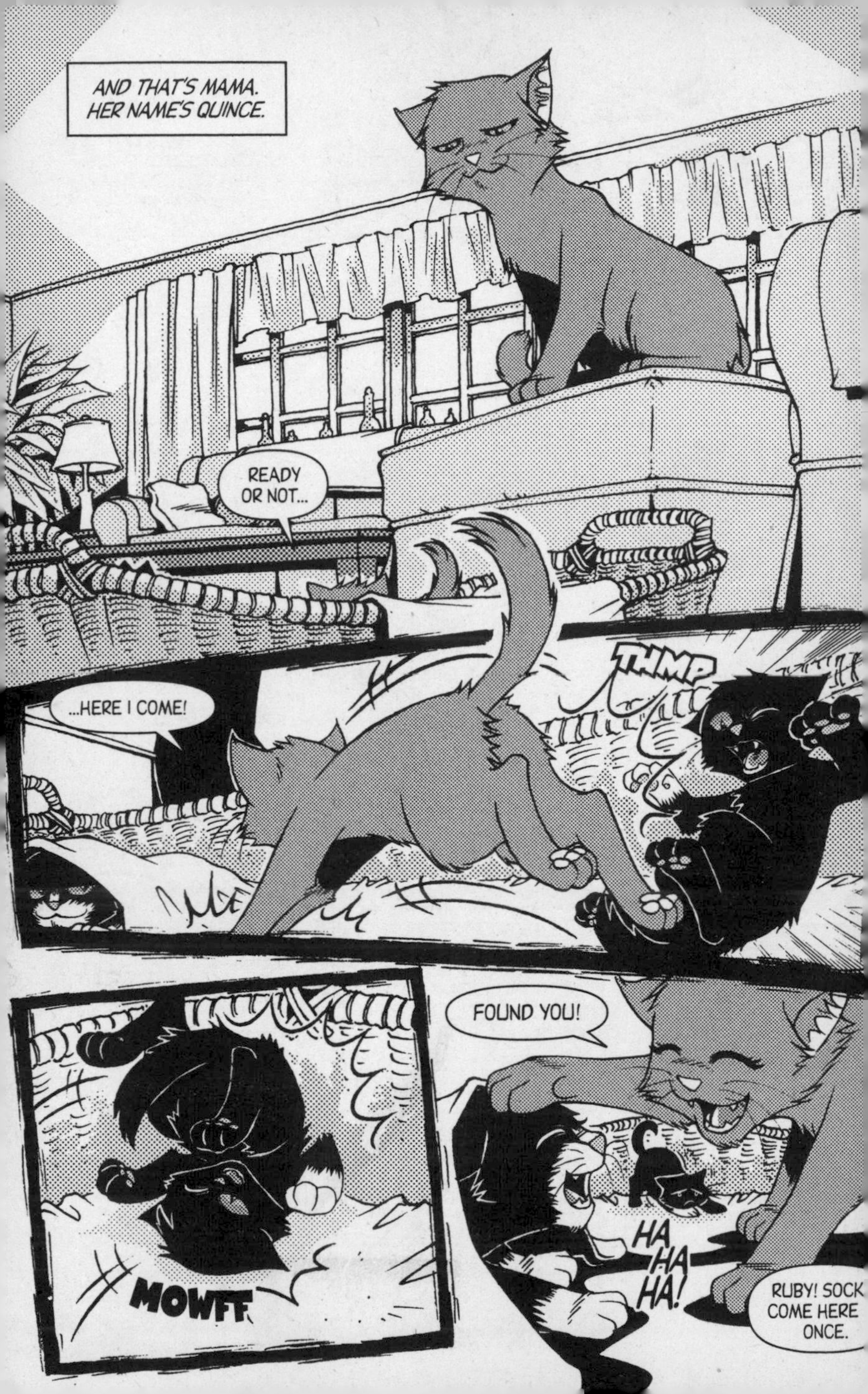
AND THAT'S MAMA. HER NAME'S QUINCE.
READY OR NOT...
...HERE I COME!
THMP
MOWFF
FOUND YOU!
HA HA HA!
RUBY! SOCK COME HERE ONCE.

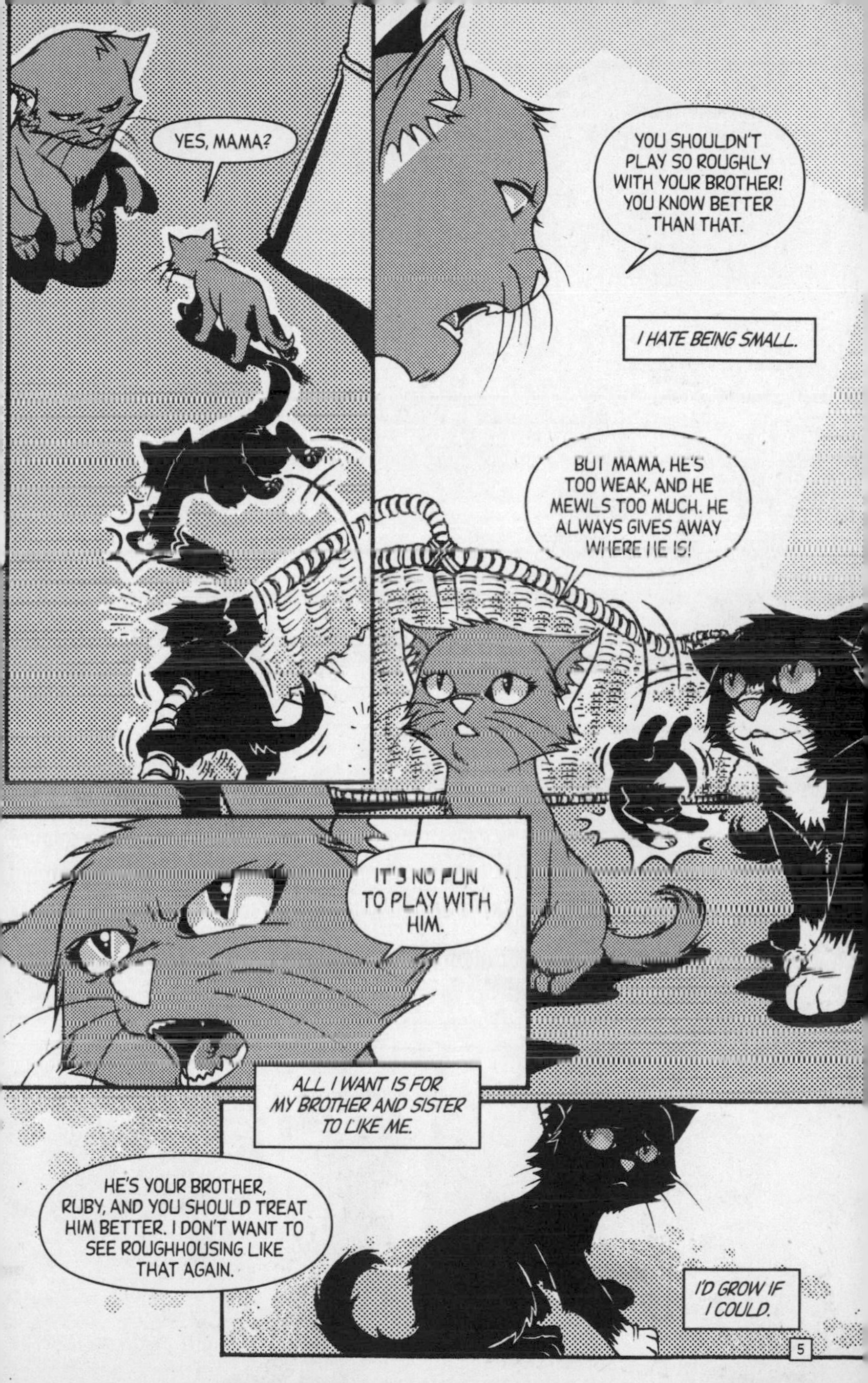
YES, MAMA?
YOU SHOULDN'T PLAY SO ROUGHLY WITH YOUR BROTHER! YOU KNOW BETTER THAN THAT.
I HATE BEING SMALL.
BUT MAMA, HE'S TOO WEAK, AND HE MEWLS TOO MUCH. HE ALWAYS GIVES AWAY WHERE HE IS!
IT'S NO FUN TO PLAY WITH HIM.
ALL I WANT IS FOR MY BROTHER AND SISTER TO LIKE ME.
HE'S YOUR BROTHER, RUBY, AND YOU SHOULD TREAT HIM BETTER. I DON'T WANT TO SEE ROUGHHOUSING LIKE THAT AGAIN.
I'D GROW IF I COULD.

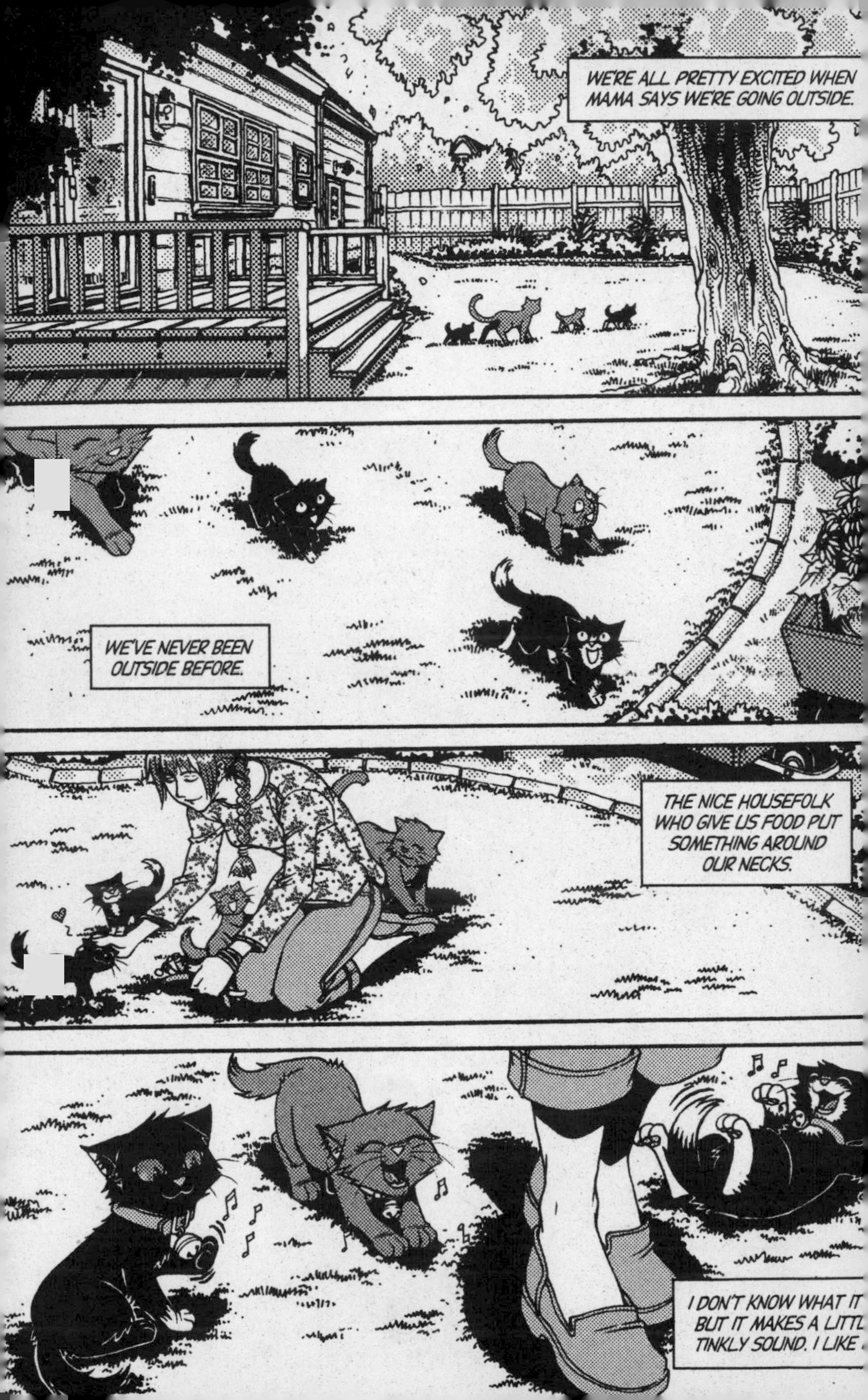
WE'RE ALL PRETTY EXCITED WHEN MAMA SAYS WE'RE GOING OUTSIDE.
WE'VE NEVER BEEN OUTSIDE BEFORE.
THE NICE HOUSEFOLK WHO GIVE US FOOD PUT SOMETHING AROUND OUR NECKS.
I DON'T KNOW WHAT IT
BUT IT MAKES A LITTL
TINKLY SOUND. I LIKE

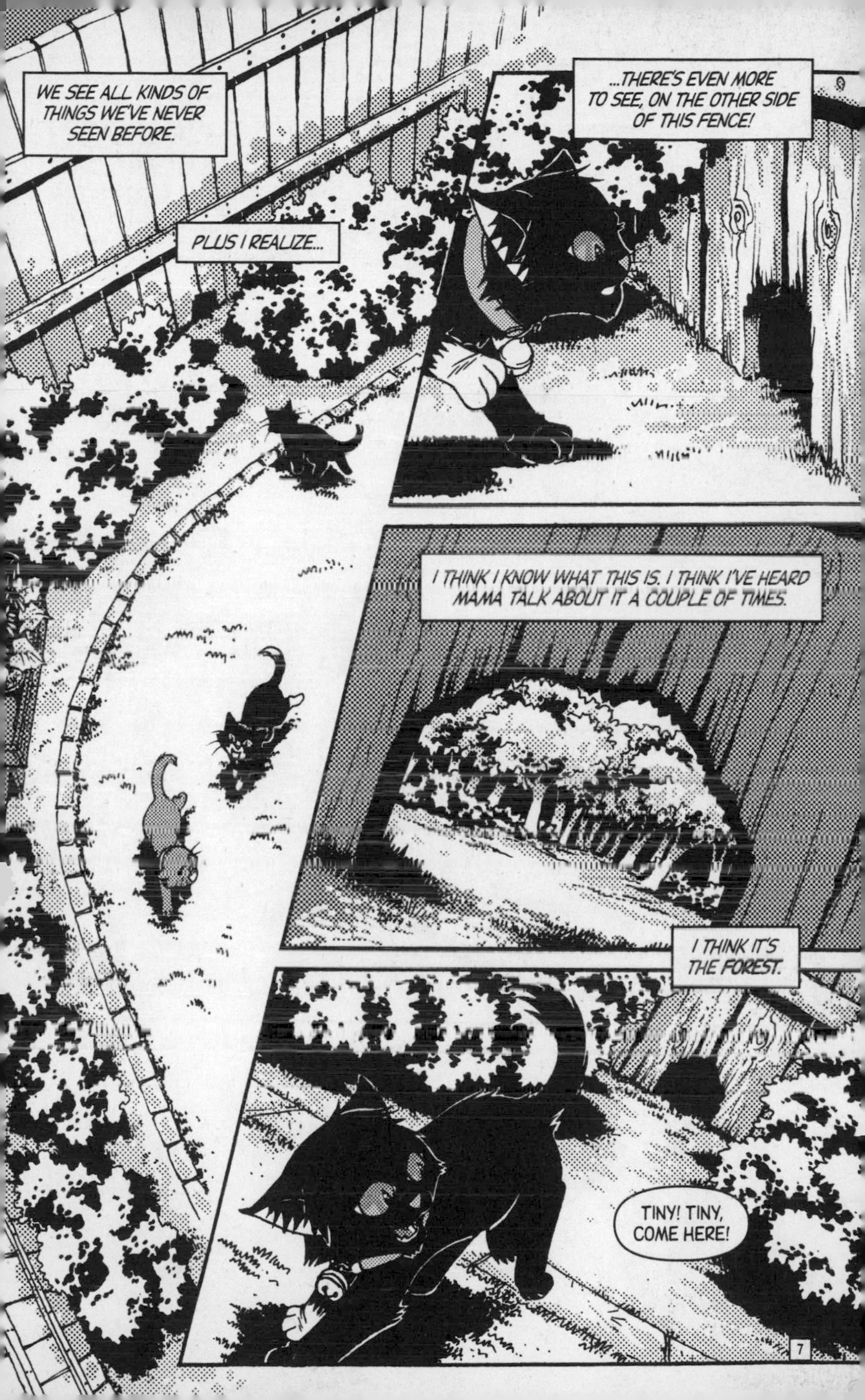
WE SEE ALL KINDS OF THINGS WE'VE NEVER SEEN BEFORE.
PLUS I REALIZE...
...THERE'S EVEN MORE TO SEE, ON THE OTHER SIDE OF THIS FENCE!
I THINK I KNOW WHAT THIS IS. I THINK I'VE HEARD MAMA TALK ABOUT IT A COUPLE OF TIMES.
I THINK IT'S THE FOREST.
TINY! TINY, COME HERE!

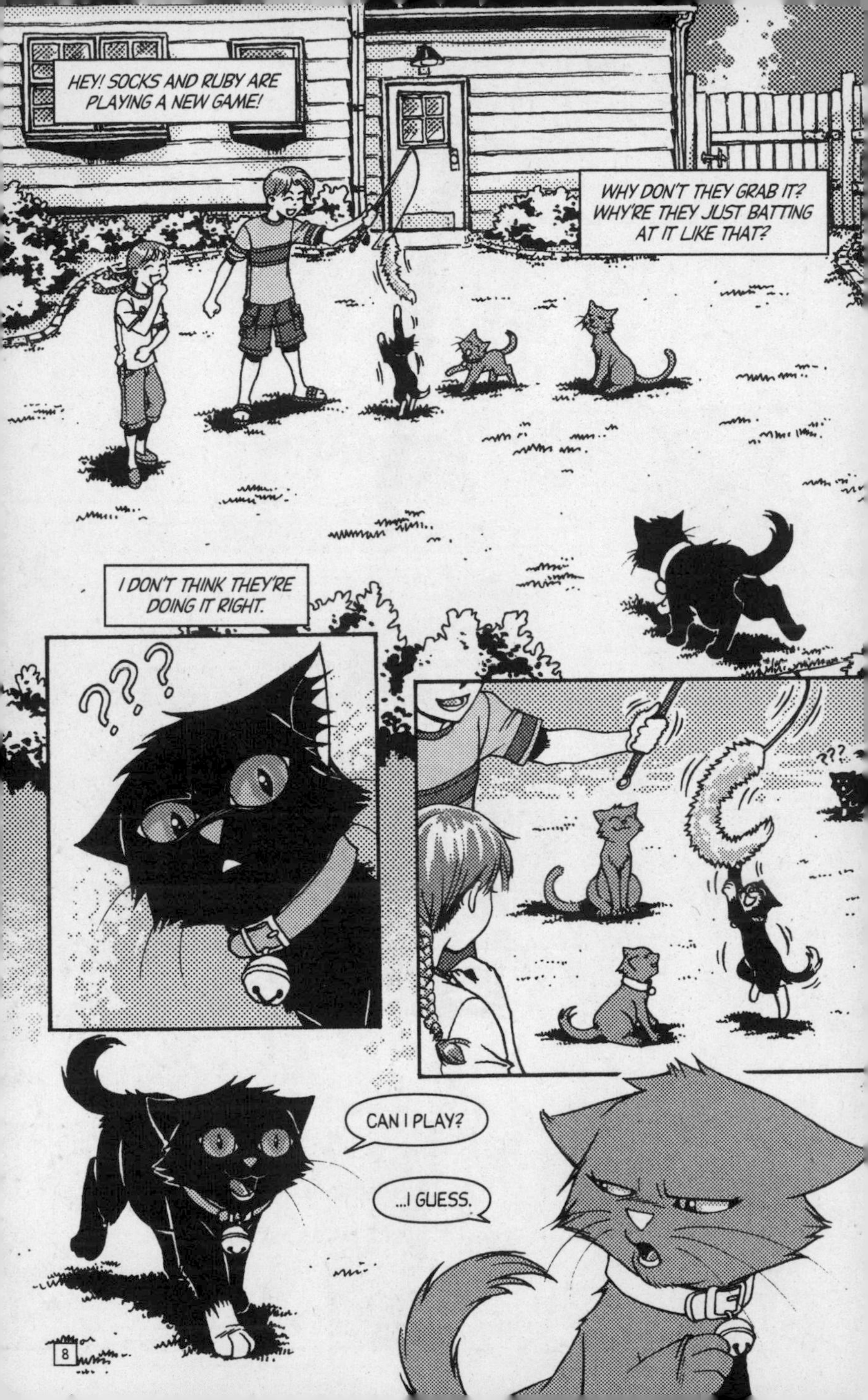
HEY! SOCKS AND RUBY ARE PLAYING A NEW GAME!
WHY DON'T THEY GRAB IT? WHY'RE THEY JUST BATTING AT IT LIKE THAT?
I DON'T THINK THEY'RE DOING IT RIGHT.
???
???
CAN I PLAY?
...I GUESS.

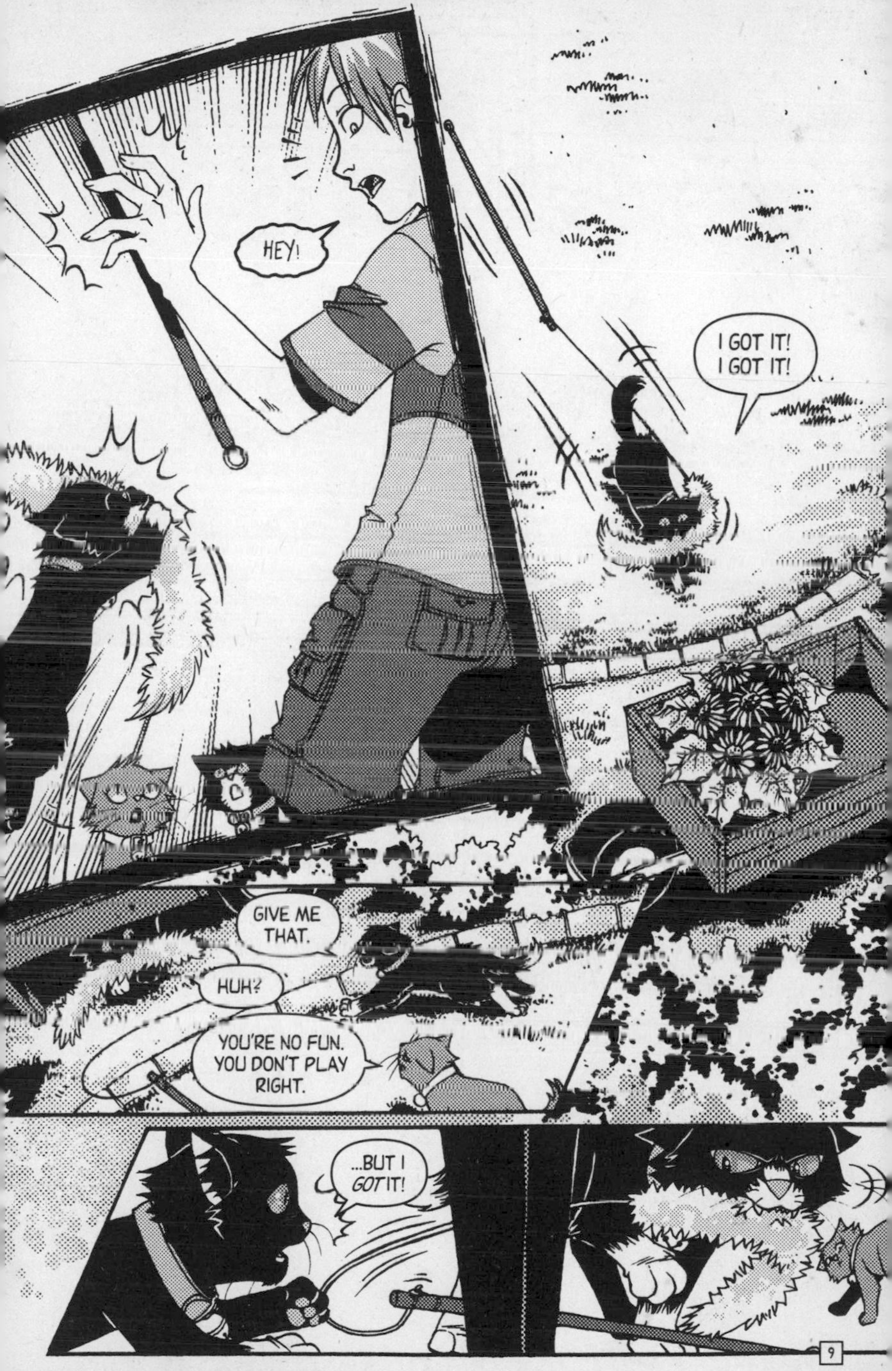
HEY!
I GOT IT! I GOT IT!
GIVE ME THAT.
HUH?
YOU'RE NO FUN. YOU DON'T PLAY RIGHT.
...BUT I *GOT* IT!

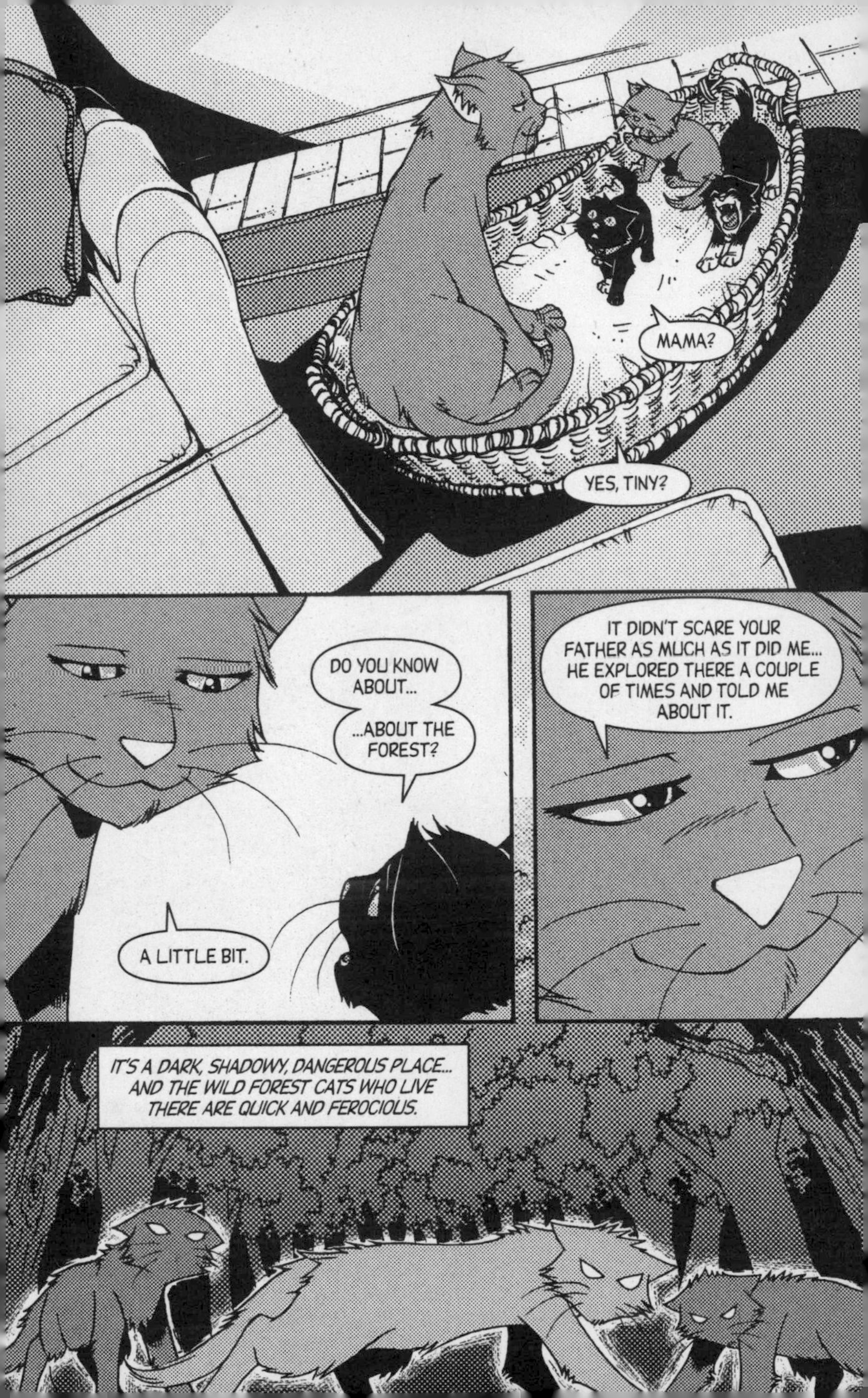
MAMA?
YES, TINY?
DO YOU KNOW ABOUT...
...ABOUT THE FOREST?
A LITTLE BIT.
IT DIDN'T SCARE YOUR FATHER AS MUCH AS IT DID ME... HE EXPLORED THERE A COUPLE OF TIMES AND TOLD ME ABOUT IT.
IT'S A DARK, SHADOWY, DANGEROUS PLACE... AND THE WILD FOREST CATS WHO LIVE THERE ARE QUICK AND FEROCIOUS.

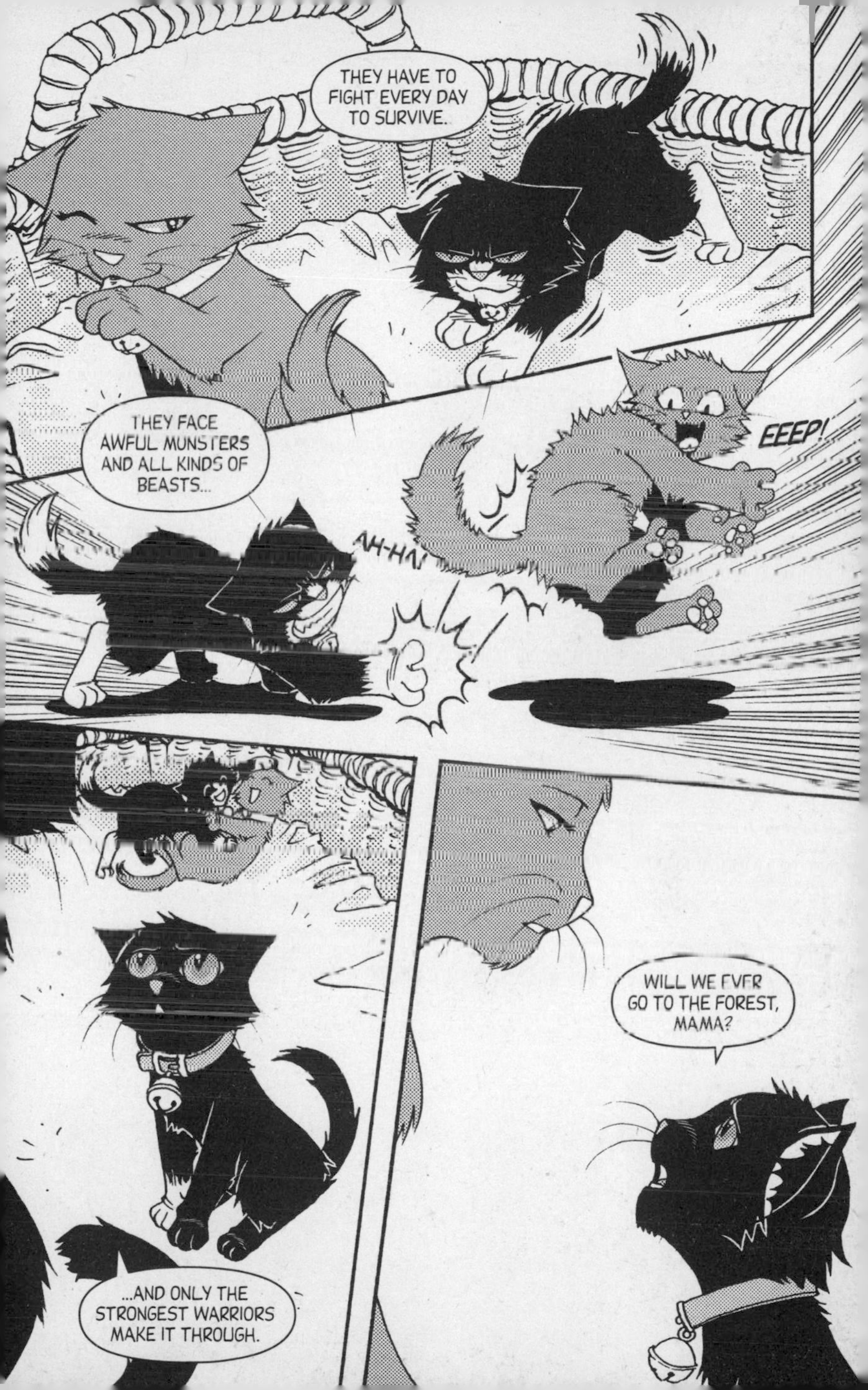
THEY HAVE TO FIGHT EVERY DAY TO SURVIVE.
THEY FACE AWFUL MONSTERS AND ALL KINDS OF BEASTS...
EEEP!
AH-HA!
...AND ONLY THE STRONGEST WARRIORS MAKE IT THROUGH.
WILL WE EVER GO TO THE FOREST, MAMA?

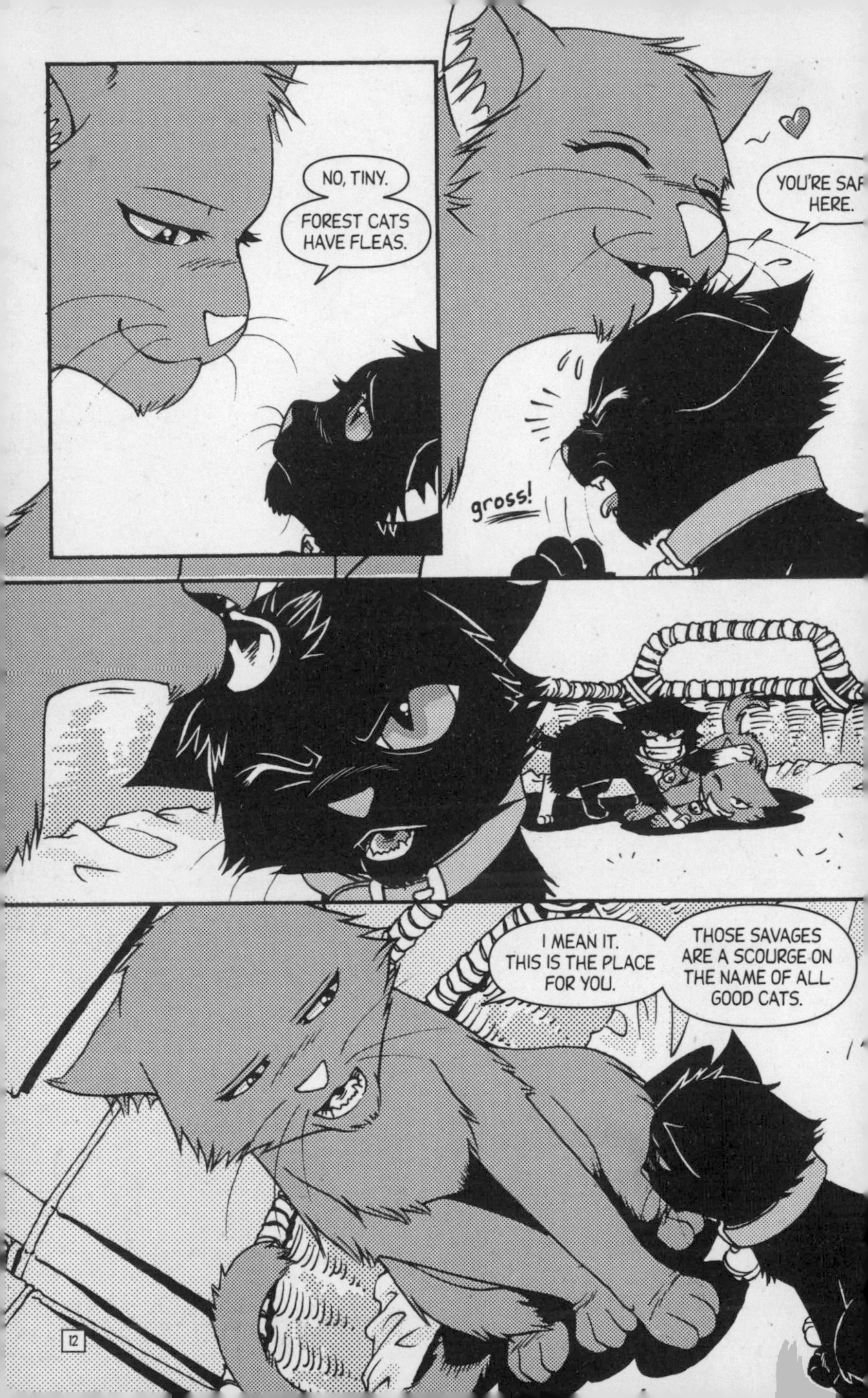
NO, TINY.
FOREST CATS HAVE FLEAS.
YOU'RE SAF HERE.
gross!
I MEAN IT. THIS IS THE PLACE FOR YOU.
THOSE SAVAGES ARE A SCOURGE ON THE NAME OF ALL GOOD CATS.

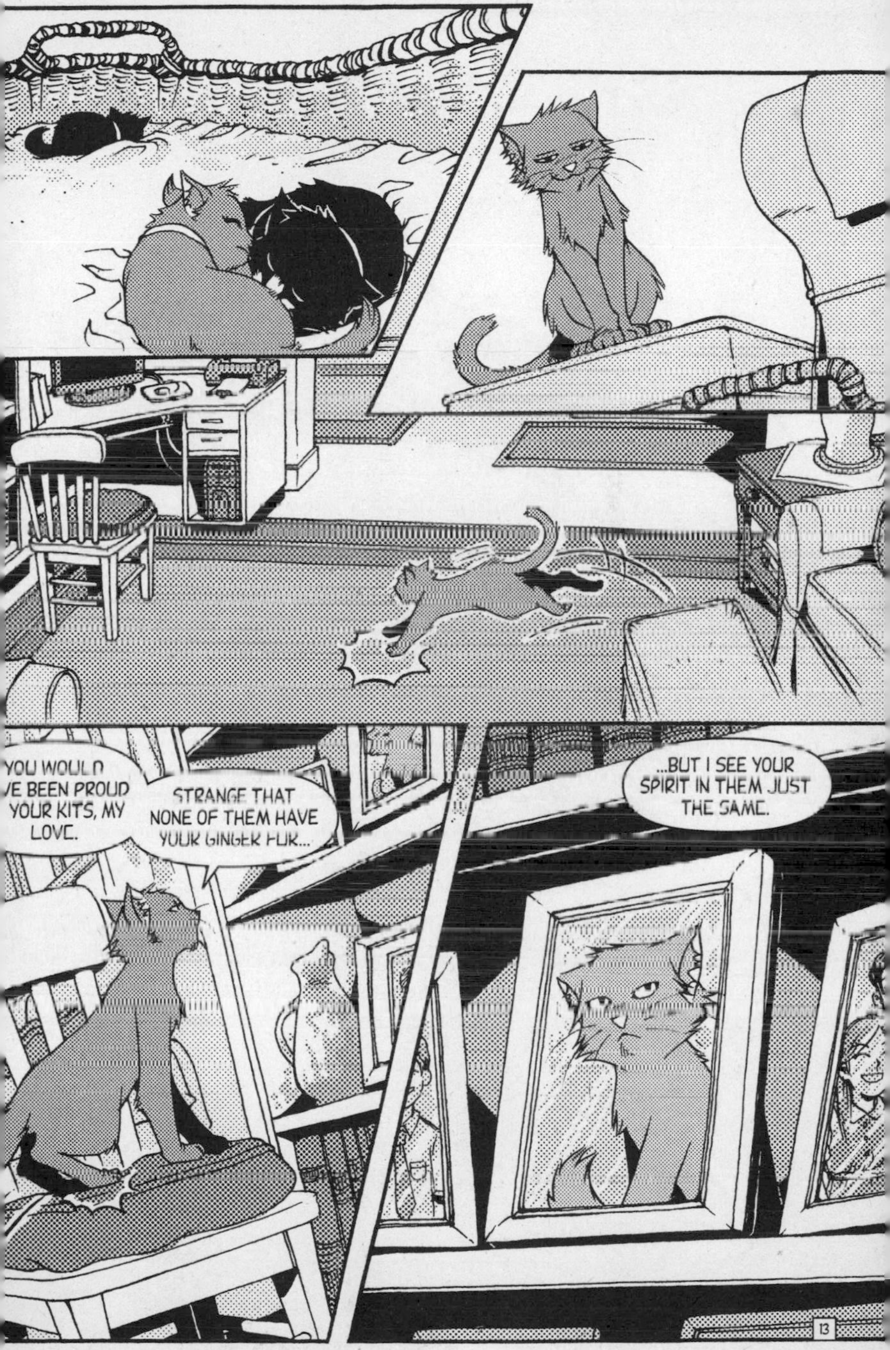
YOU WOULD VE BEEN PROUD YOUR KITS, MY LOVE.
STRANGE THAT NONE OF THEM HAVE YOUR GINGER FUR...
...BUT I SEE YOUR SPIRIT IN THEM JUST THE SAME.

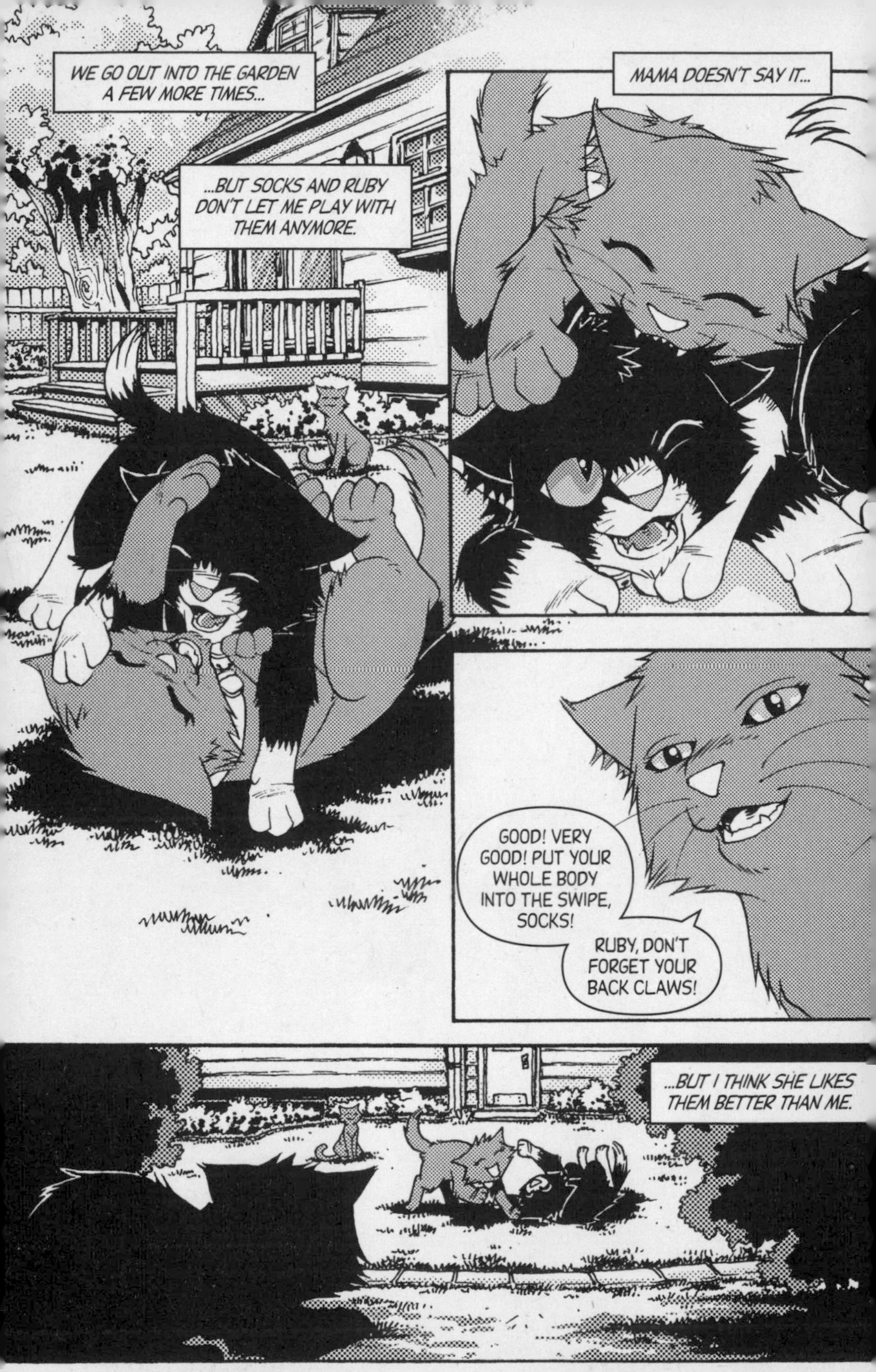
WE GO OUT INTO THE GARDEN A FEW MORE TIMES...
...BUT SOCKS AND RUBY DON'T LET ME PLAY WITH THEM ANYMORE.
MAMA DOESN'T SAY IT...
GOOD! VERY GOOD! PUT YOUR WHOLE BODY INTO THE SWIPE, SOCKS!
RUBY, DON'T FORGET YOUR BACK CLAWS!
...BUT I THINK SHE LIKES THEM BETTER THAN ME.

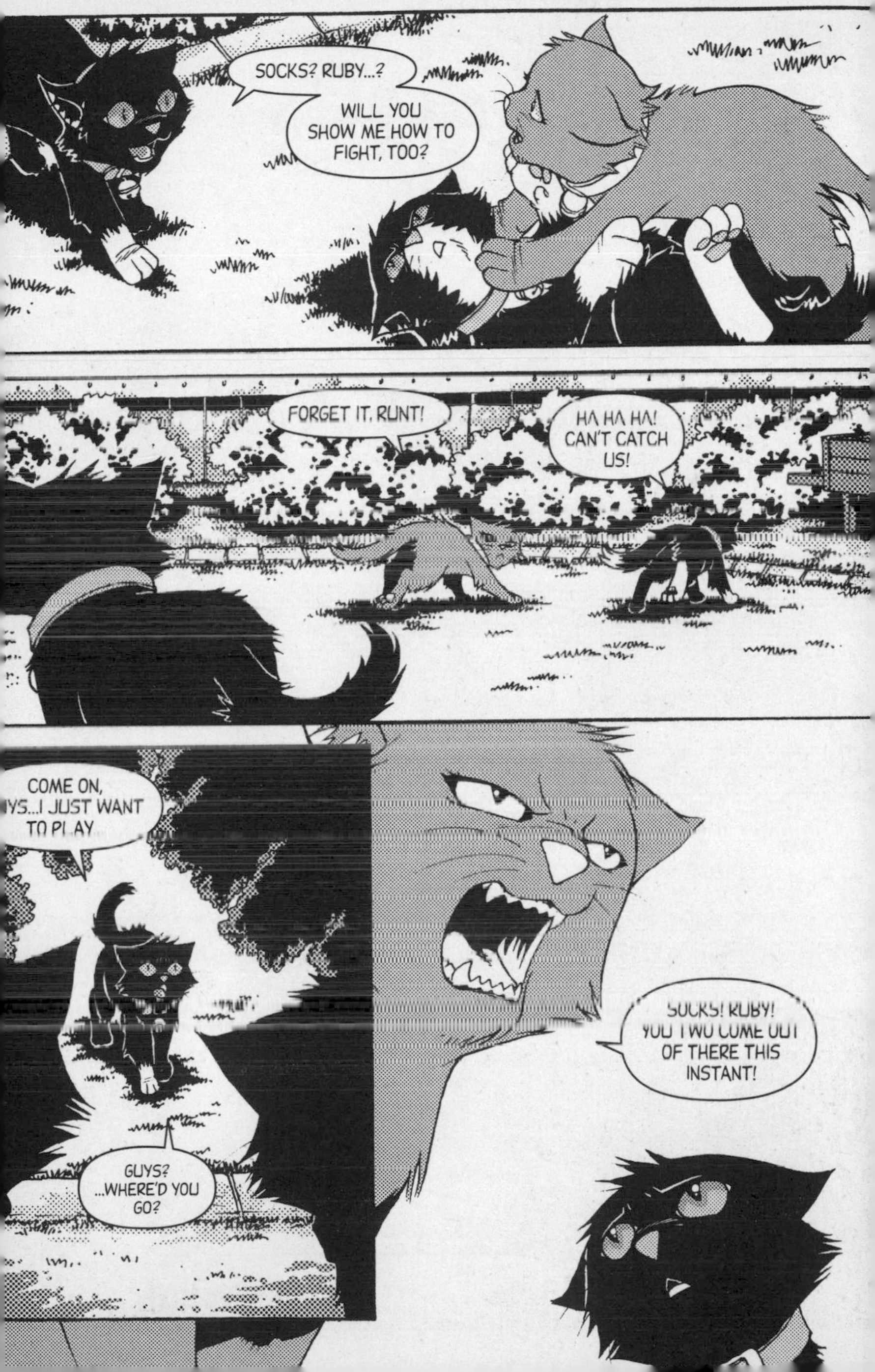
SOCKS? RUBY...?
WILL YOU SHOW ME HOW TO FIGHT, TOO?
FORGET IT, RUNT!
HA HA HA! CAN'T CATCH US!
COME ON, YS...I JUST WANT TO PLAY.
GUYS? ...WHERE'D YOU GO?
SOCKS! RUBY! YOU TWO COME OUT OF THERE THIS INSTANT!

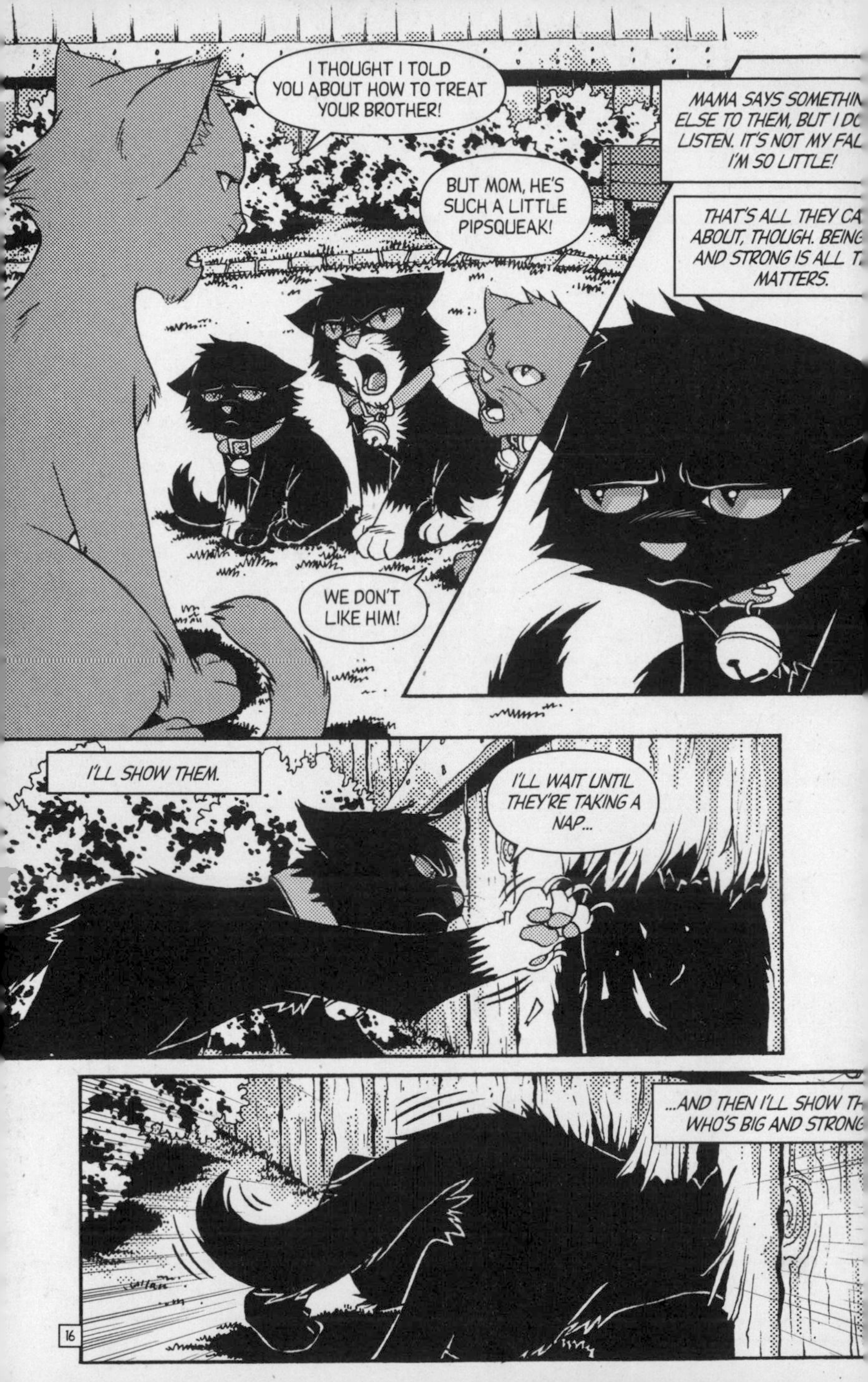
I THOUGHT I TOLD YOU ABOUT HOW TO TREAT YOUR BROTHER!
BUT MOM, HE'S SUCH A LITTLE PIPSQUEAK!
WE DON'T LIKE HIM!
MAMA SAYS SOMETHIN ELSE TO THEM, BUT I DO LISTEN. IT'S NOT MY FAL I'M SO LITTLE!
THAT'S ALL THEY CA ABOUT, THOUGH. BEING AND STRONG IS ALL T MATTERS.
I'LL SHOW THEM.
I'LL WAIT UNTIL THEY'RE TAKING A NAP...
...AND THEN I'LL SHOW TH WHO'S BIG AND STRONG

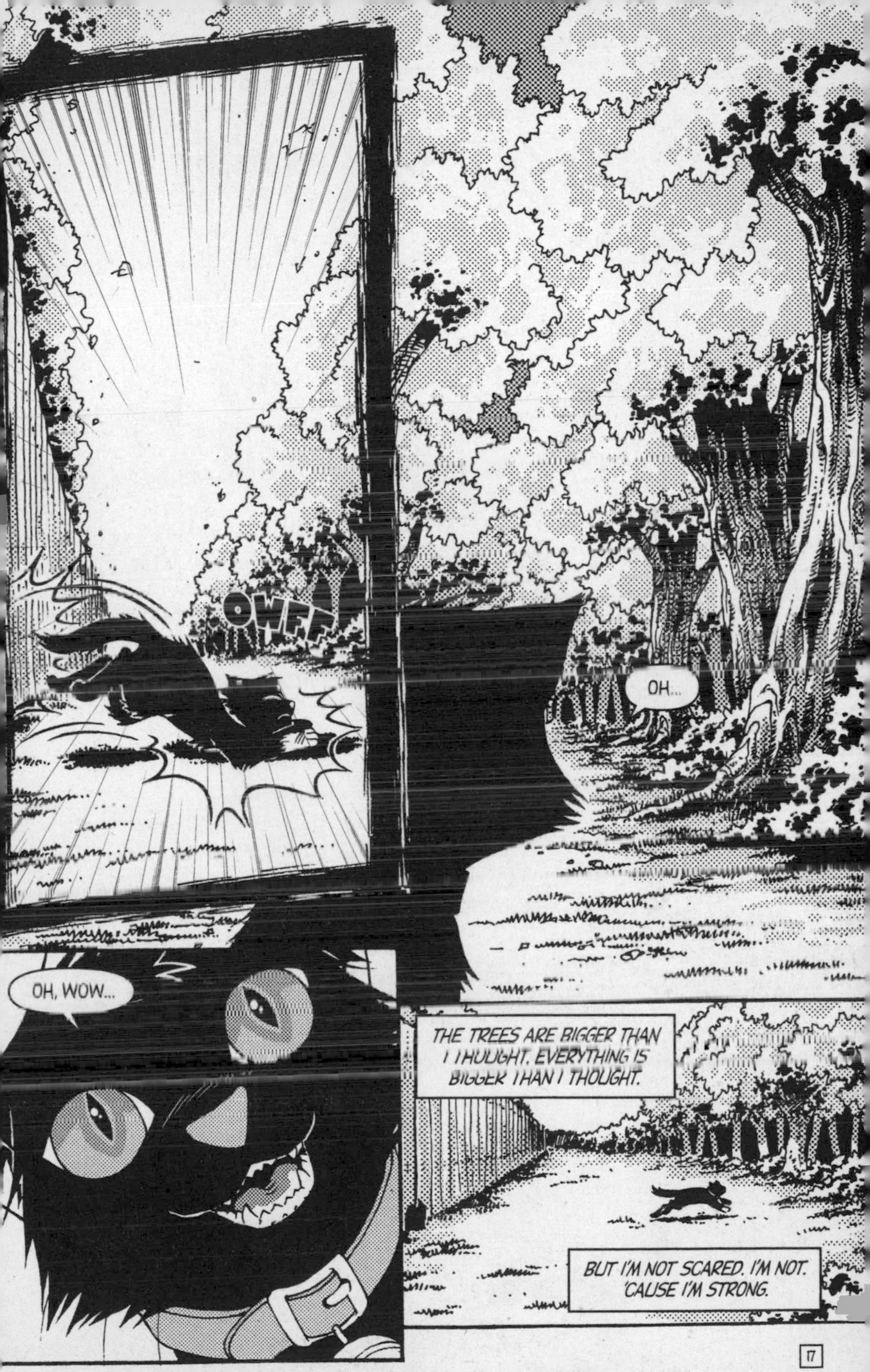
OWFF
OH...
OH, WOW...
THE TREES ARE BIGGER THAN I THOUGHT. EVERYTHING IS BIGGER THAN I THOUGHT.
BUT I'M NOT SCARED. I'M NOT. 'CAUSE I'M STRONG.

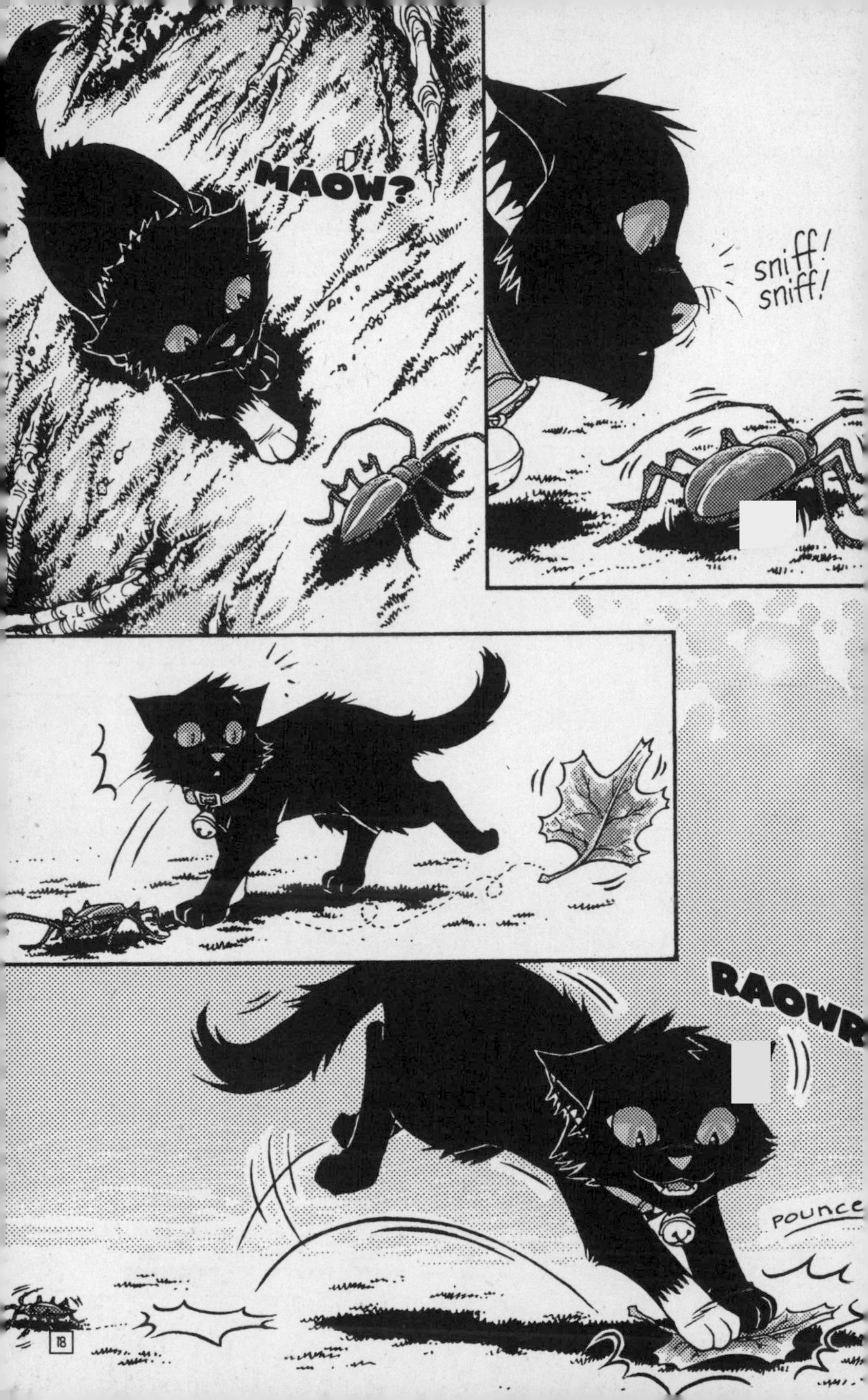
MAOW?
sniff!
sniff!
RAOWR
pounce

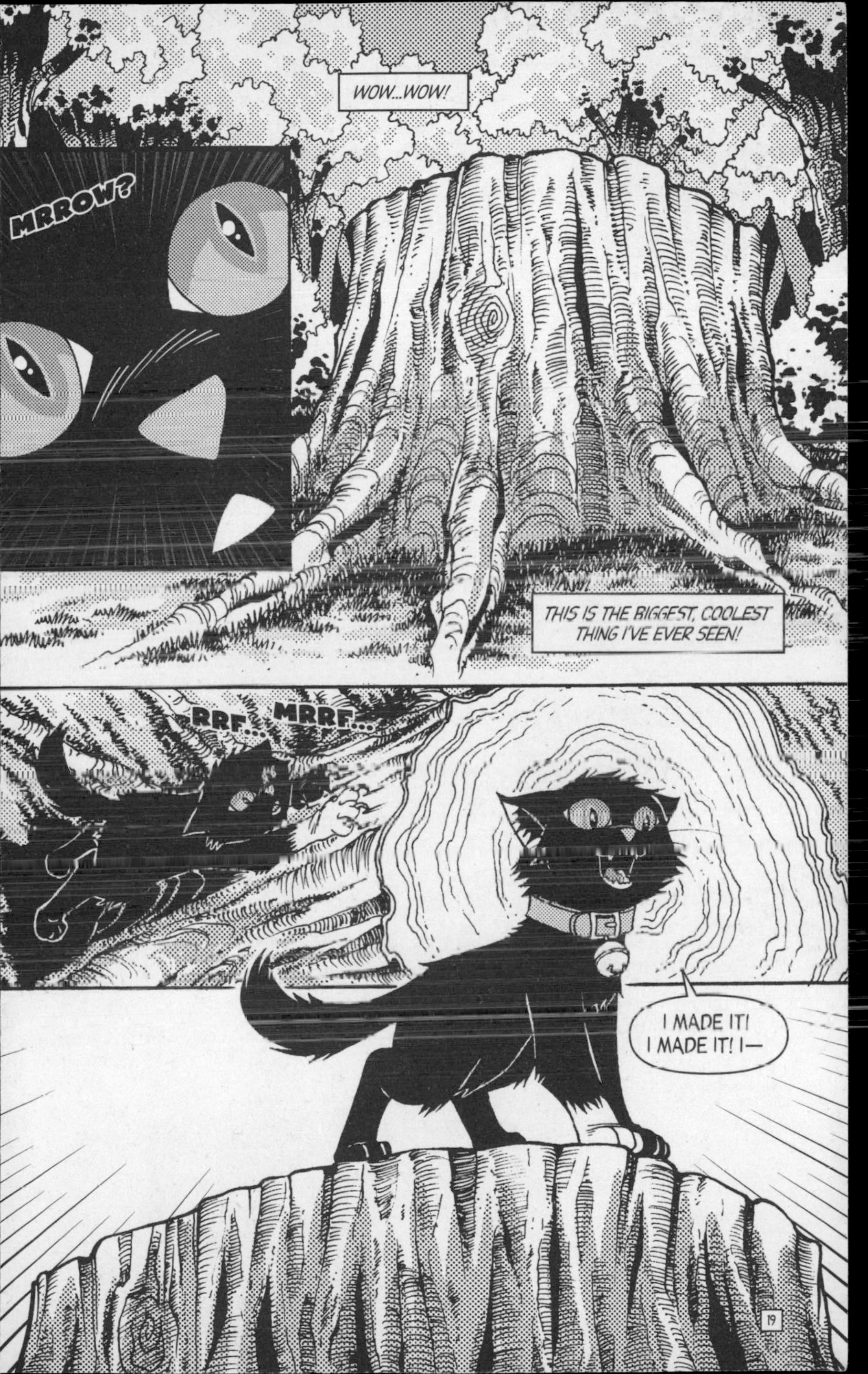
MRROW?
WOW...WOW!
THIS IS THE BIGGEST, COOLEST THING I'VE EVER SEEN!
MRRF... MRRF...
I MADE IT! I MADE IT! I—

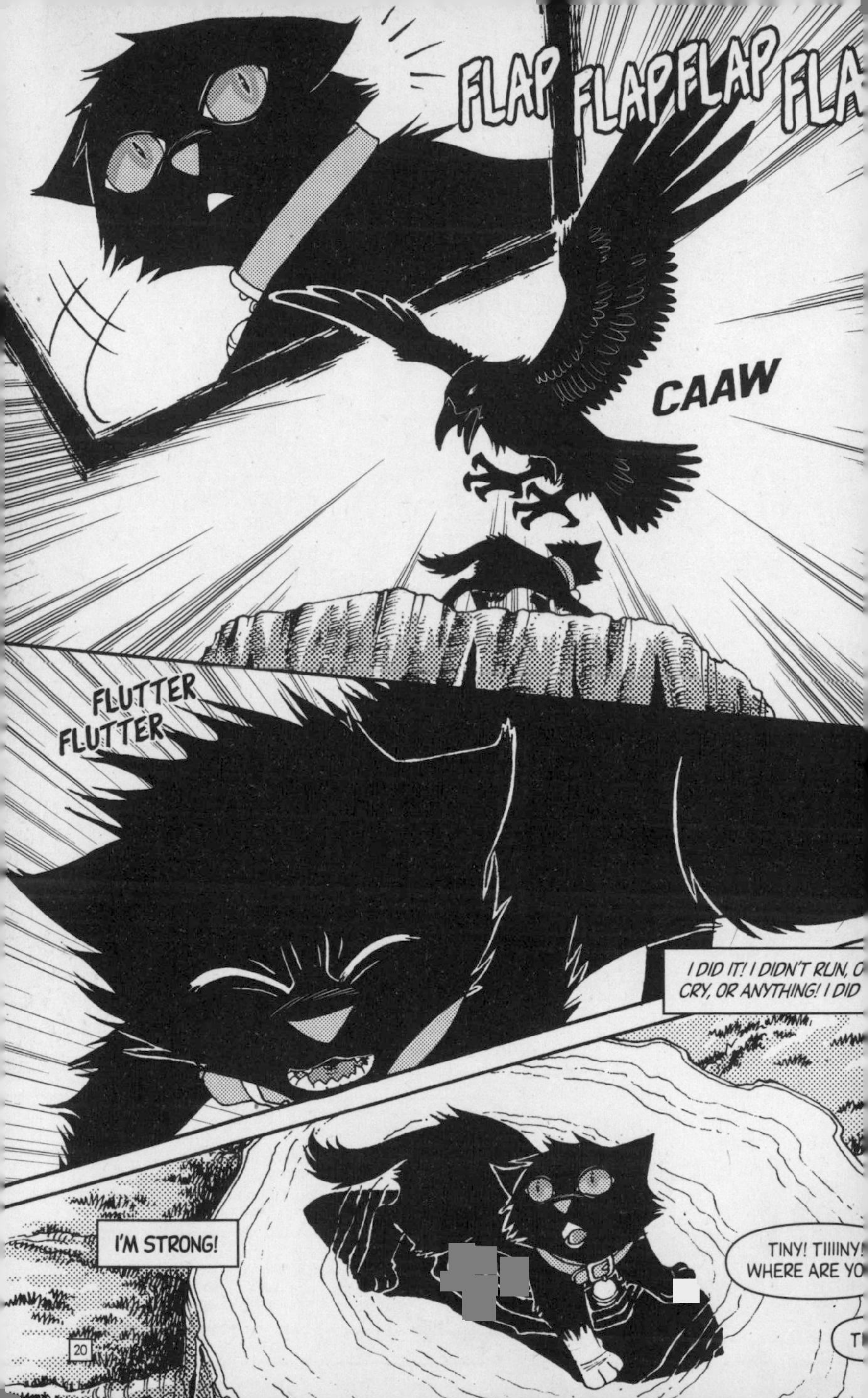
FLAP FLAPFLAP FLA
CAAW
FLUTTER
FLUTTER
I DID IT! I DIDN'T RUN, O
CRY, OR ANYTHING! I DID
I'M STRONG!
TINY! TIIIINY!
WHERE ARE YO
T

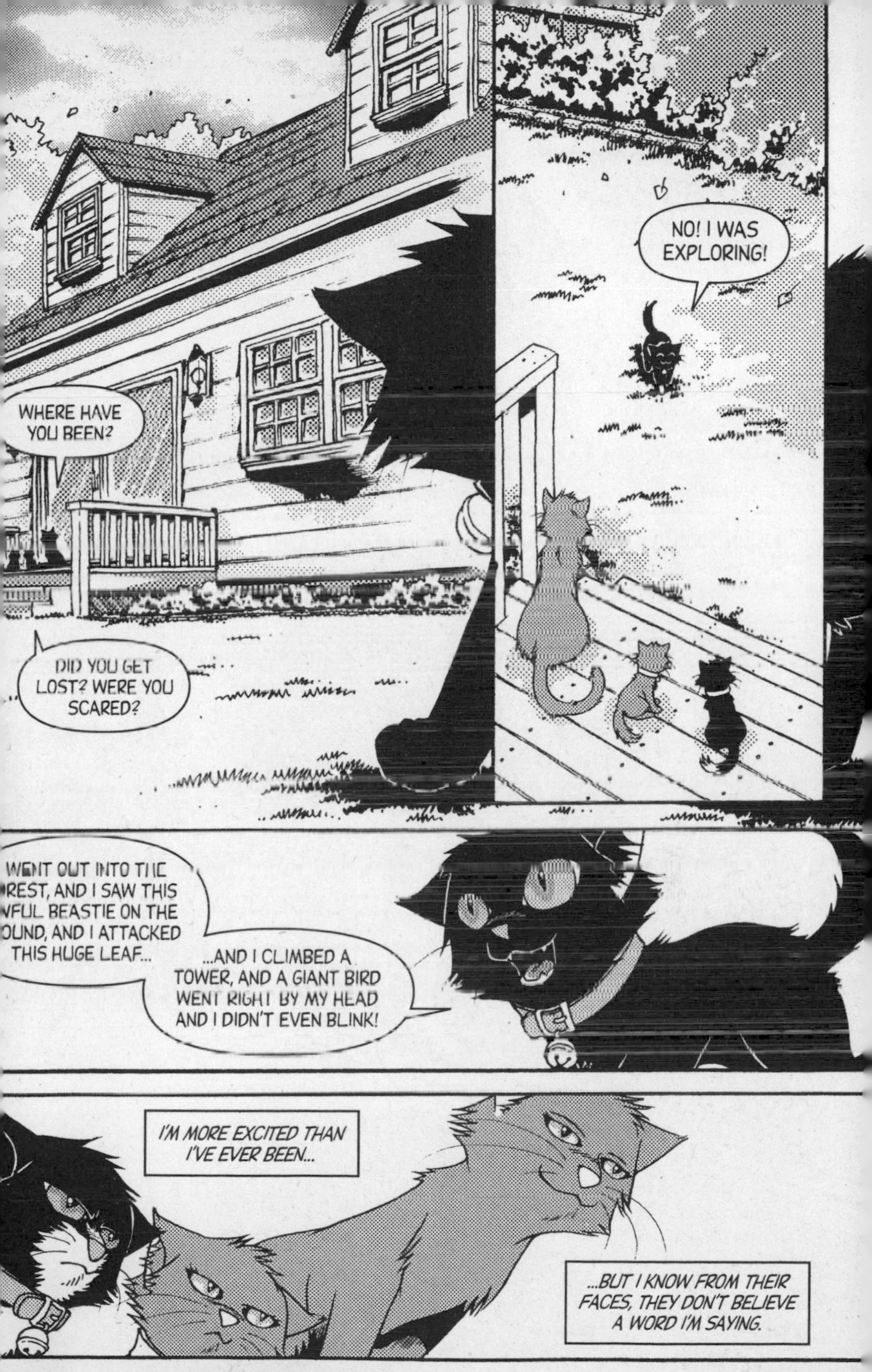
WHERE HAVE YOU BEEN?
DID YOU GET LOST? WERE YOU SCARED?
NO! I WAS EXPLORING!
WENT OUT INTO THE REST, AND I SAW THIS WFUL BEASTIE ON THE OUND, AND I ATTACKED THIS HUGE LEAF...
...AND I CLIMBED A TOWER, AND A GIANT BIRD WENT RIGHT BY MY HEAD AND I DIDN'T EVEN BLINK!
I'M MORE EXCITED THAN I'VE EVER BEEN...
...BUT I KNOW FROM THEIR FACES, THEY DON'T BELIEVE A WORD I'M SAYING.

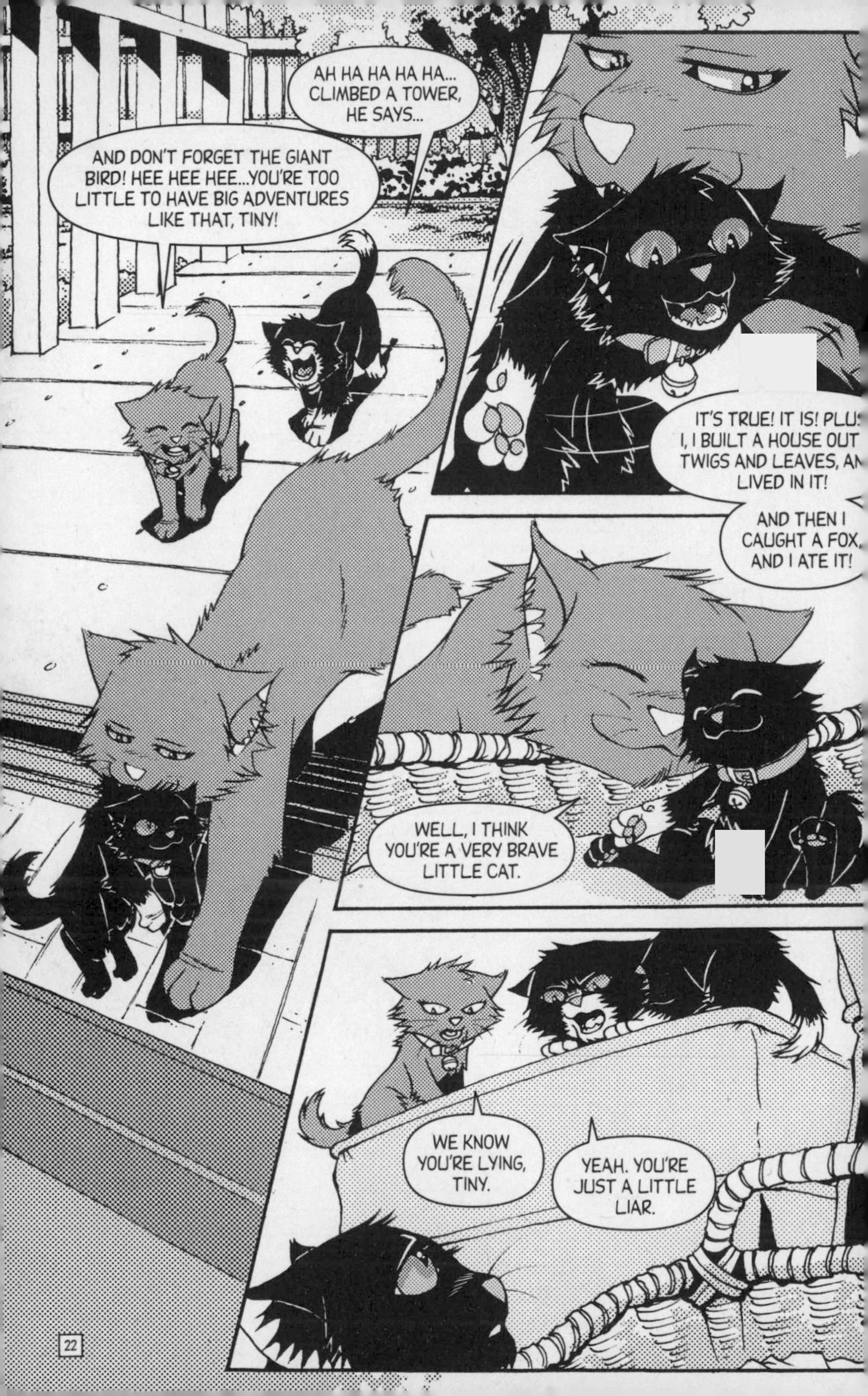
AH HA HA HA HA... CLIMBED A TOWER, HE SAYS...
AND DON'T FORGET THE GIANT BIRD! HEE HEE HEE...YOU'RE TOO LITTLE TO HAVE BIG ADVENTURES LIKE THAT, TINY!
IT'S TRUE! IT IS! PLU I, I BUILT A HOUSE OUT TWIGS AND LEAVES, AN LIVED IN IT!
AND THEN I CAUGHT A FOX, AND I ATE IT!
WELL, I THINK YOU'RE A VERY BRAVE LITTLE CAT.
WE KNOW YOU'RE LYING, TINY.
YEAH. YOU'RE JUST A LITTLE LIAR.

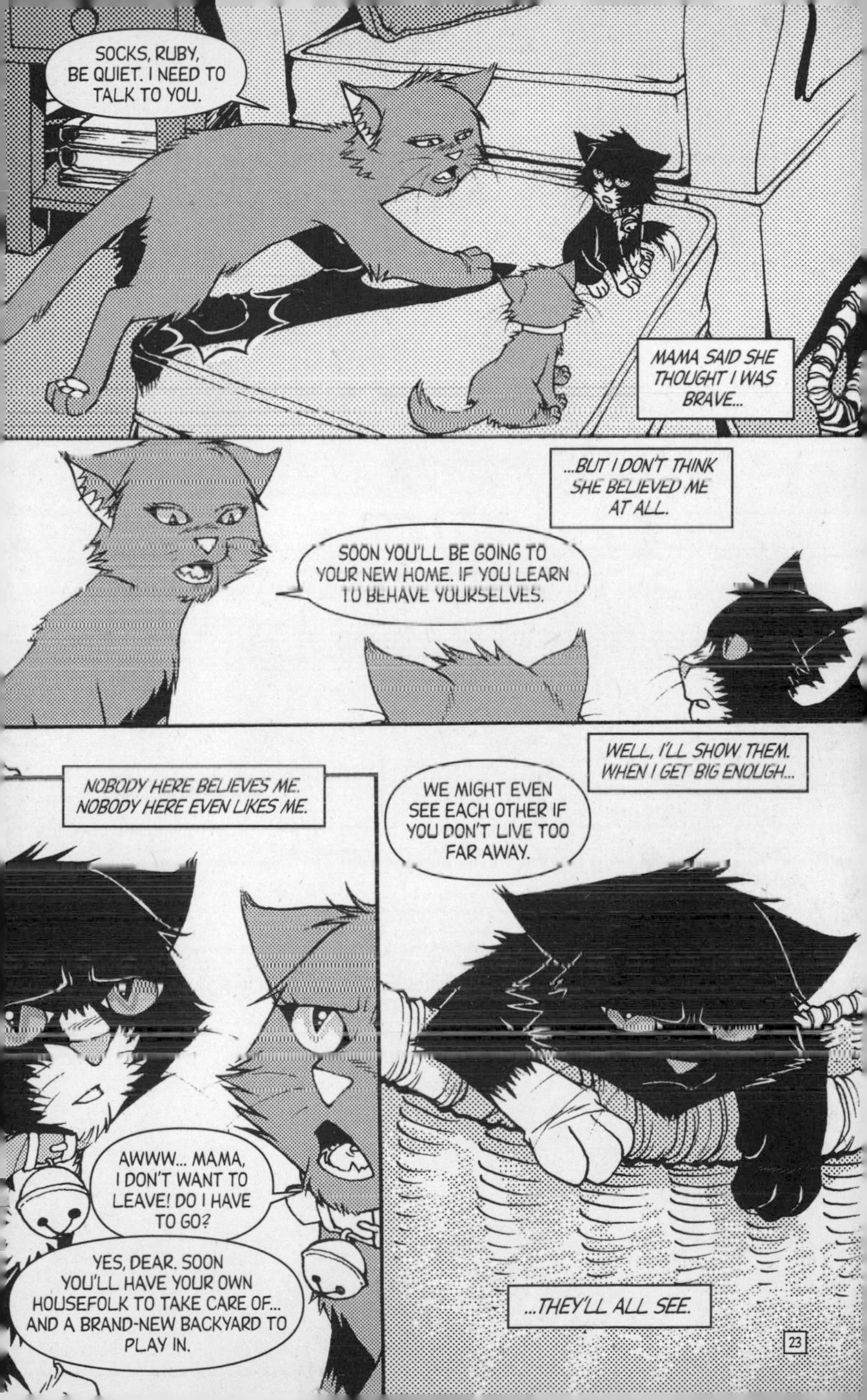
SOCKS, RUBY, BE QUIET. I NEED TO TALK TO YOU.
MAMA SAID SHE THOUGHT I WAS BRAVE...
...BUT I DON'T THINK SHE BELIEVED ME AT ALL.
SOON YOU'LL BE GOING TO YOUR NEW HOME. IF YOU LEARN TO BEHAVE YOURSELVES.
NOBODY HERE BELIEVES ME. NOBODY HERE EVEN LIKES ME.
AWWW... MAMA, I DON'T WANT TO LEAVE! DO I HAVE TO GO?
YES, DEAR. SOON YOU'LL HAVE YOUR OWN HOUSEFOLK TO TAKE CARE OF... AND A BRAND-NEW BACKYARD TO PLAY IN.
WE MIGHT EVEN SEE EACH OTHER IF YOU DON'T LIVE TOO FAR AWAY.
WELL, I'LL SHOW THEM. WHEN I GET BIG ENOUGH...
...THEY'LL ALL SEE.

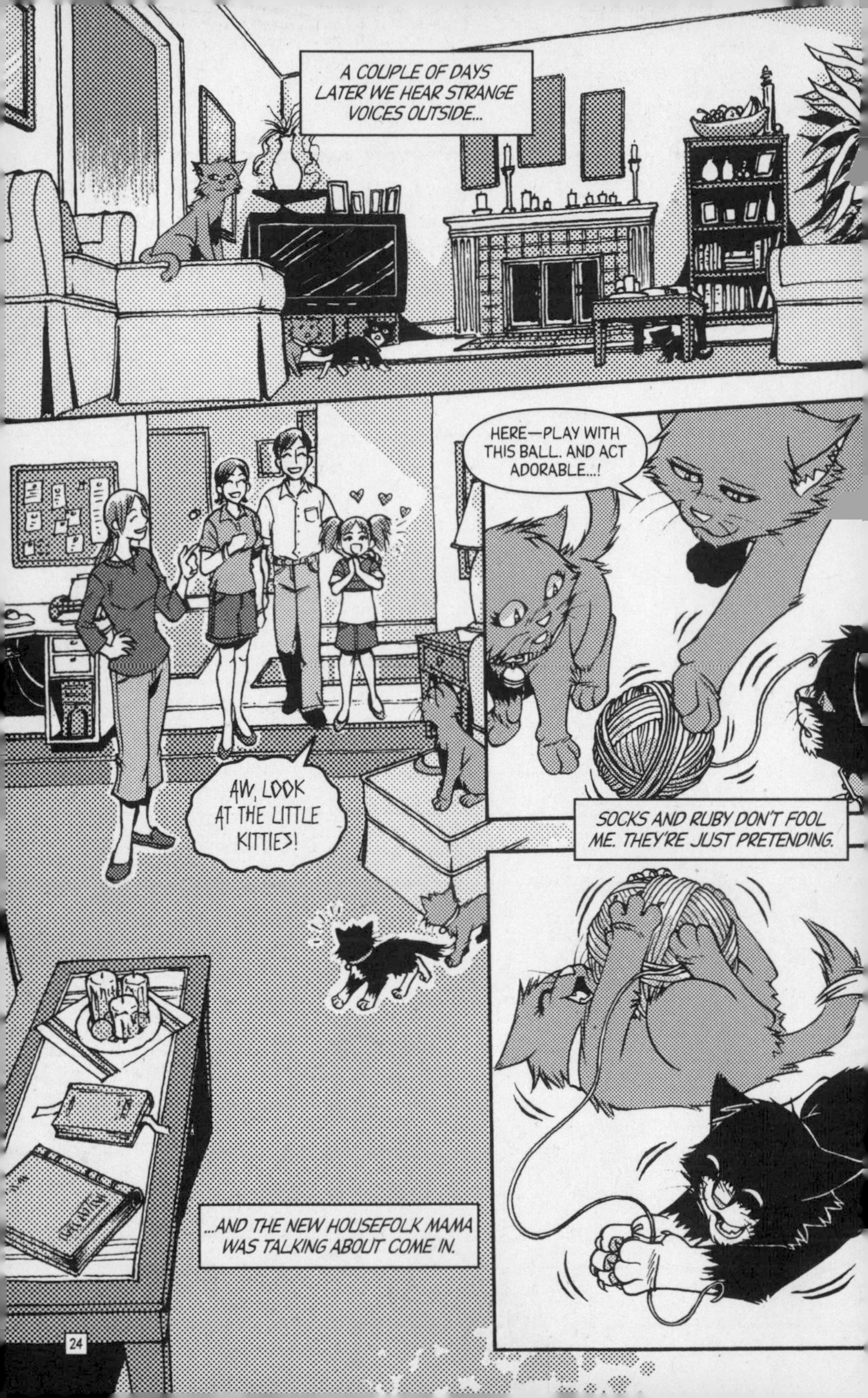

A COUPLE OF DAYS LATER WE HEAR STRANGE VOICES OUTSIDE...
AW, LOOK AT THE LITTLE KITTIES!
...AND THE NEW HOUSEFOLK MAMA WAS TALKING ABOUT COME IN.
HERE—PLAY WITH THIS BALL. AND ACT ADORABLE...!
SOCKS AND RUBY DON'T FOOL ME. THEY'RE JUST PRETENDING.

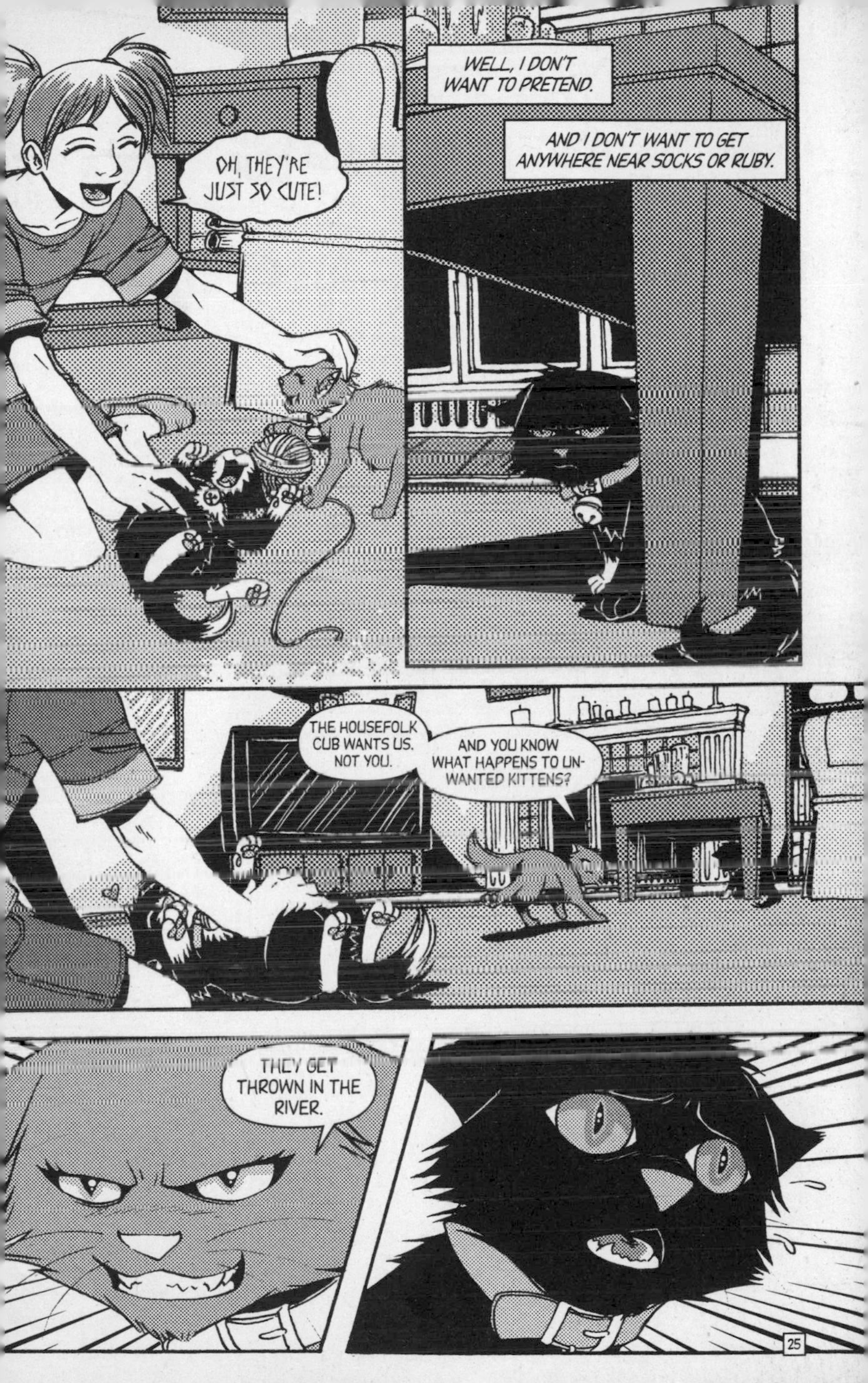
OH, THEY'RE JUST SO CUTE!
WELL, I DON'T WANT TO PRETEND.
AND I DON'T WANT TO GET ANYWHERE NEAR SOCKS OR RUBY.
THE HOUSEFOLK CUB WANTS US. NOT YOU.
AND YOU KNOW WHAT HAPPENS TO UN-WANTED KITTENS?
THEY GET THROWN IN THE RIVER.

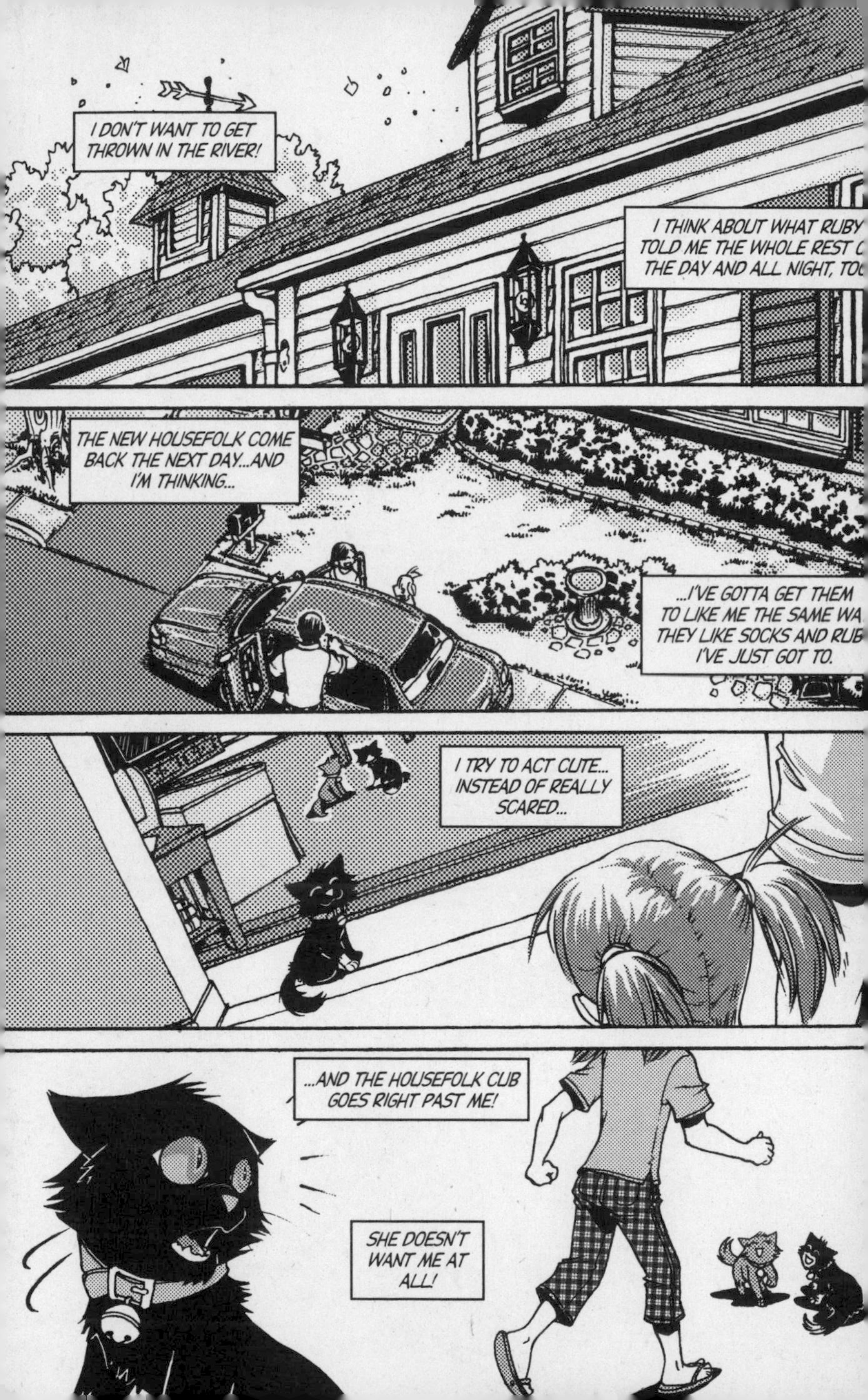
I DON'T WANT TO GET THROWN IN THE RIVER!
I THINK ABOUT WHAT RUBY TOLD ME THE WHOLE REST O THE DAY AND ALL NIGHT, TO
THE NEW HOUSEFOLK COME BACK THE NEXT DAY...AND I'M THINKING...
...I'VE GOTTA GET THEM TO LIKE ME THE SAME WA THEY LIKE SOCKS AND RUB I'VE JUST GOT TO.
I TRY TO ACT CUTE... INSTEAD OF REALLY SCARED...
...AND THE HOUSEFOLK CUB GOES RIGHT PAST ME!
SHE DOESN'T WANT ME AT ALL!

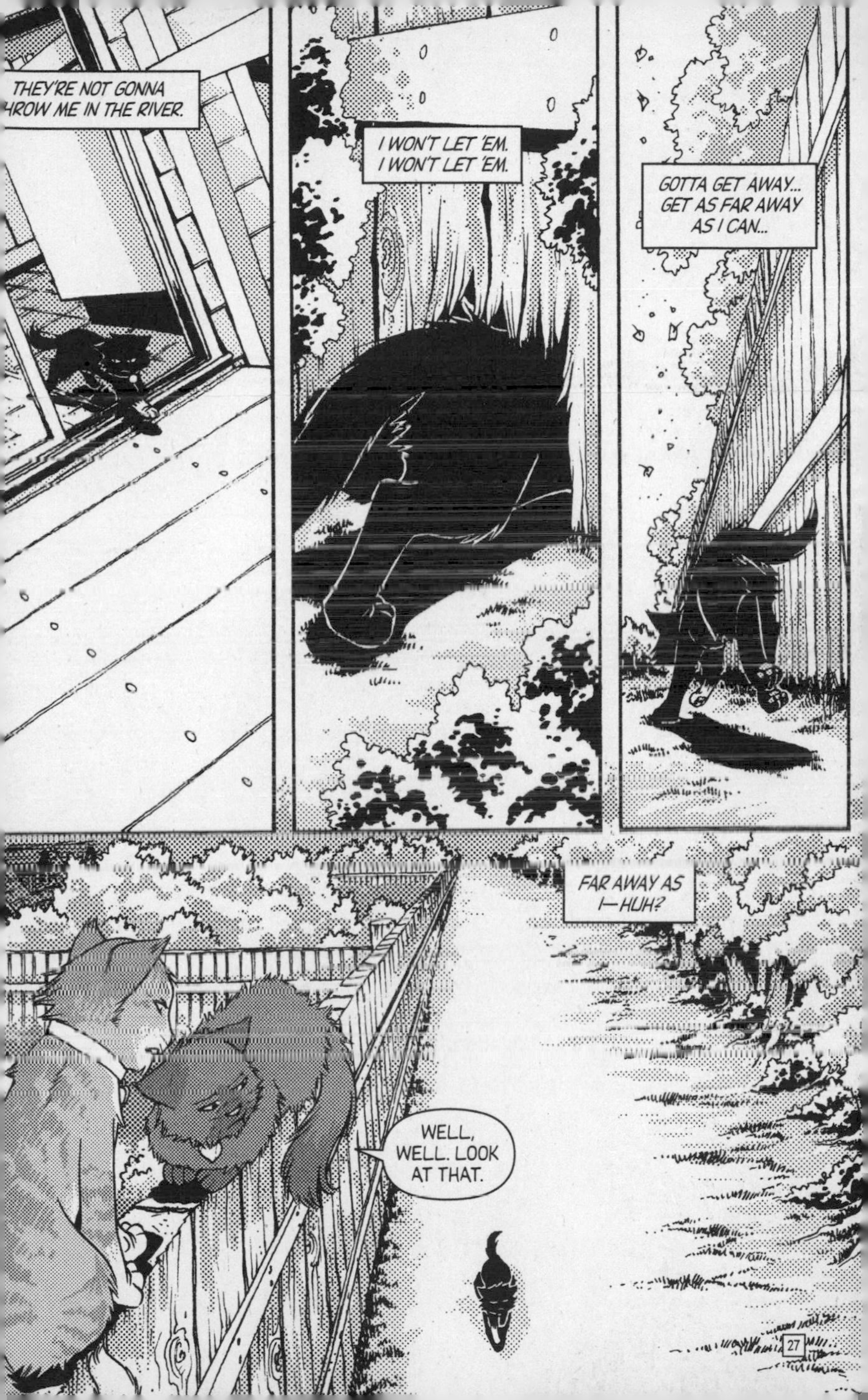
THEY'RE NOT GONNA
THROW ME IN THE RIVER.
I WON'T LET 'EM.
I WON'T LET 'EM.
GOTTA GET AWAY... GET AS FAR AWAY AS I CAN...
FAR AWAY AS I—HUH?
WELL, WELL. LOOK AT THAT.

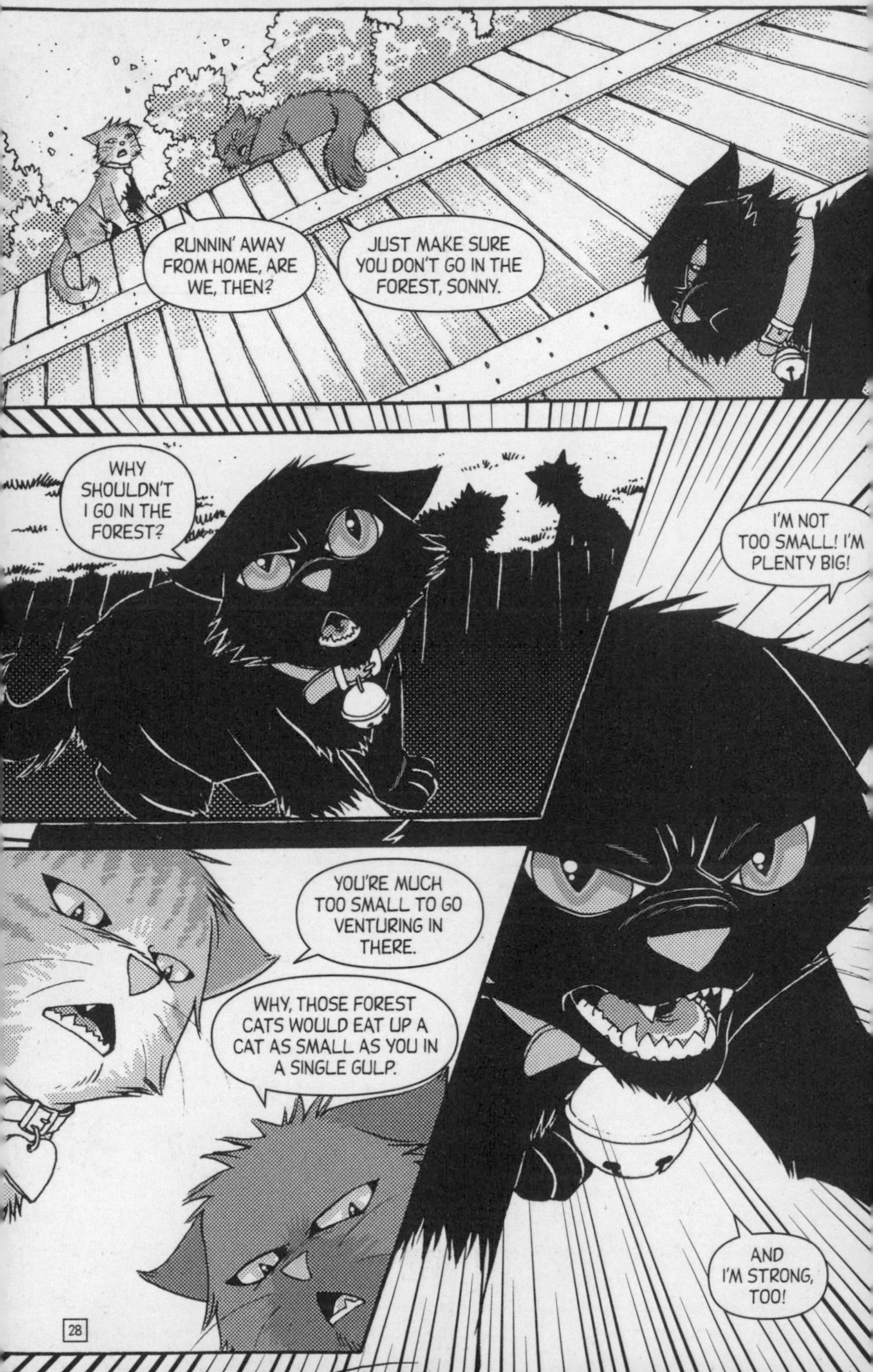
RUNNIN' AWAY FROM HOME, ARE WE, THEN?
JUST MAKE SURE YOU DON'T GO IN THE FOREST, SONNY.
WHY SHOULDN'T I GO IN THE FOREST?
YOU'RE MUCH TOO SMALL TO GO VENTURING IN THERE.
WHY, THOSE FOREST CATS WOULD EAT UP A CAT AS SMALL AS YOU IN A SINGLE GULP.
I'M NOT TOO SMALL! I'M PLENTY BIG!
AND I'M STRONG, TOO!

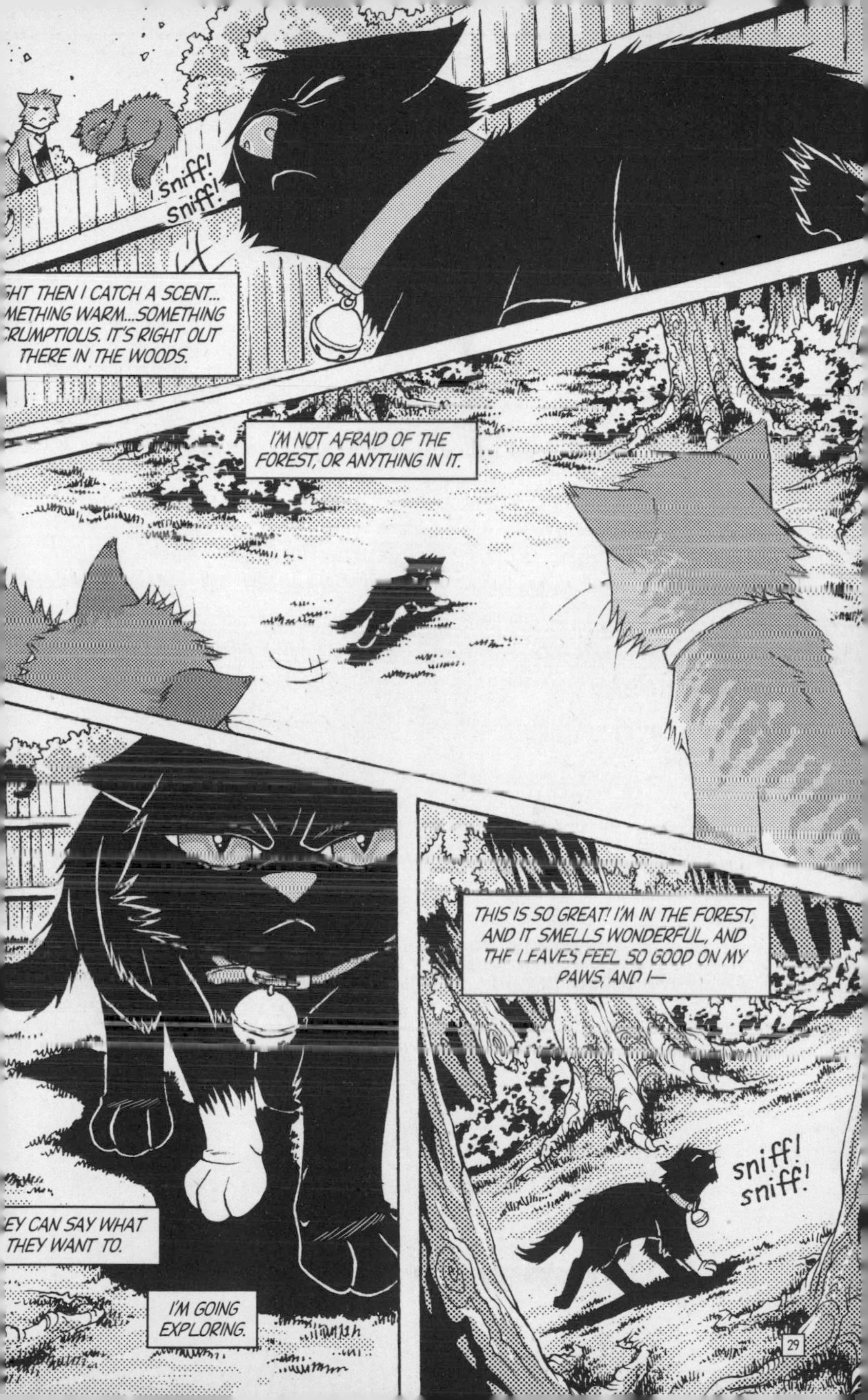
sniff! sniff!
GHT THEN I CATCH A SCENT... METHING WARM...SOMETHING CRUMPTIOUS. IT'S RIGHT OUT THERE IN THE WOODS.
I'M NOT AFRAID OF THE FOREST, OR ANYTHING IN IT.
EY CAN SAY WHAT THEY WANT TO.
I'M GOING EXPLORING.
THIS IS SO GREAT! I'M IN THE FOREST, AND IT SMELLS WONDERFUL, AND THE LEAVES FEEL SO GOOD ON MY PAWS, AND I—
sniff! sniff!

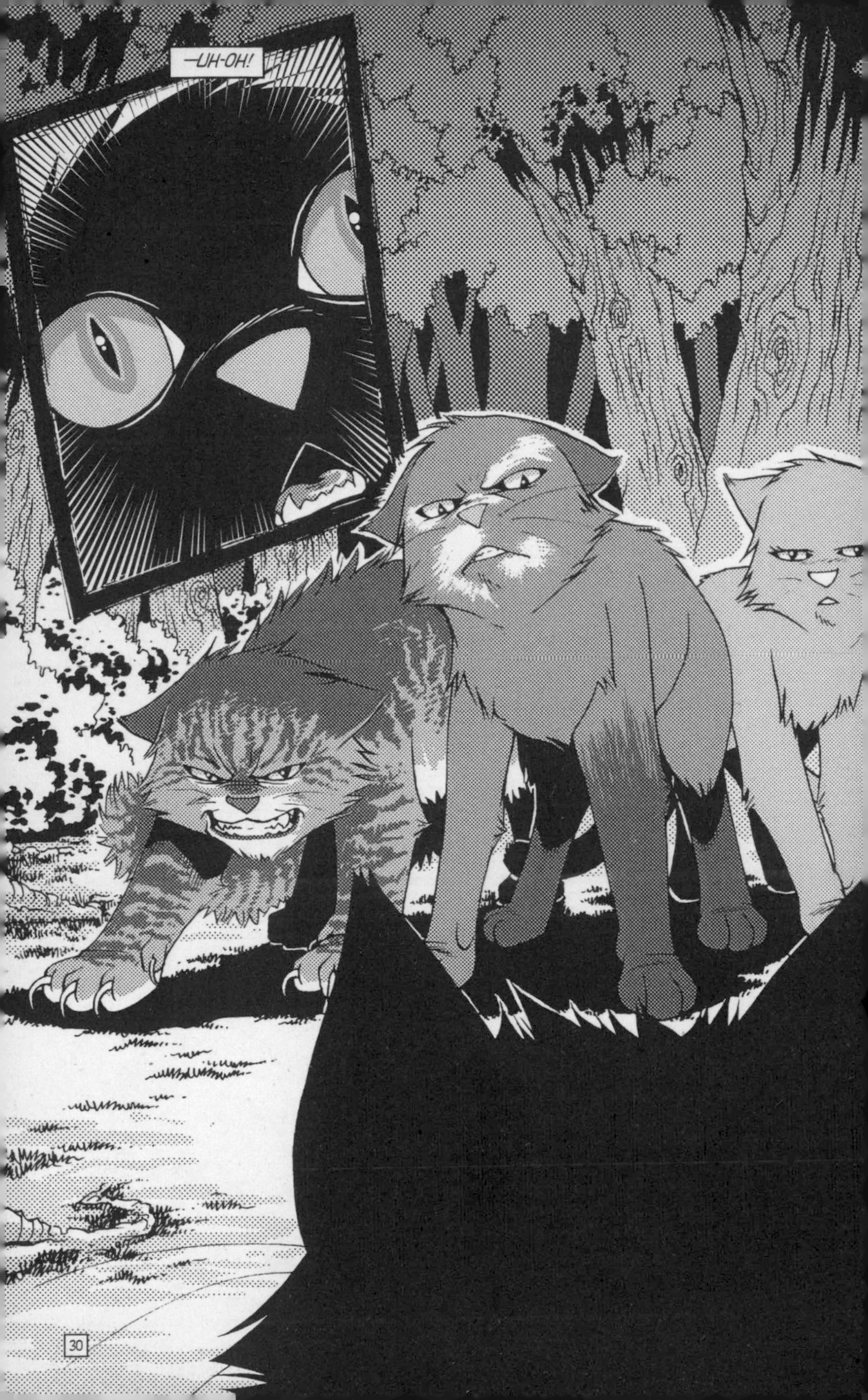
—UH-OH!

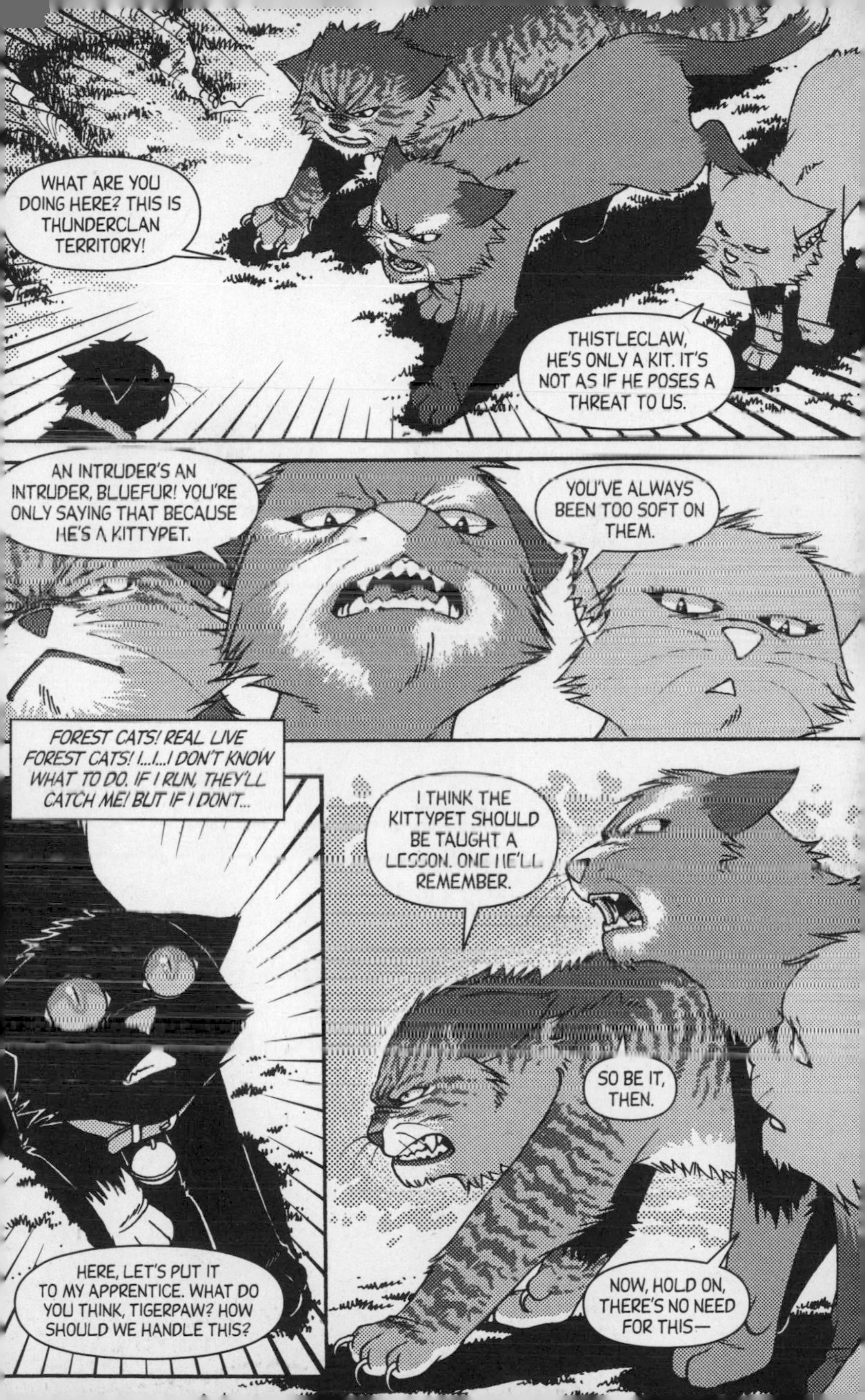
WHAT ARE YOU DOING HERE? THIS IS THUNDERCLAN TERRITORY!
THISTLECLAW, HE'S ONLY A KIT. IT'S NOT AS IF HE POSES A THREAT TO US.
AN INTRUDER'S AN INTRUDER, BLUEFUR! YOU'RE ONLY SAYING THAT BECAUSE HE'S A KITTYPET.
YOU'VE ALWAYS BEEN TOO SOFT ON THEM.
FOREST CATS! REAL LIVE FOREST CATS! I...I...I DON'T KNOW WHAT TO DO. IF I RUN, THEY'LL CATCH ME! BUT IF I DON'T...
HERE, LET'S PUT IT TO MY APPRENTICE. WHAT DO YOU THINK, TIGERPAW? HOW SHOULD WE HANDLE THIS?
I THINK THE KITTYPET SHOULD BE TAUGHT A LESSON. ONE HE'LL REMEMBER.
SO BE IT, THEN.
NOW, HOLD ON, THERE'S NO NEED FOR THIS—

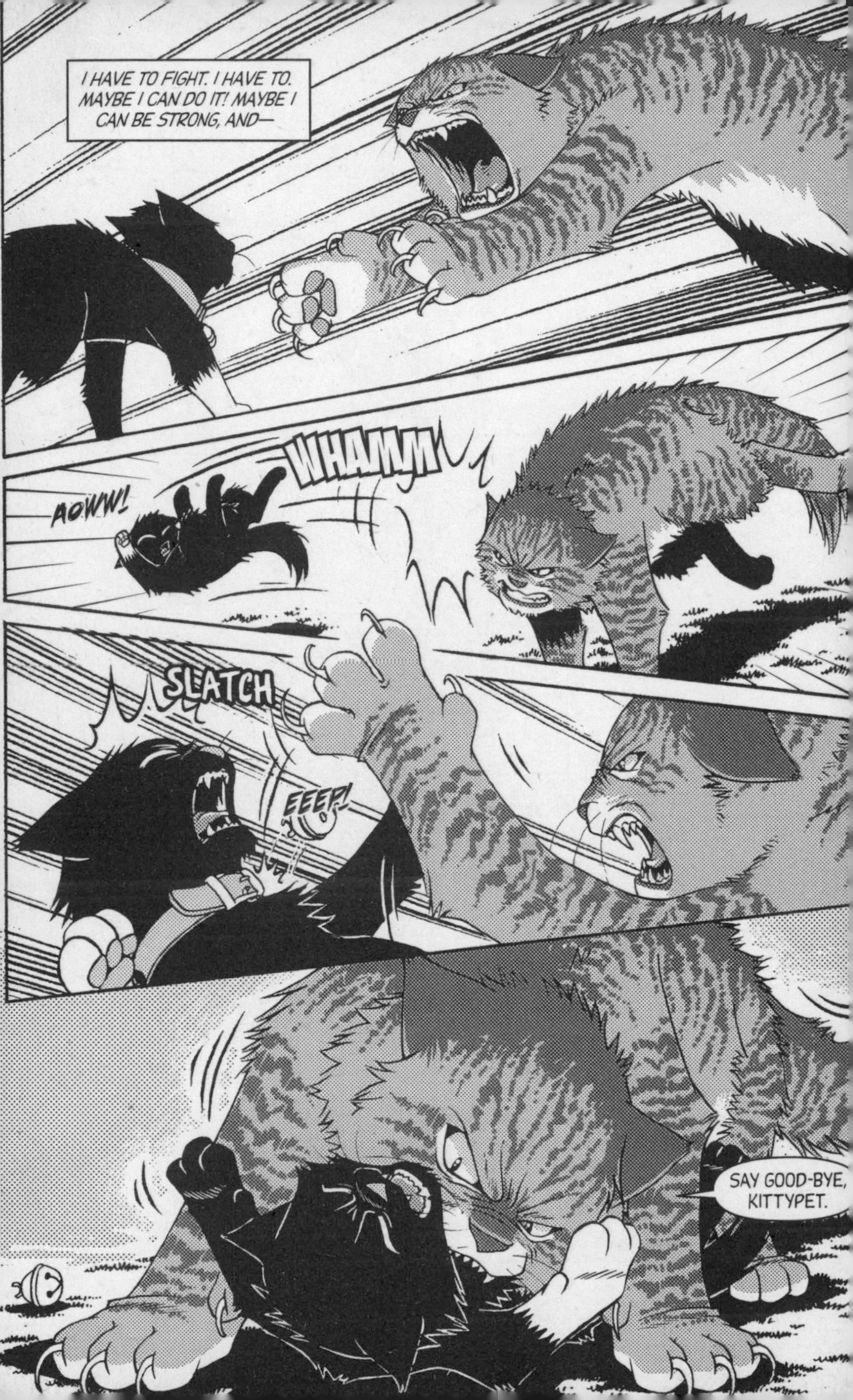
I HAVE TO FIGHT. I HAVE TO. MAYBE I CAN DO IT! MAYBE I CAN BE STRONG, AND—
AOWW!
WHAMM
SLATCH
EEEP!
SAY GOOD-BYE, KITTYPET.

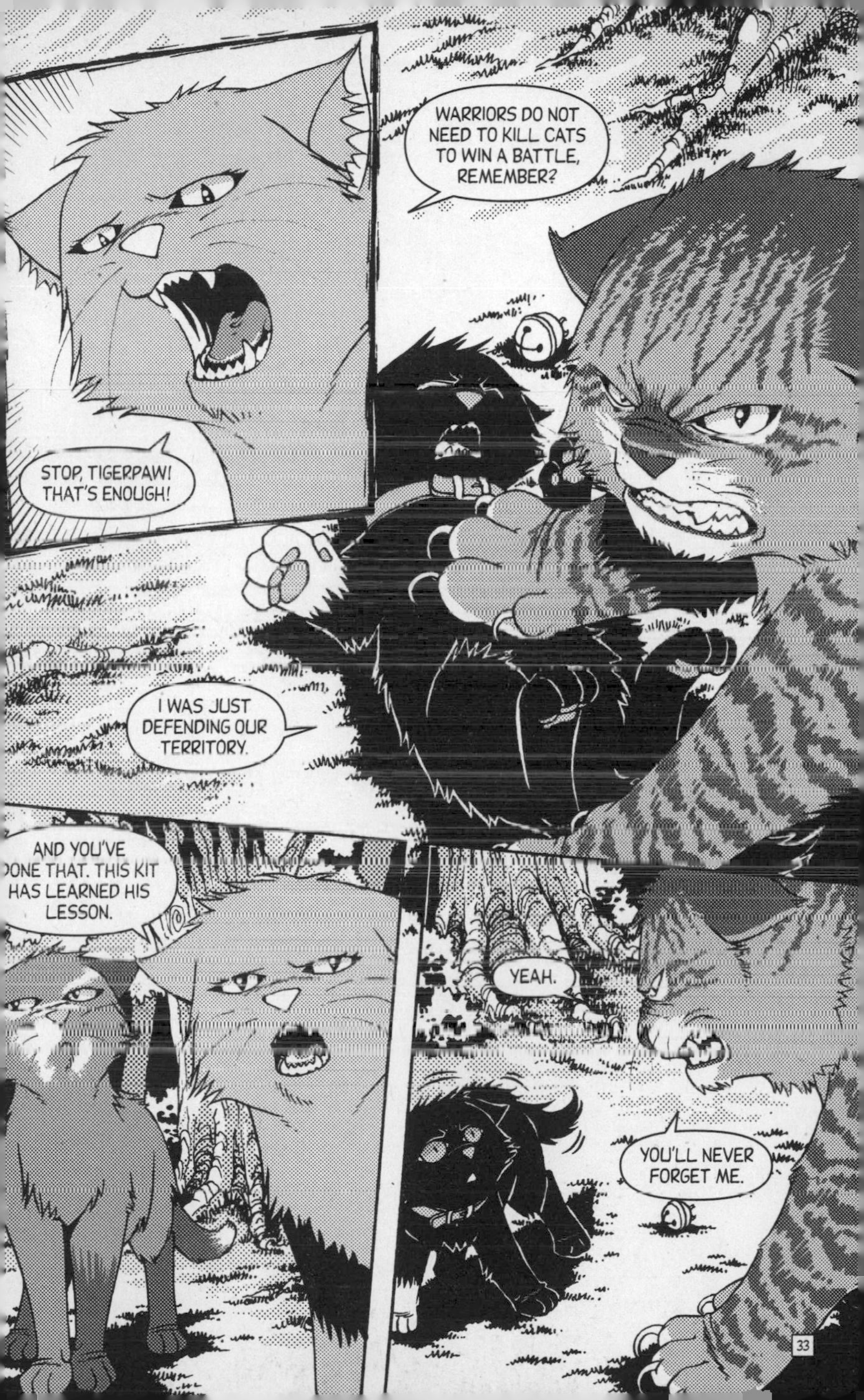
STOP, TIGERPAW! THAT'S ENOUGH!
WARRIORS DO NOT NEED TO KILL CATS TO WIN A BATTLE, REMEMBER?
I WAS JUST DEFENDING OUR TERRITORY.
AND YOU'VE DONE THAT. THIS KIT HAS LEARNED HIS LESSON.
YEAH.
YOU'LL NEVER FORGET ME.

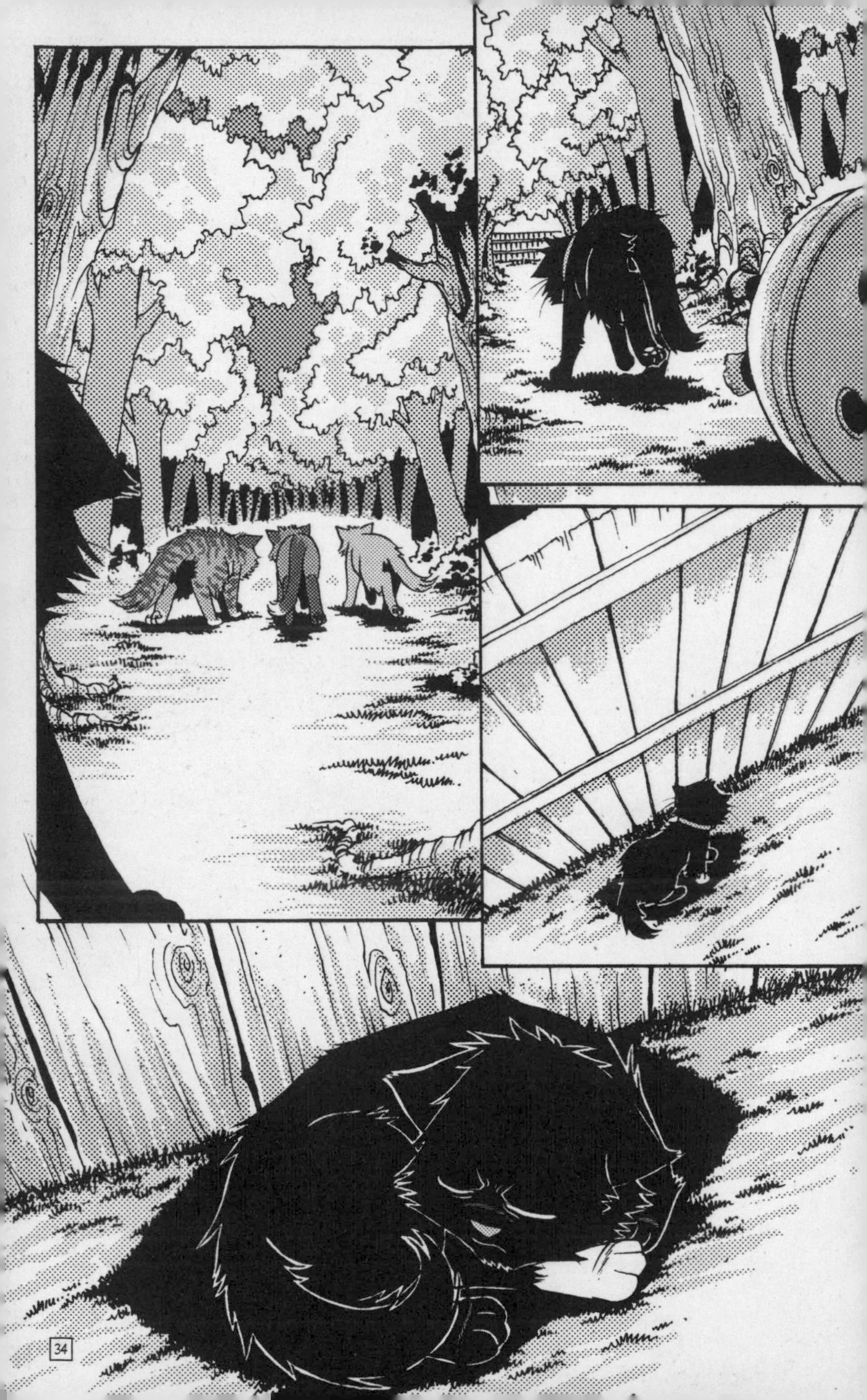

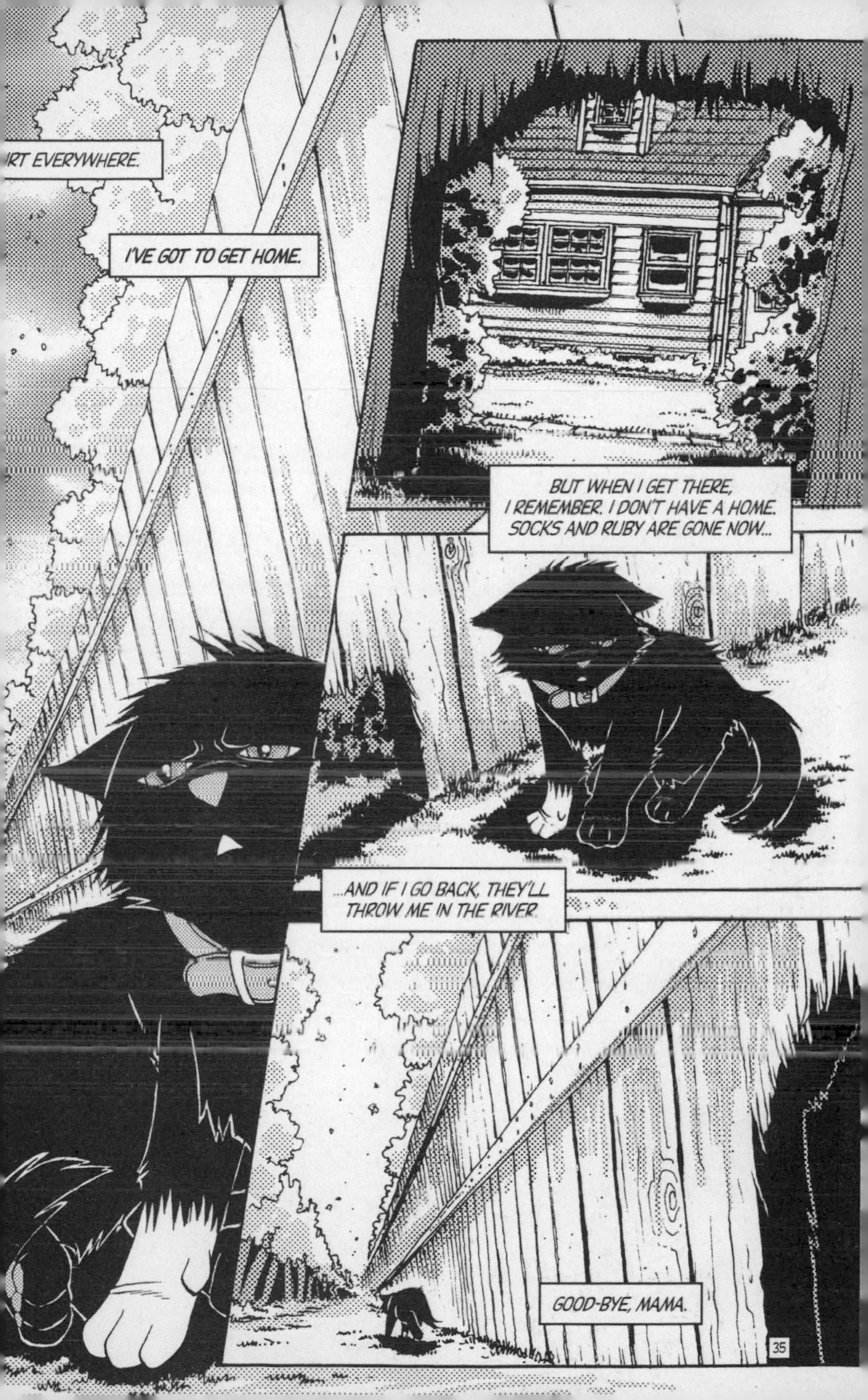
IRT EVERYWHERE.
I'VE GOT TO GET HOME.
BUT WHEN I GET THERE, I REMEMBER. I DON'T HAVE A HOME. SOCKS AND RUBY ARE GONE NOW...
...AND IF I GO BACK, THEY'LL THROW ME IN THE RIVER.
GOOD-BYE, MAMA.

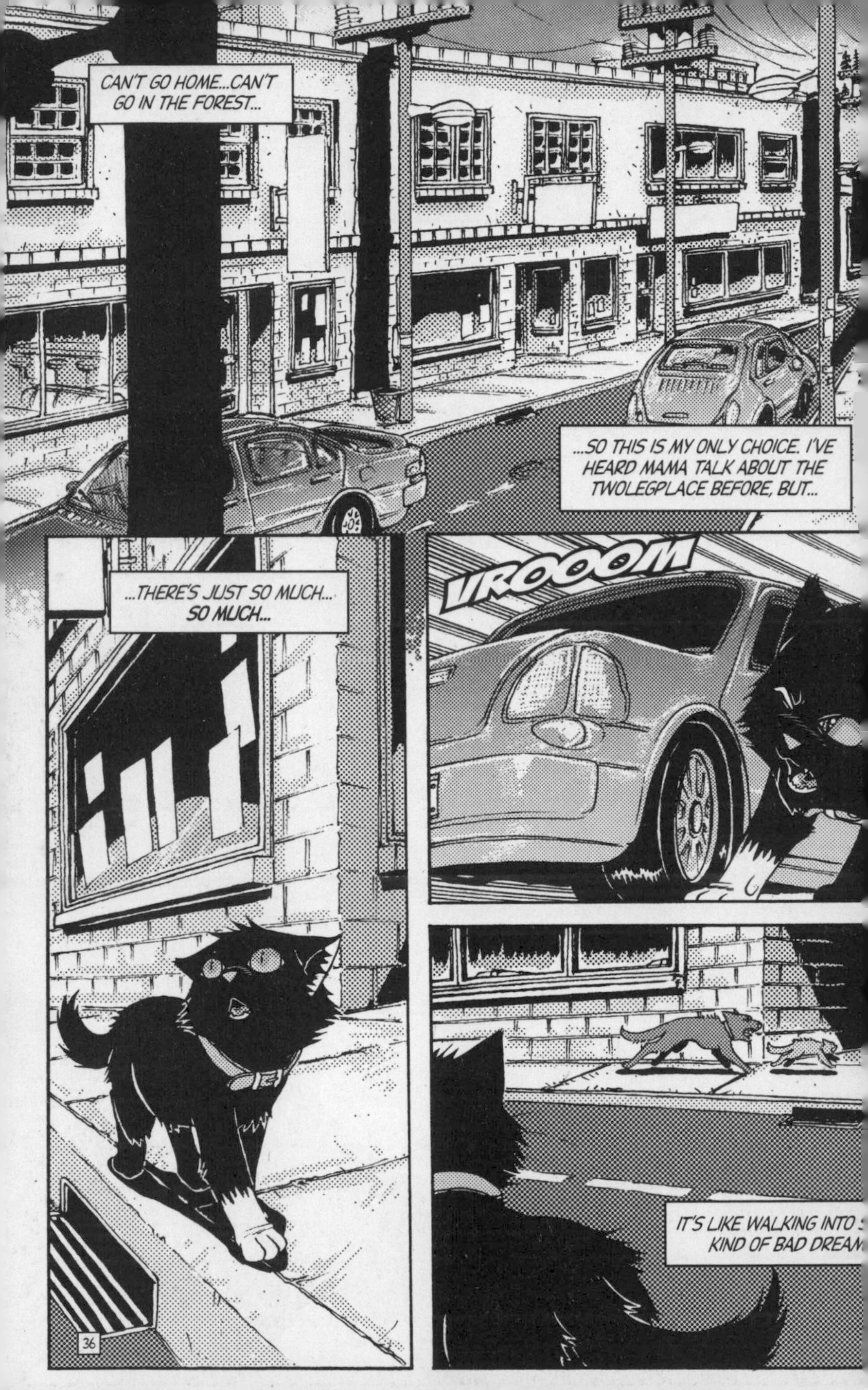
CAN'T GO HOME...CAN'T GO IN THE FOREST...
...SO THIS IS MY ONLY CHOICE. I'VE HEARD MAMA TALK ABOUT THE TWOLEGPLACE BEFORE, BUT...
...THERE'S JUST SO MUCH... SO MUCH...
VROOOOM
IT'S LIKE WALKING INTO
KIND OF BAD DREAM

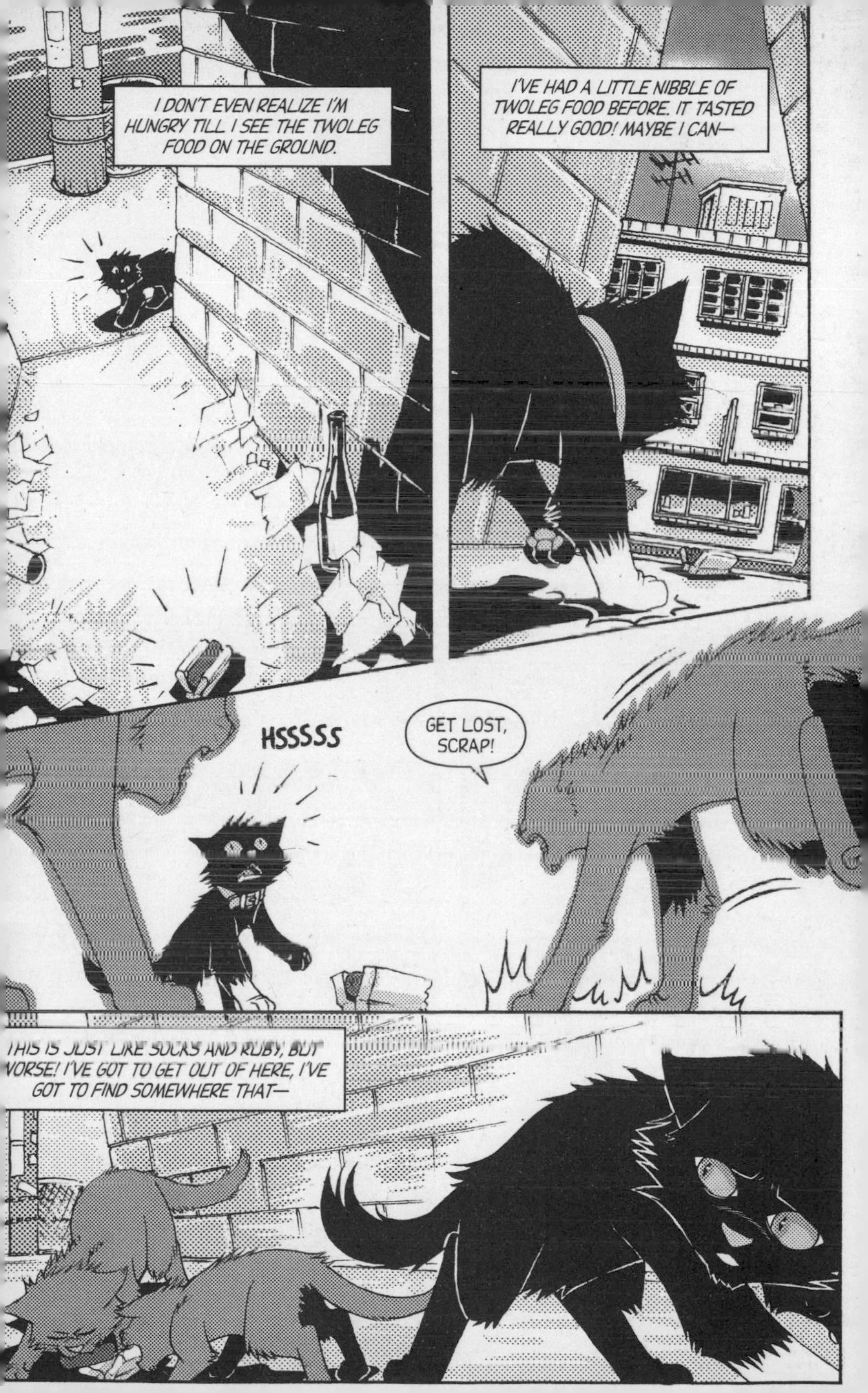
I DON'T EVEN REALIZE I'M HUNGRY TILL I SEE THE TWOLEG FOOD ON THE GROUND.
I'VE HAD A LITTLE NIBBLE OF TWOLEG FOOD BEFORE. IT TASTED REALLY GOOD! MAYBE I CAN—
HSSSSS
GET LOST, SCRAP!
THIS IS JUST LIKE SOCKS AND RUBY, BUT WORSE! I'VE GOT TO GET OUT OF HERE, I'VE GOT TO FIND SOMEWHERE THAT—

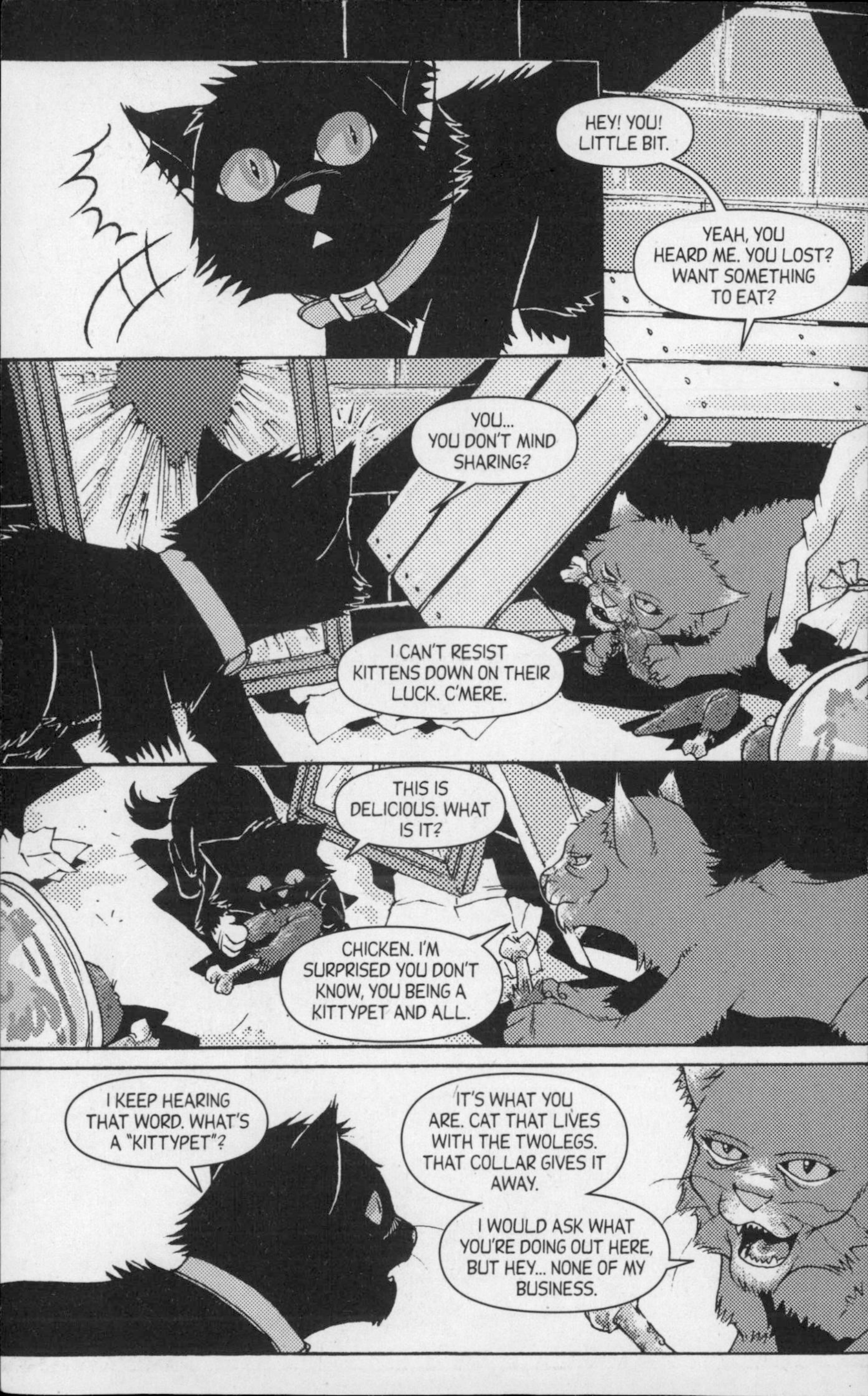
HEY! YOU! LITTLE BIT.
YEAH, YOU HEARD ME. YOU LOST? WANT SOMETHING TO EAT?
YOU... YOU DON'T MIND SHARING?
I CAN'T RESIST KITTENS DOWN ON THEIR LUCK. C'MERE.
THIS IS DELICIOUS. WHAT IS IT?
CHICKEN. I'M SURPRISED YOU DON'T KNOW, YOU BEING A KITTYPET AND ALL.
I KEEP HEARING THAT WORD. WHAT'S A "KITTYPET"?
IT'S WHAT YOU ARE. CAT THAT LIVES WITH THE TWOLEGS. THAT COLLAR GIVES IT AWAY.
I WOULD ASK WHAT YOU'RE DOING OUT HERE, BUT HEY... NONE OF MY BUSINESS.

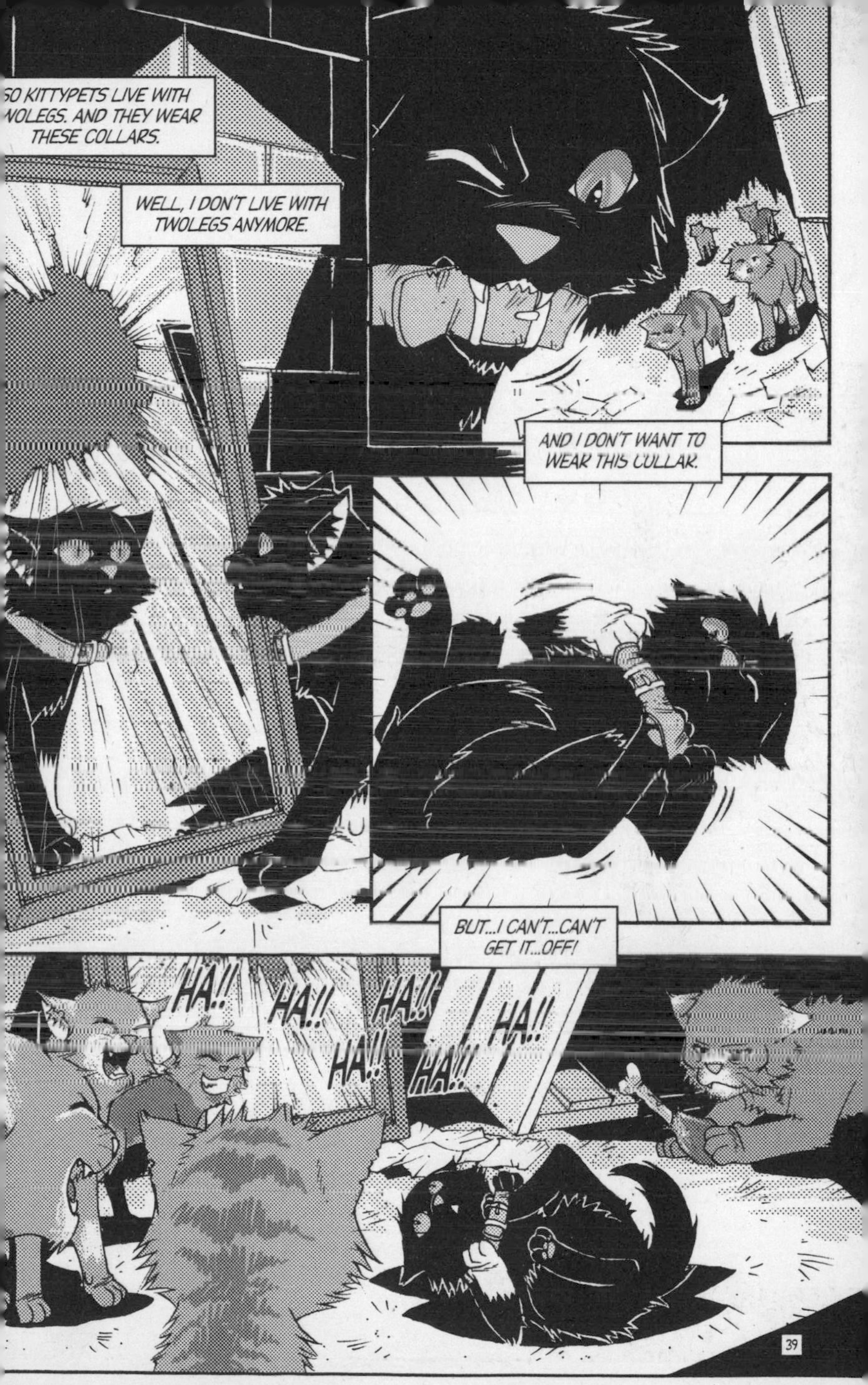
SO KITTYPETS LIVE WITH TWOLEGS. AND THEY WEAR THESE COLLARS.
WELL, I DON'T LIVE WITH TWOLEGS ANYMORE.
AND I DON'T WANT TO WEAR THIS COLLAR.
BUT...I CAN'T...CAN'T GET IT...OFF!
HA!!
HA!!
HA!!
HA!!
HA!!
HA!!

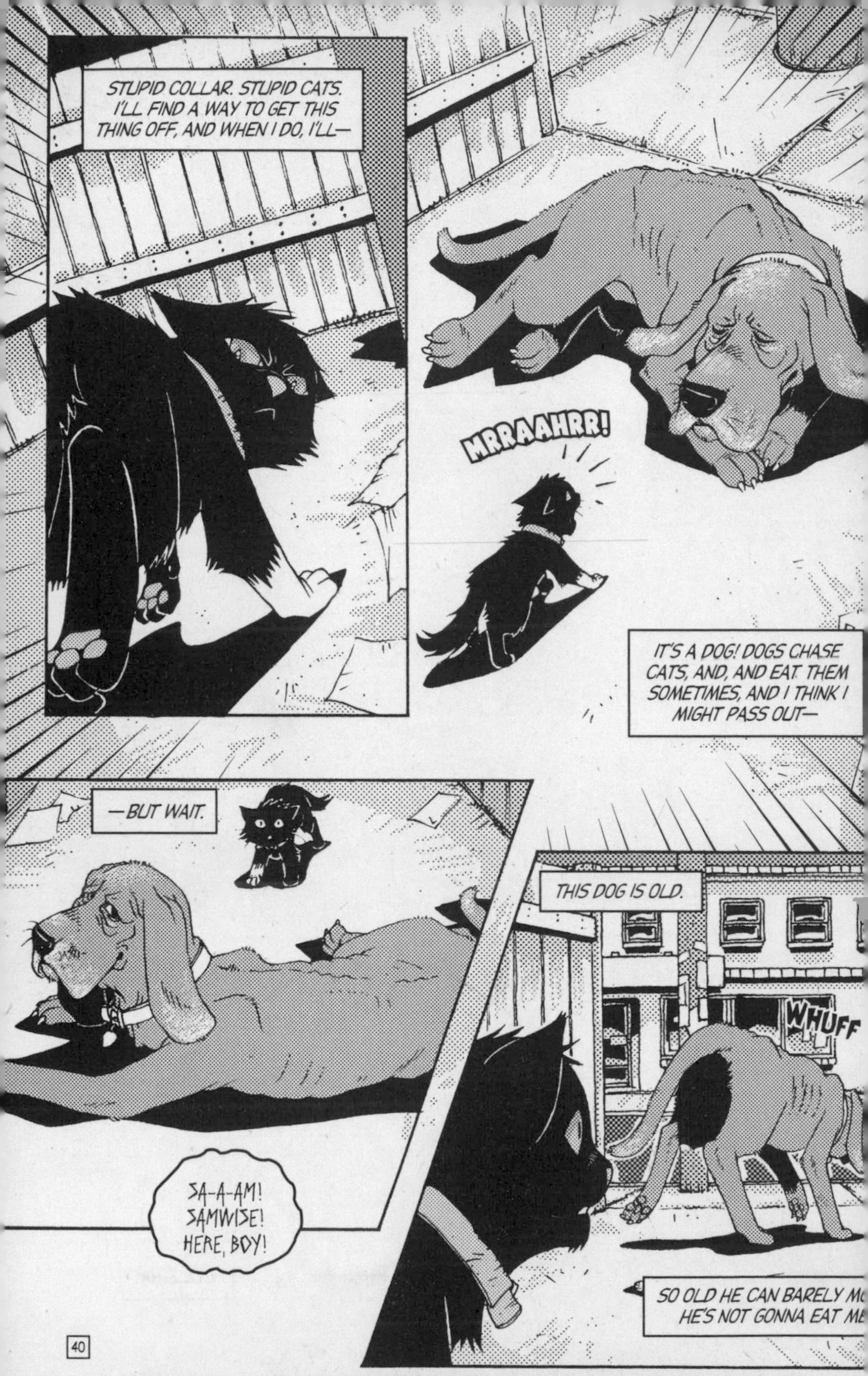
STUPID COLLAR. STUPID CATS. I'LL FIND A WAY TO GET THIS THING OFF, AND WHEN I DO, I'LL—
MRRAAHRR!
IT'S A DOG! DOGS CHASE CATS, AND, AND EAT THEM SOMETIMES, AND I THINK I MIGHT PASS OUT—
—BUT WAIT.
SA-A-AM! SAMWISE! HERE, BOY!
THIS DOG IS OLD.
WHUFF
SO OLD HE CAN BARELY M
HE'S NOT GONNA EAT M

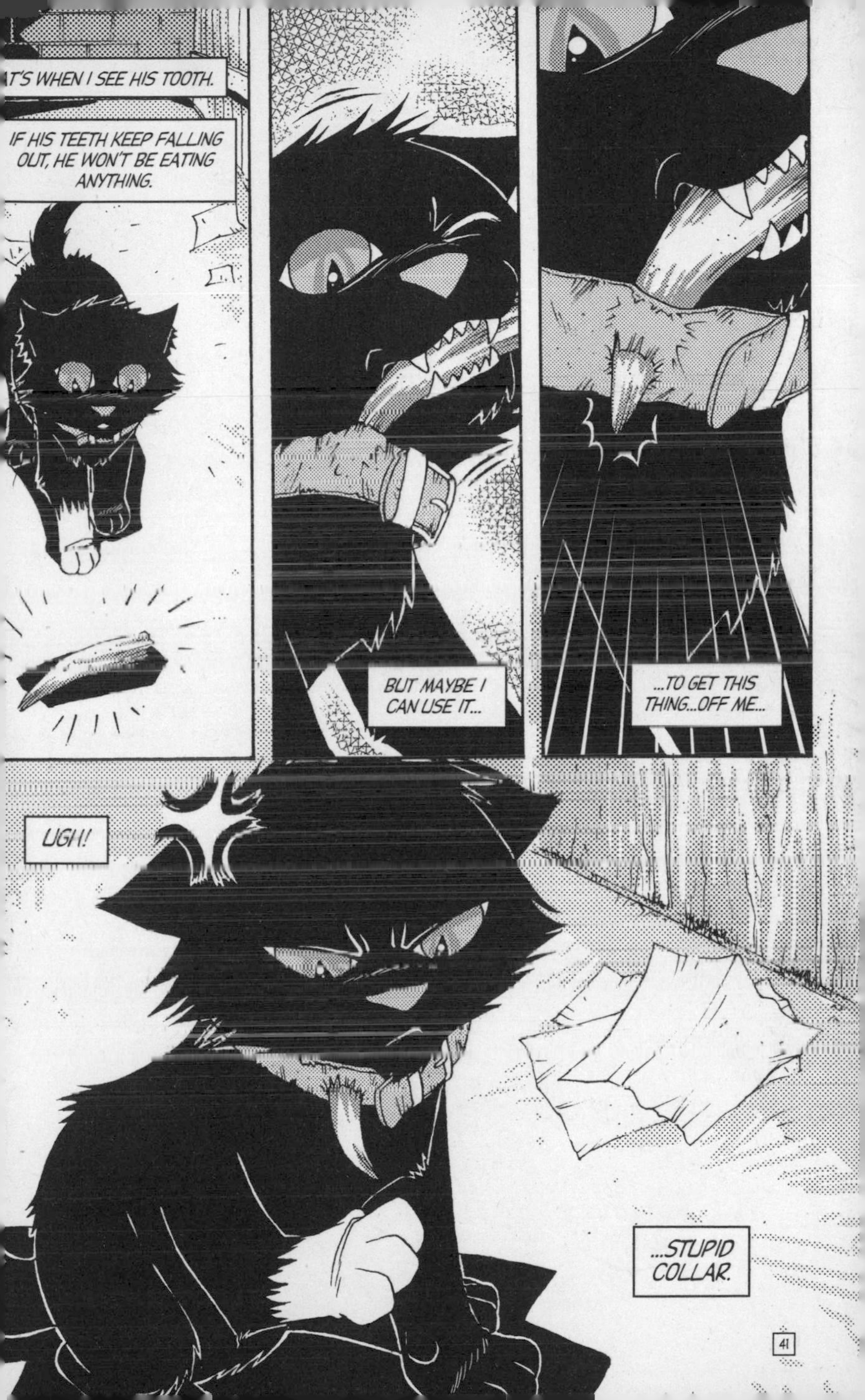

T'S WHEN I SEE HIS TOOTH.
IF HIS TEETH KEEP FALLING OUT, HE WON'T BE EATING ANYTHING.
BUT MAYBE I CAN USE IT...
...TO GET THIS THING...OFF ME...
UGH!
...STUPID COLLAR.

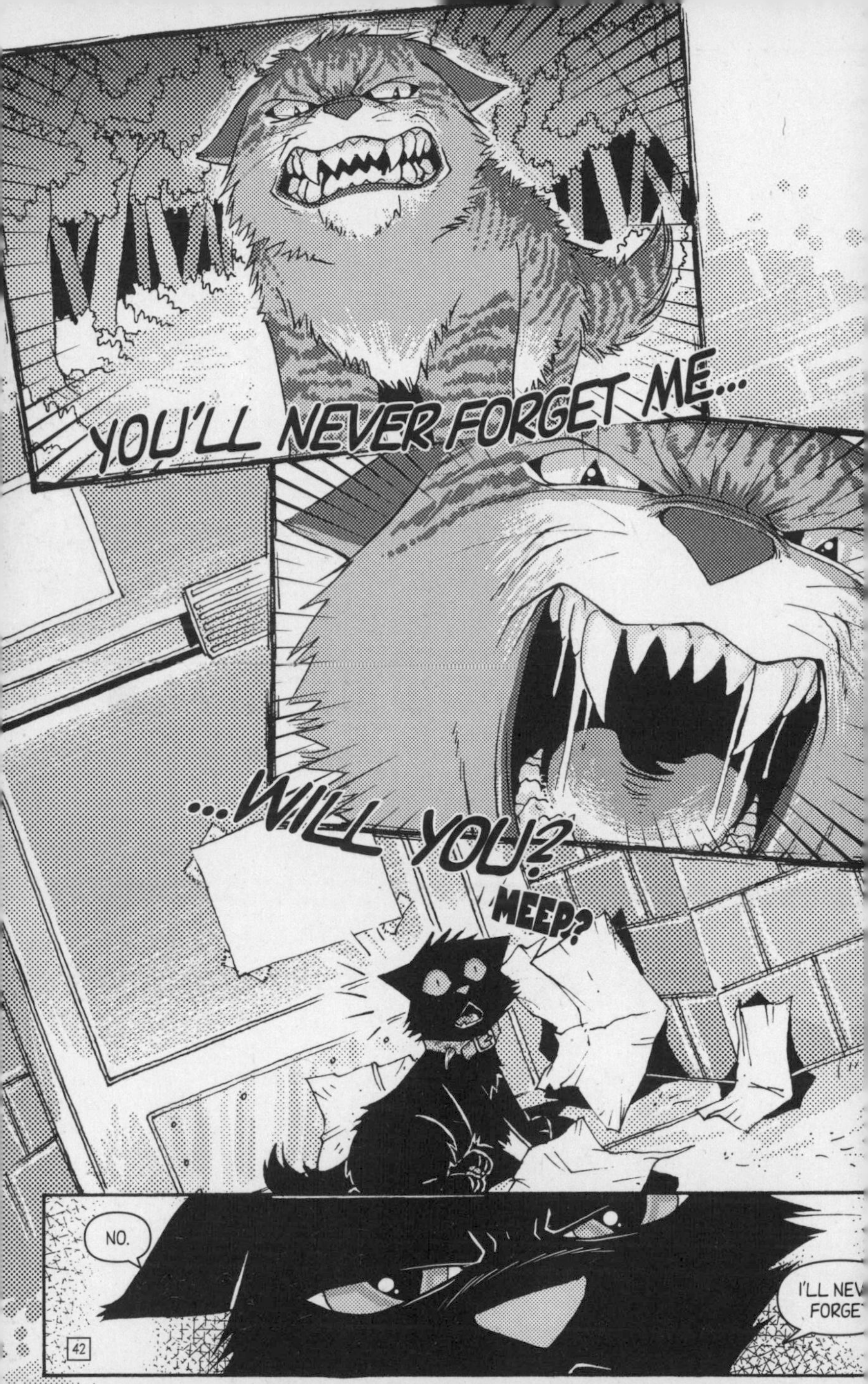
YOU'LL NEVER FORGET ME...
...WILL YOU?
MEEP?
NO.
I'LL NEV
FORGE

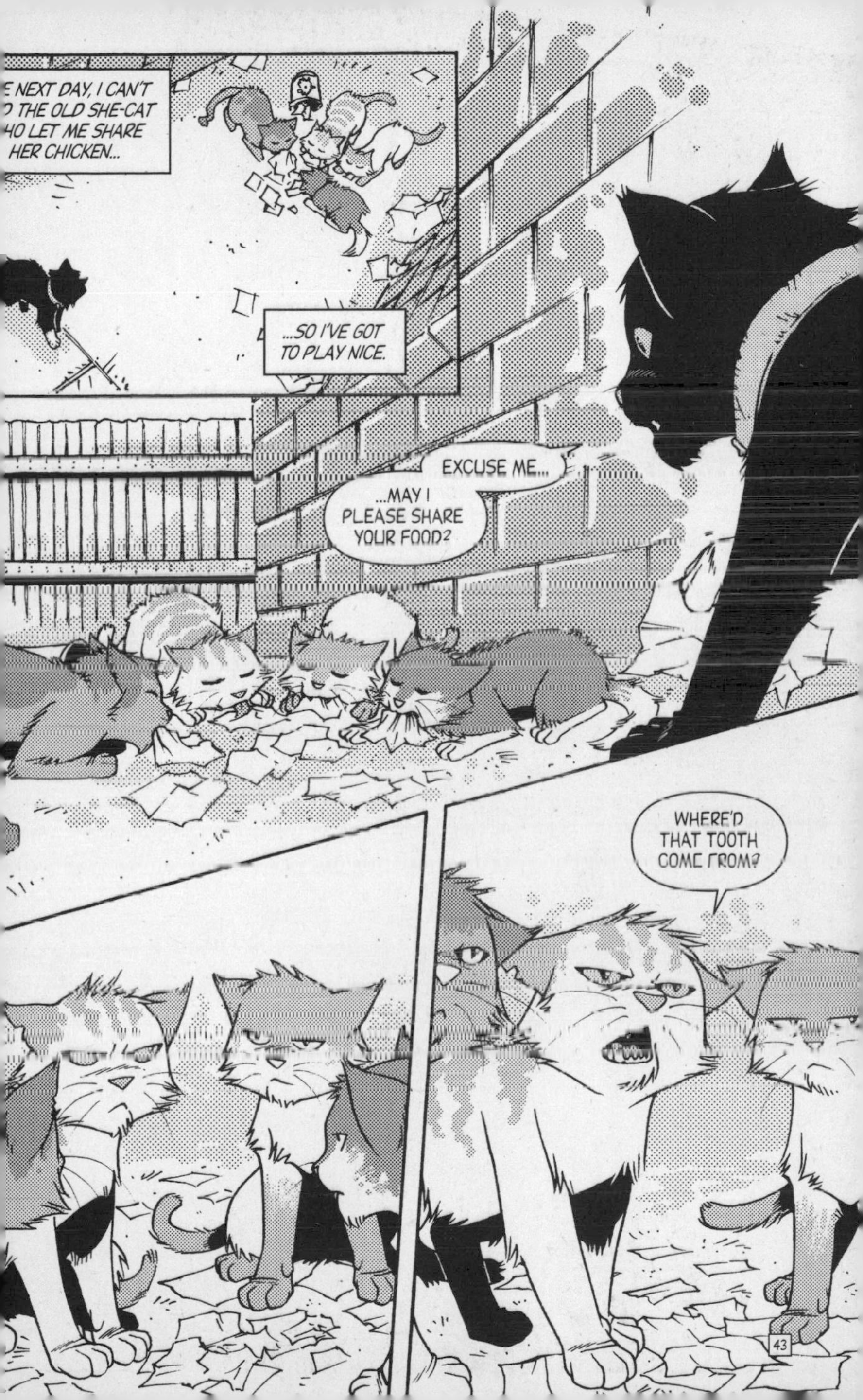
E NEXT DAY, I CAN'T
D THE OLD SHE-CAT
HO LET ME SHARE
HER CHICKEN...
...SO I'VE GOT
TO PLAY NICE.
EXCUSE ME...
...MAY I
PLEASE SHARE
YOUR FOOD?
WHERE'D
THAT TOOTH
COME FROM?

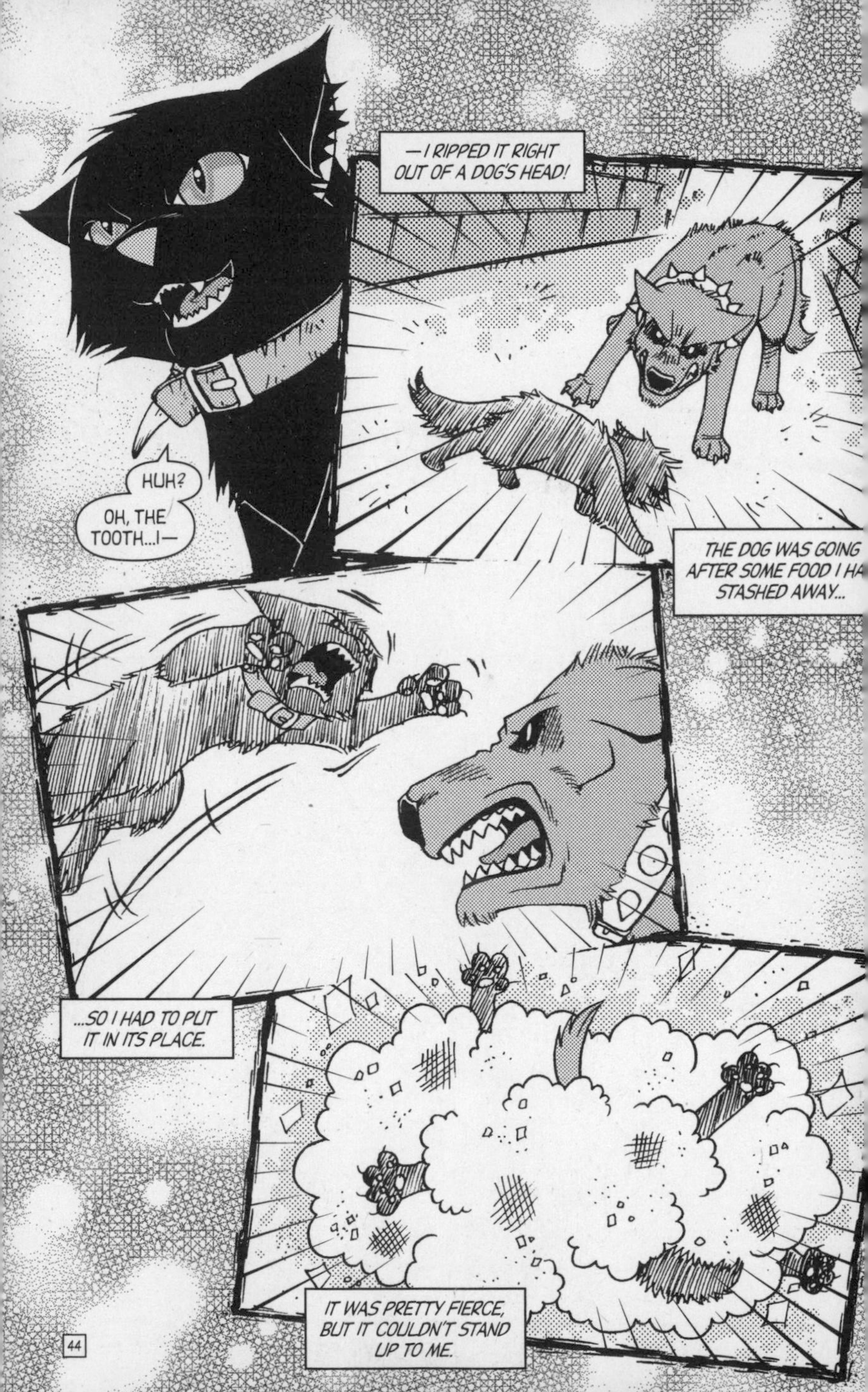
HUH? OH, THE TOOTH...I—
—I RIPPED IT RIGHT OUT OF A DOG'S HEAD!
THE DOG WAS GOING AFTER SOME FOOD I HA STASHED AWAY...
...SO I HAD TO PUT IT IN ITS PLACE.
IT WAS PRETTY FIERCE, BUT IT COULDN'T STAND UP TO ME.

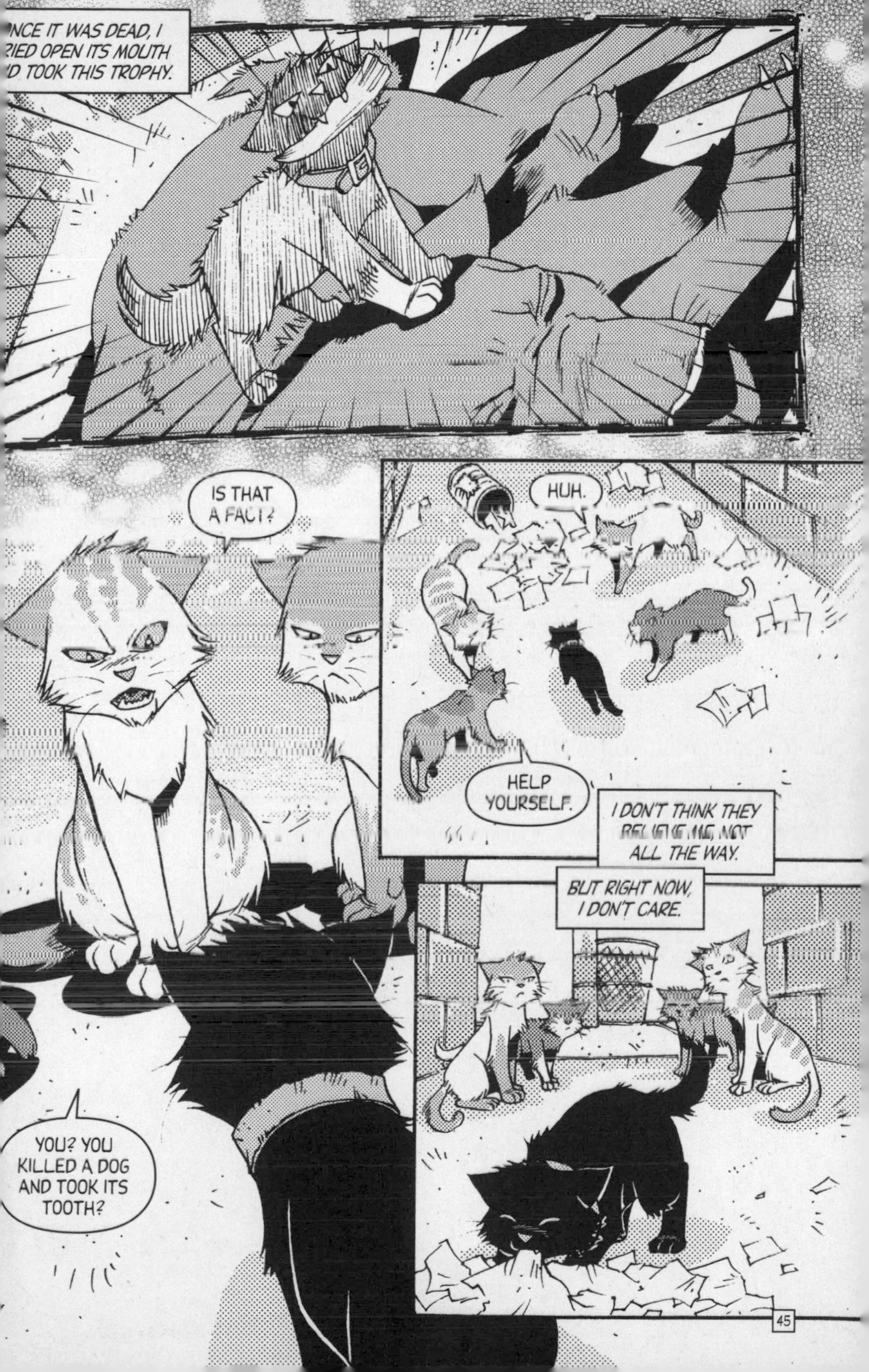

NCE IT WAS DEAD, I
RIED OPEN ITS MOUTH
D TOOK THIS TROPHY.
IS THAT A FACT?
YOU? YOU KILLED A DOG AND TOOK ITS TOOTH?
HUH.
HELP YOURSELF.
I DON'T THINK THEY BELIEVE ME, NOT ALL THE WAY.
BUT RIGHT NOW, I DON'T CARE.

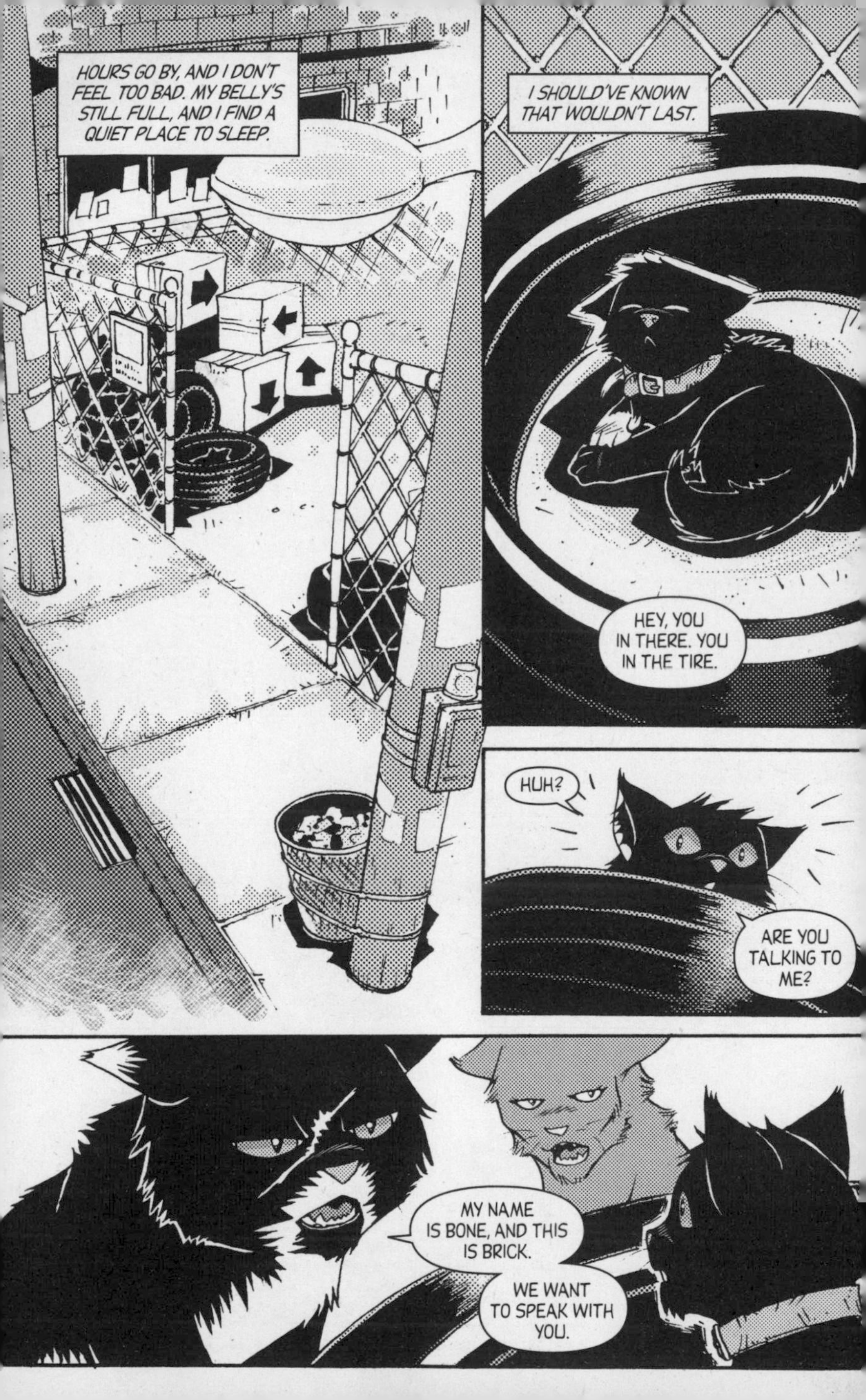
HOURS GO BY, AND I DON'T FEEL TOO BAD. MY BELLY'S STILL FULL, AND I FIND A QUIET PLACE TO SLEEP.
I SHOULD'VE KNOWN THAT WOULDN'T LAST.
HEY, YOU IN THERE. YOU IN THE TIRE.
HUH?
ARE YOU TALKING TO ME?
MY NAME IS BONE, AND THIS IS BRICK.
WE WANT TO SPEAK WITH YOU.

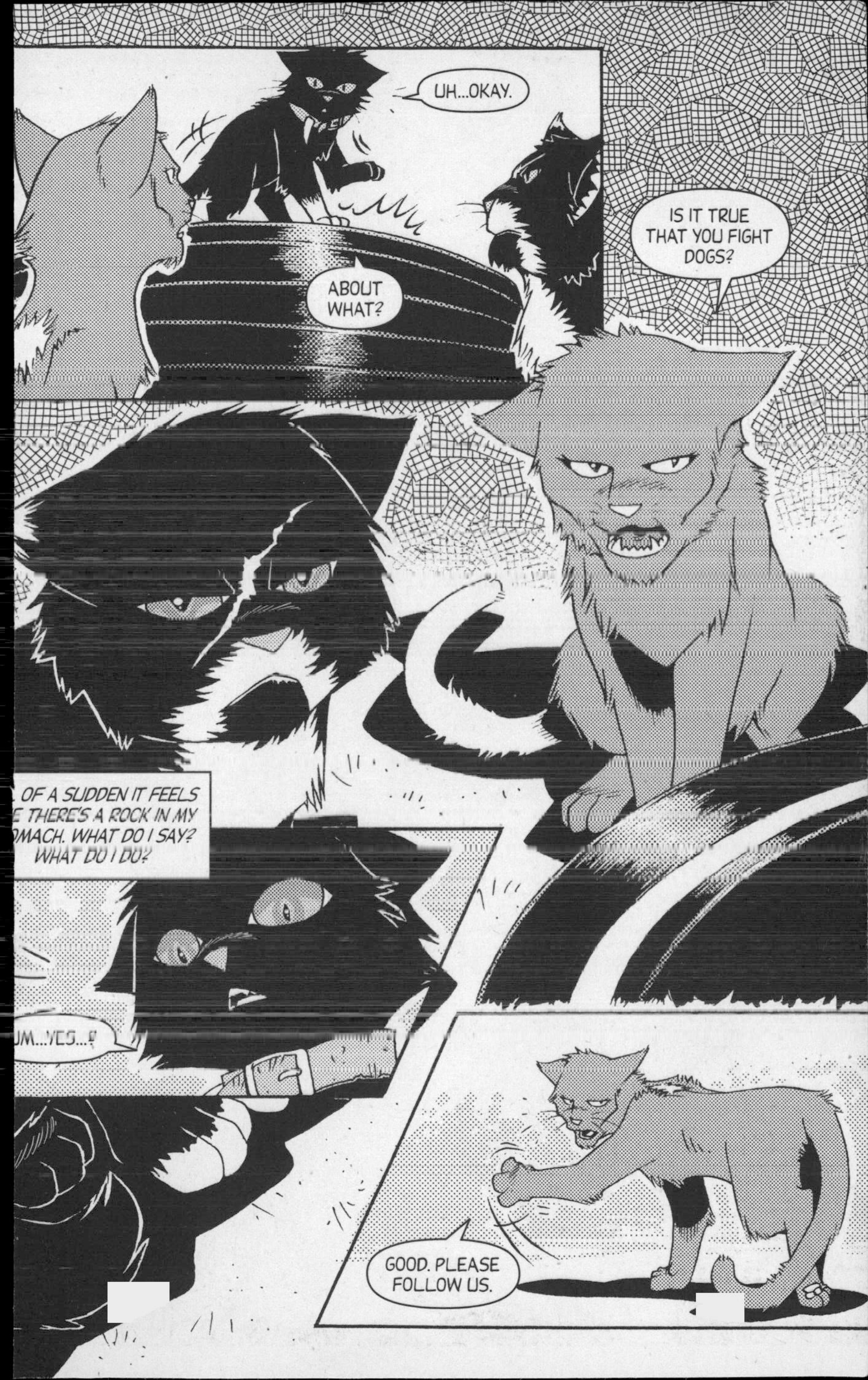
UH...OKAY.
ABOUT WHAT?
IS IT TRUE THAT YOU FIGHT DOGS?
OF A SUDDEN IT FEELS E THERE'S A ROCK IN MY OMACH. WHAT DO I SAY? WHAT DO I DO?
UM...YES...?
GOOD. PLEASE FOLLOW US.

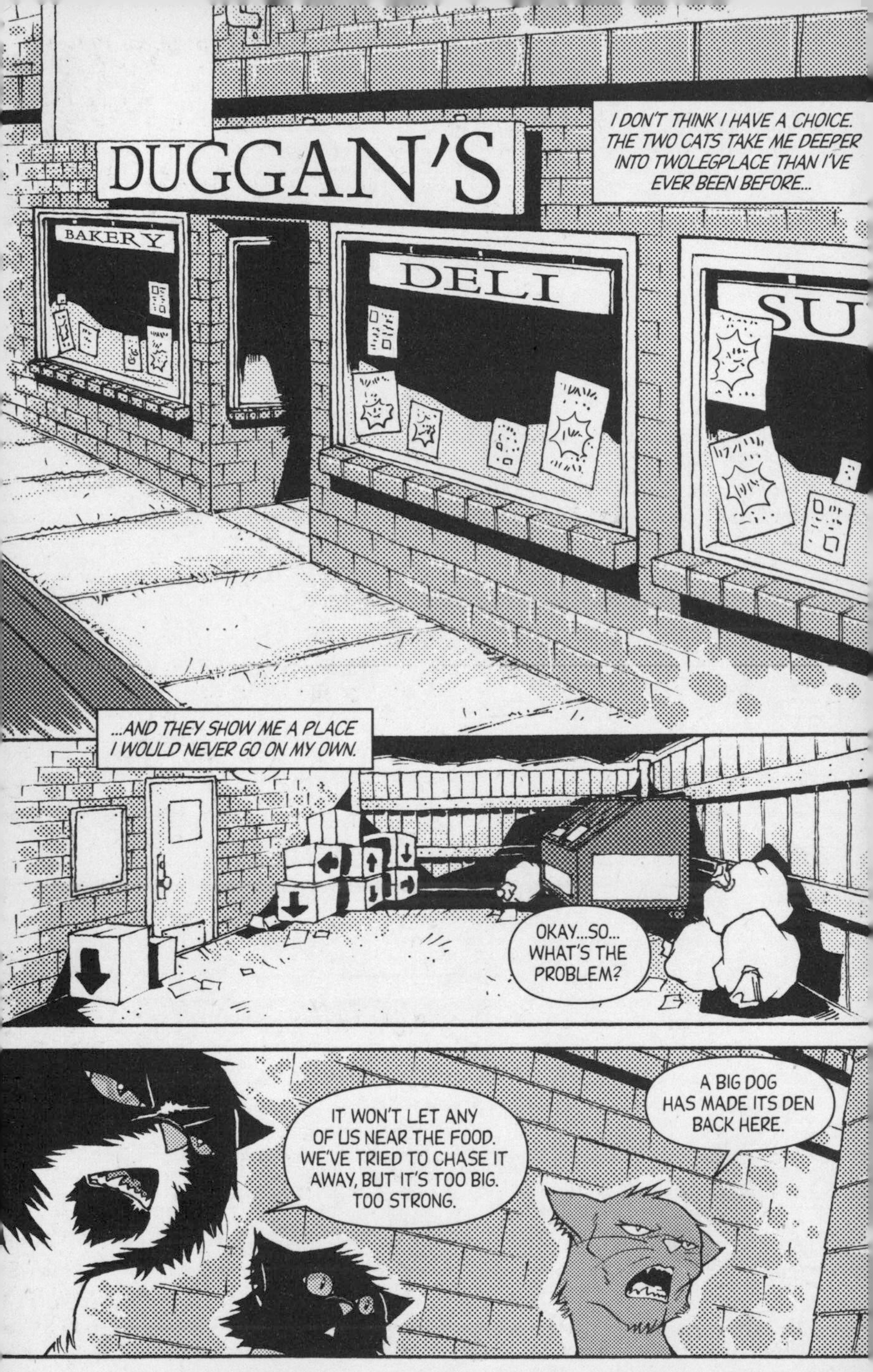
DUGGAN'S
BAKERY
DELI
SU
I DON'T THINK I HAVE A CHOICE. THE TWO CATS TAKE ME DEEPER INTO TWOLEGPLACE THAN I'VE EVER BEEN BEFORE...
...AND THEY SHOW ME A PLACE I WOULD NEVER GO ON MY OWN.
OKAY...SO... WHAT'S THE PROBLEM?
IT WON'T LET ANY OF US NEAR THE FOOD. WE'VE TRIED TO CHASE IT AWAY, BUT IT'S TOO BIG. TOO STRONG.
A BIG DOG HAS MADE ITS DEN BACK HERE.

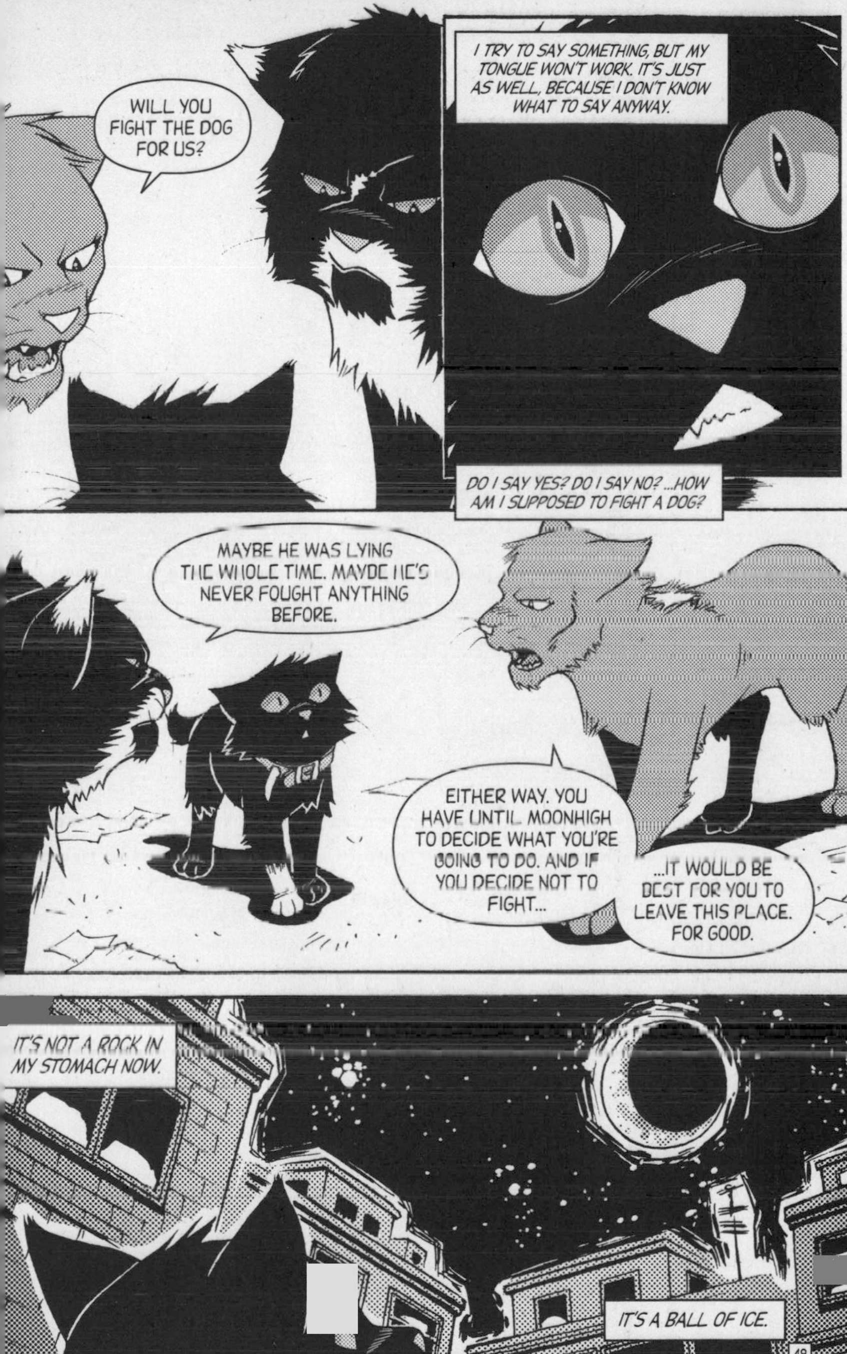
WILL YOU FIGHT THE DOG FOR US?
I TRY TO SAY SOMETHING, BUT MY TONGUE WON'T WORK. IT'S JUST AS WELL, BECAUSE I DON'T KNOW WHAT TO SAY ANYWAY.
DO I SAY YES? DO I SAY NO? ...HOW AM I SUPPOSED TO FIGHT A DOG?
MAYBE HE WAS LYING THE WHOLE TIME. MAYBE HE'S NEVER FOUGHT ANYTHING BEFORE.
EITHER WAY. YOU HAVE UNTIL MOONHIGH TO DECIDE WHAT YOU'RE GOING TO DO. AND IF YOU DECIDE NOT TO FIGHT...
...IT WOULD BE BEST FOR YOU TO LEAVE THIS PLACE. FOR GOOD.
IT'S NOT A ROCK IN MY STOMACH NOW.
IT'S A BALL OF ICE.

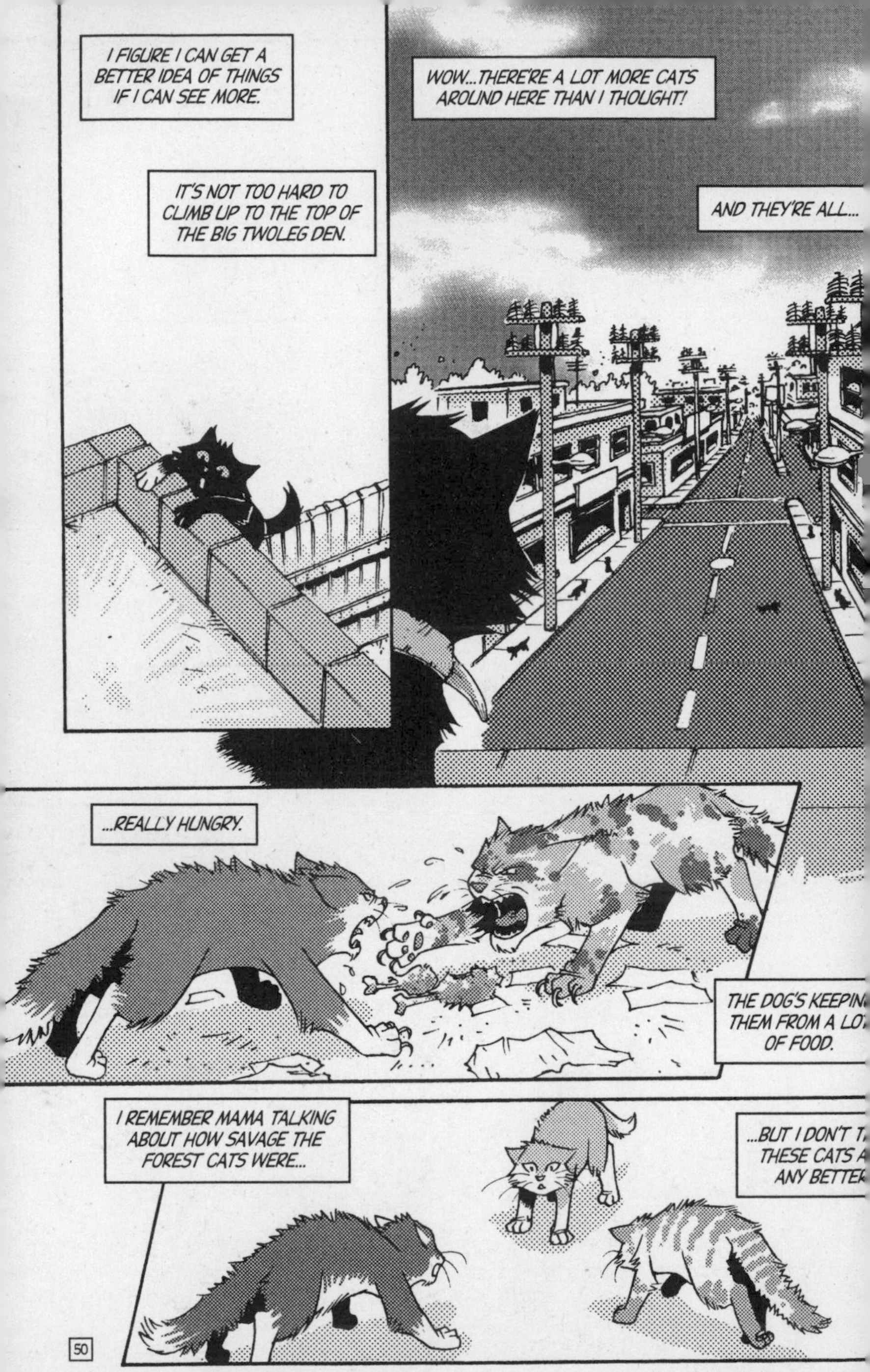
I FIGURE I CAN GET A BETTER IDEA OF THINGS IF I CAN SEE MORE.
IT'S NOT TOO HARD TO CLIMB UP TO THE TOP OF THE BIG TWOLEG DEN.
WOW...THERE'RE A LOT MORE CATS AROUND HERE THAN I THOUGHT!
AND THEY'RE ALL...
...REALLY HUNGRY.
THE DOG'S KEEPIN
THEM FROM A LO
OF FOOD.
I REMEMBER MAMA TALKING ABOUT HOW SAVAGE THE FOREST CATS WERE...
...BUT I DON'T T
THESE CATS A
ANY BETTER

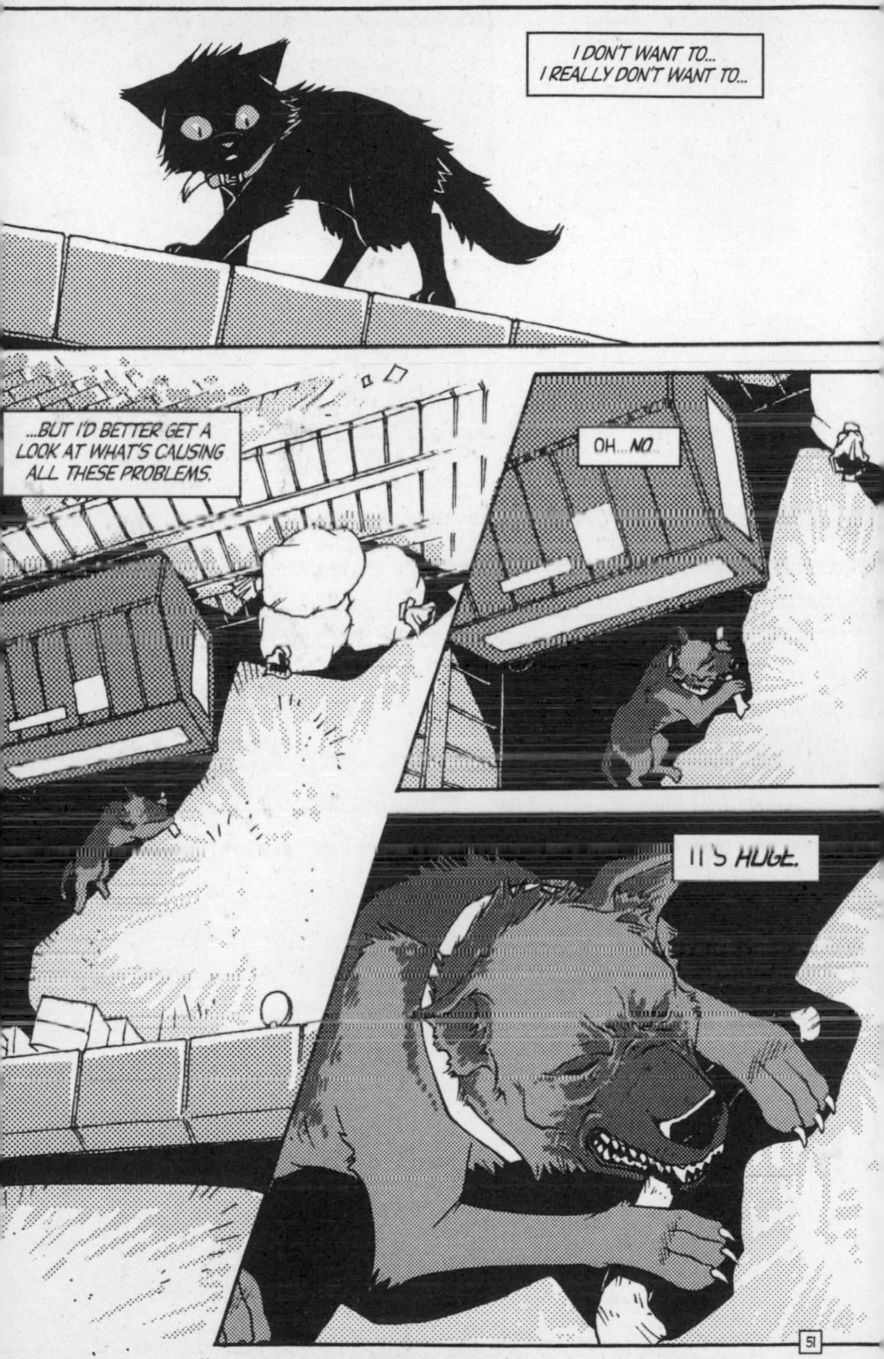
I DON'T WANT TO...
I REALLY DON'T WANT TO...
...BUT I'D BETTER GET A LOOK AT WHAT'S CAUSING ALL THESE PROBLEMS.
OH...NO.
IT'S HUGE.

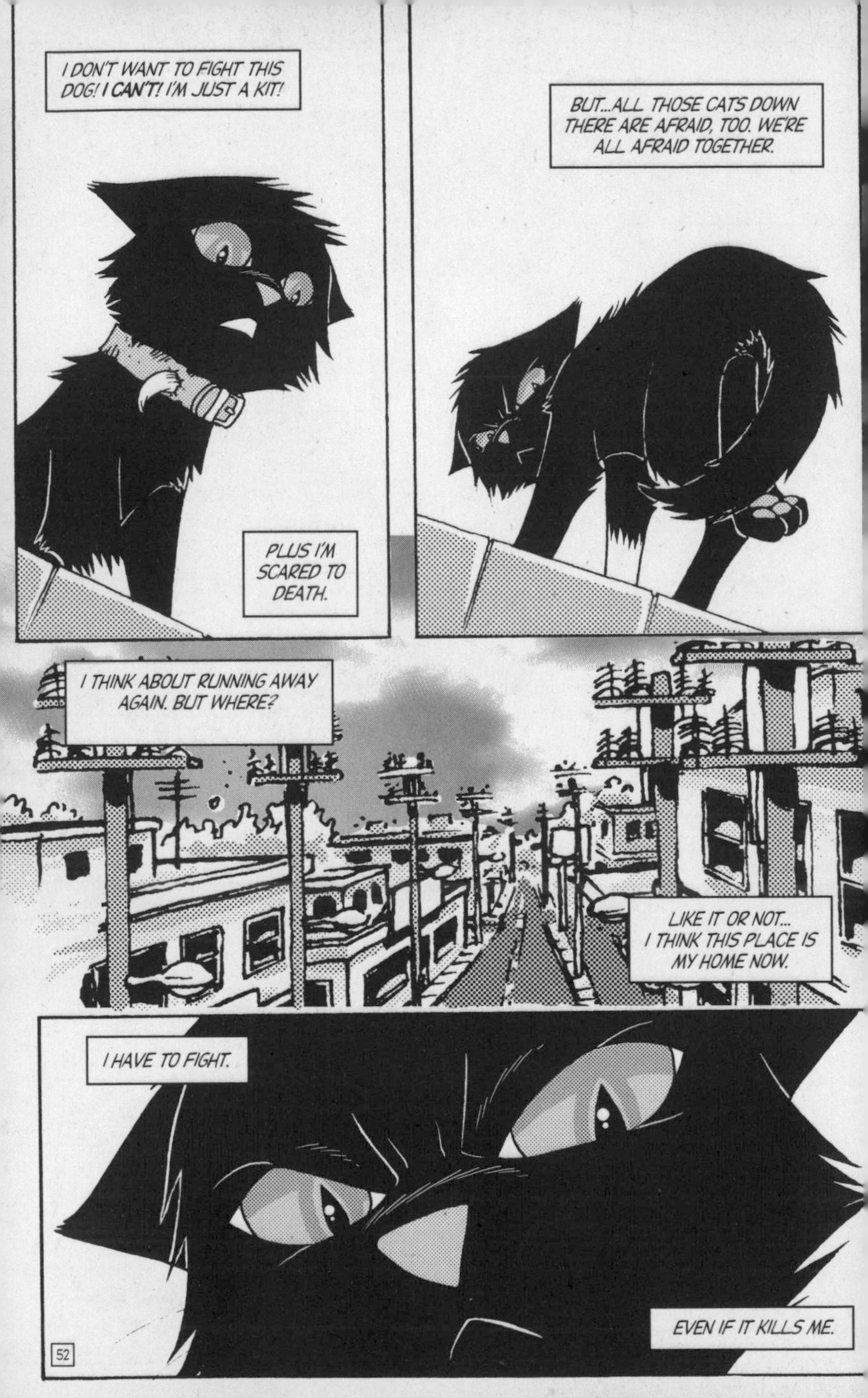

I DON'T WANT TO FIGHT THIS DOG! I CAN'T! I'M JUST A KIT!
PLUS I'M SCARED TO DEATH.
BUT...ALL THOSE CATS DOWN THERE ARE AFRAID, TOO. WE'RE ALL AFRAID TOGETHER.
I THINK ABOUT RUNNING AWAY AGAIN. BUT WHERE?
LIKE IT OR NOT... I THINK THIS PLACE IS MY HOME NOW.
I HAVE TO FIGHT.
EVEN IF IT KILLS ME.

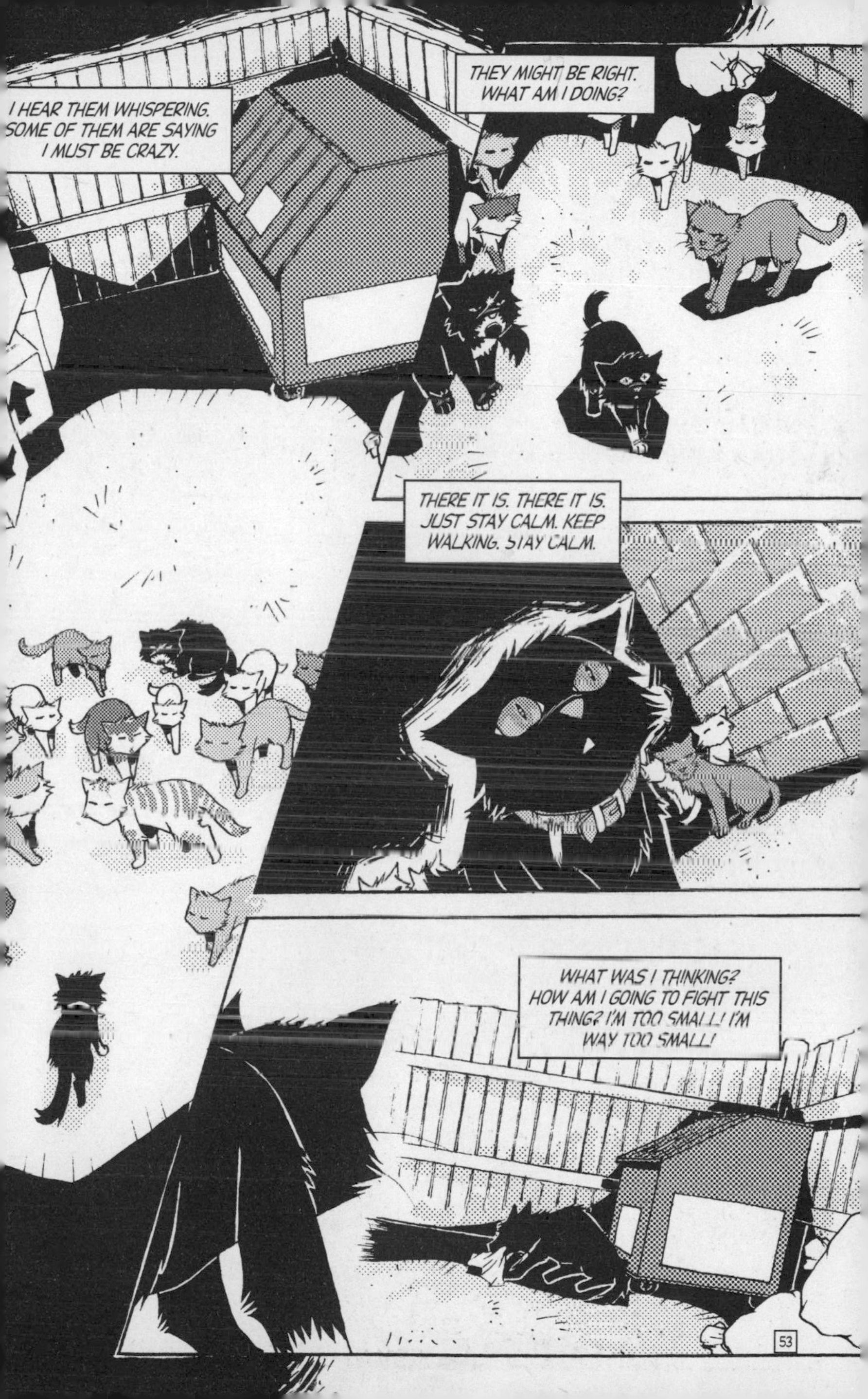
I HEAR THEM WHISPERING. SOME OF THEM ARE SAYING I MUST BE CRAZY.
THEY MIGHT BE RIGHT. WHAT AM I DOING?
THERE IT IS. THERE IT IS. JUST STAY CALM. KEEP WALKING. STAY CALM.
WHAT WAS I THINKING? HOW AM I GOING TO FIGHT THIS THING? I'M TOO SMALL! I'M WAY TOO SMALL!

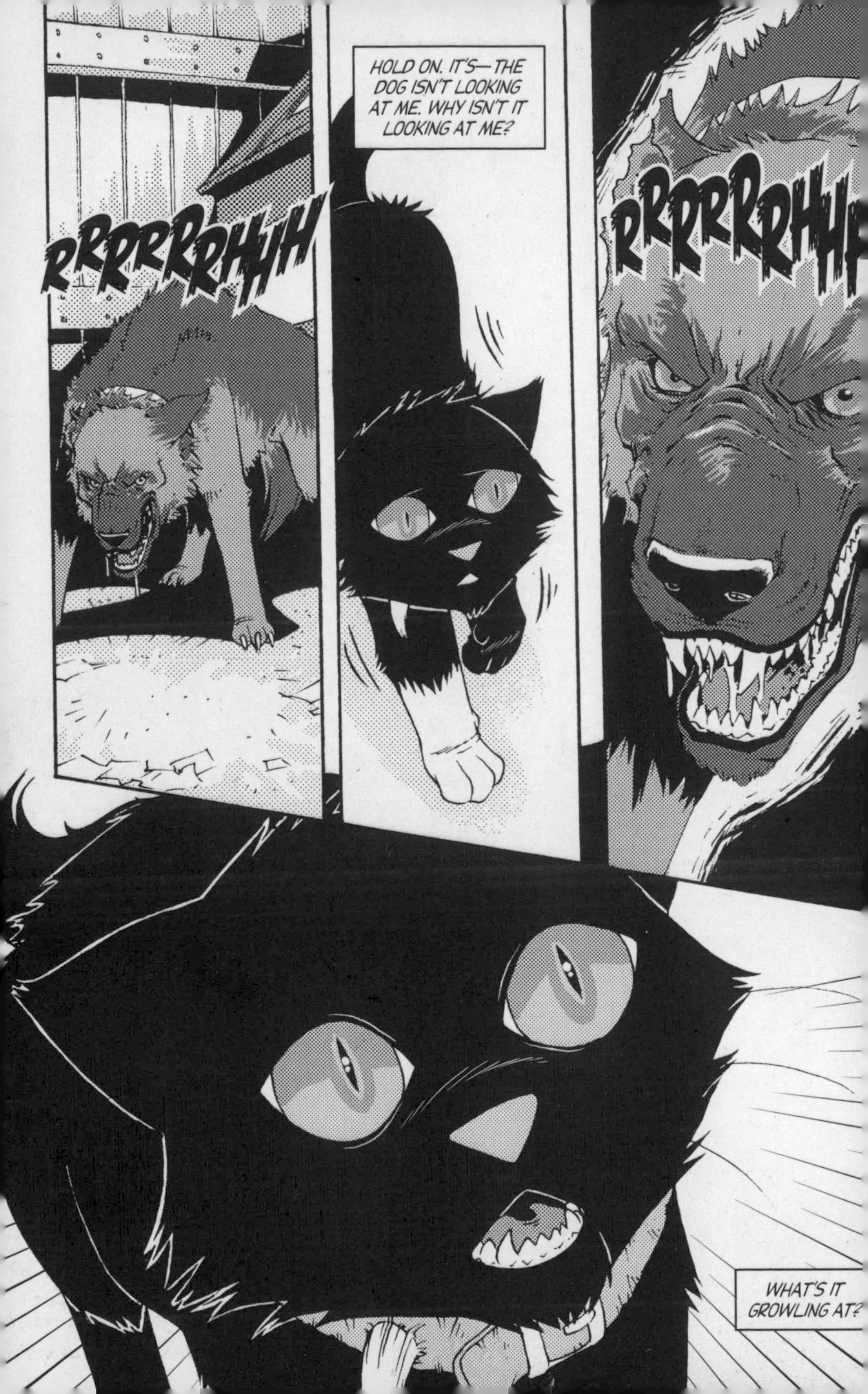
RRRRRRHHH
HOLD ON. IT'S—THE DOG ISN'T LOOKING AT ME. WHY ISN'T IT LOOKING AT ME?
RRRRRRHHH
WHAT'S IT GROWLING AT?

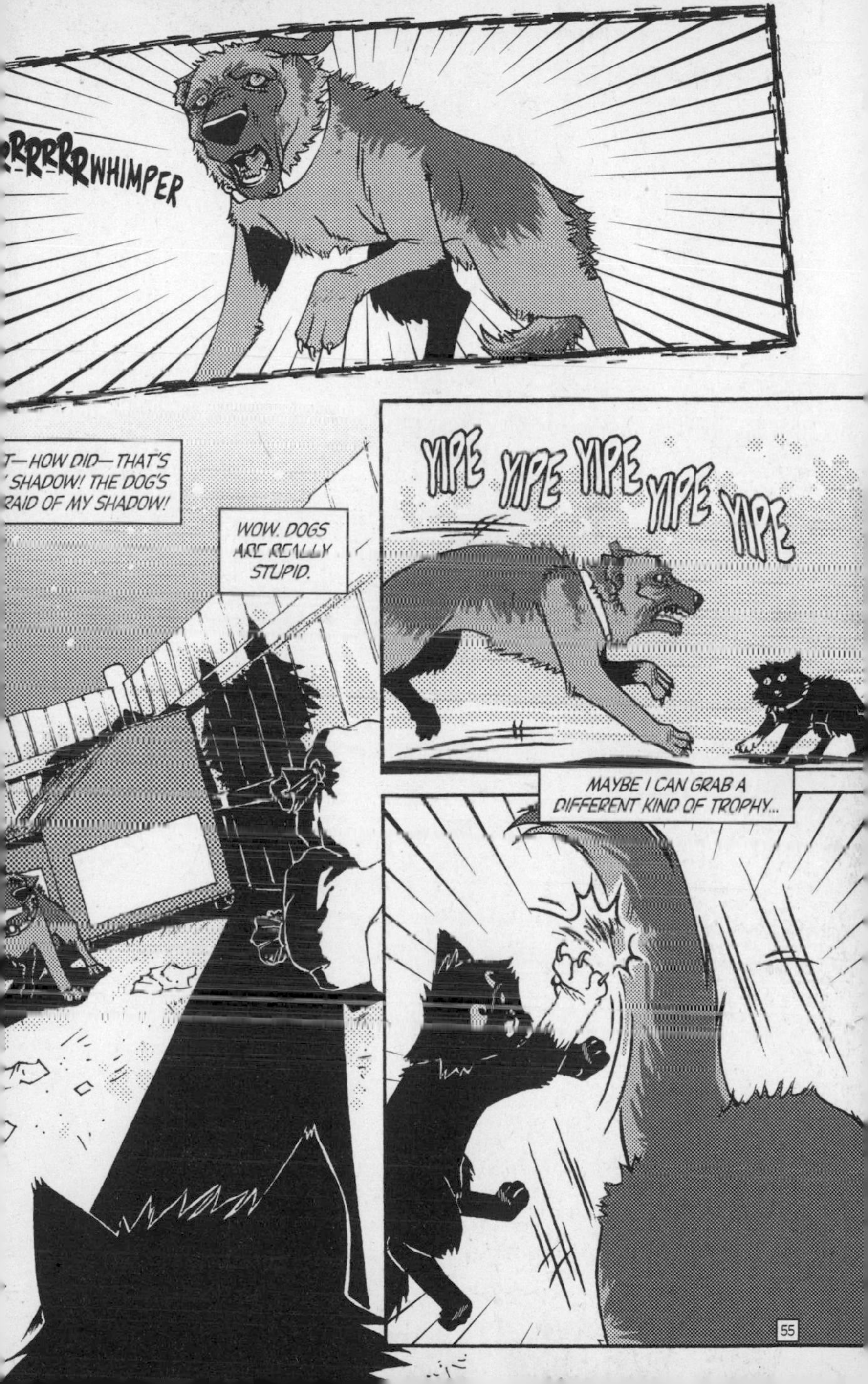
RRRRRRWHIMPER
T—HOW DID—THAT'S
' SHADOW! THE DOG'S
RAID OF MY SHADOW!
WOW. DOGS ARE REALLY STUPID.
YIPE YIPE YIPE YIPE YIPE
MAYBE I CAN GRAB A DIFFERENT KIND OF TROPHY...

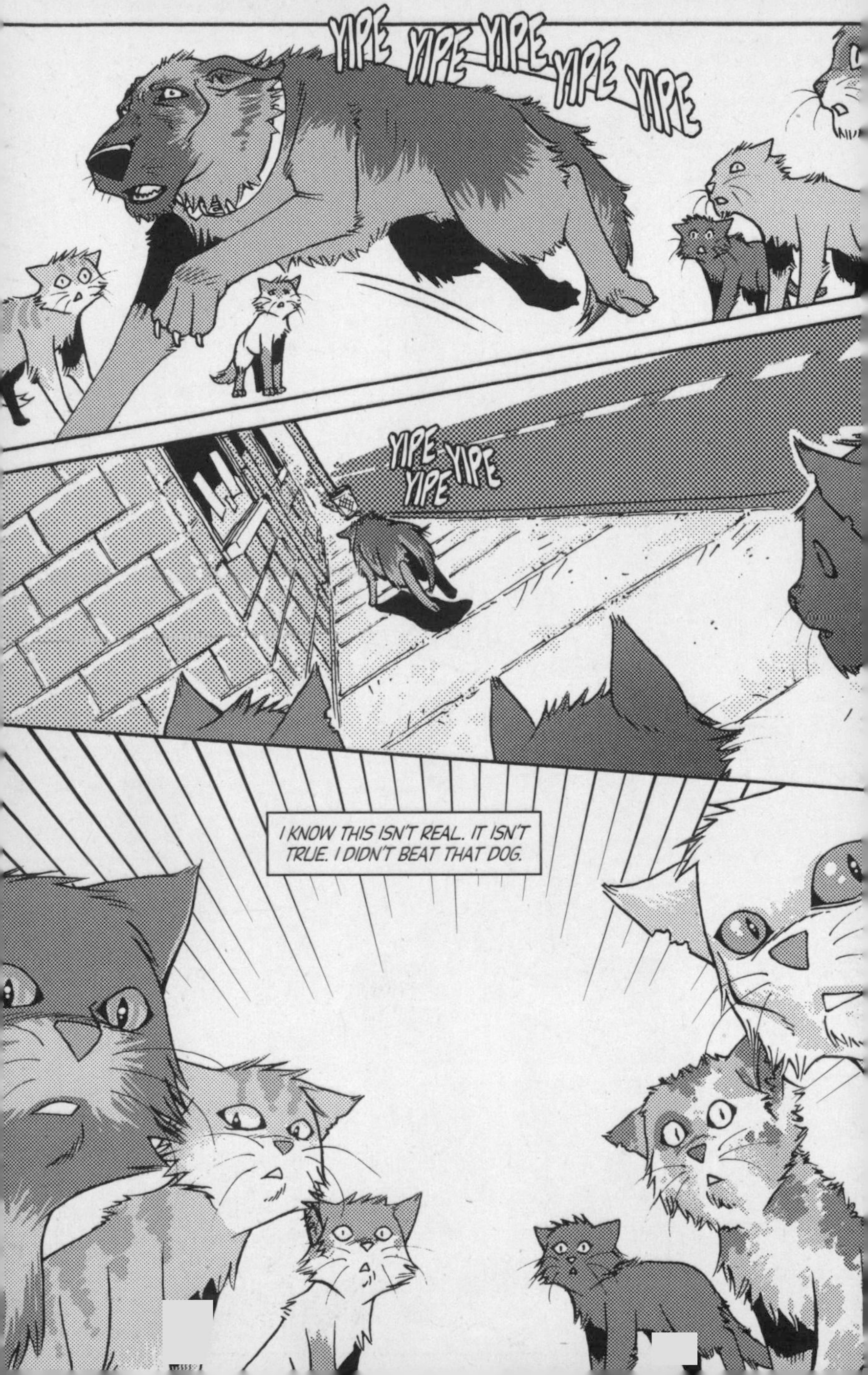
YIPE YIPE YIPE YIPE YIPE
YIPE YIPE YIPE
I KNOW THIS ISN'T REAL. IT ISN'T TRUE. I DIDN'T BEAT THAT DOG.

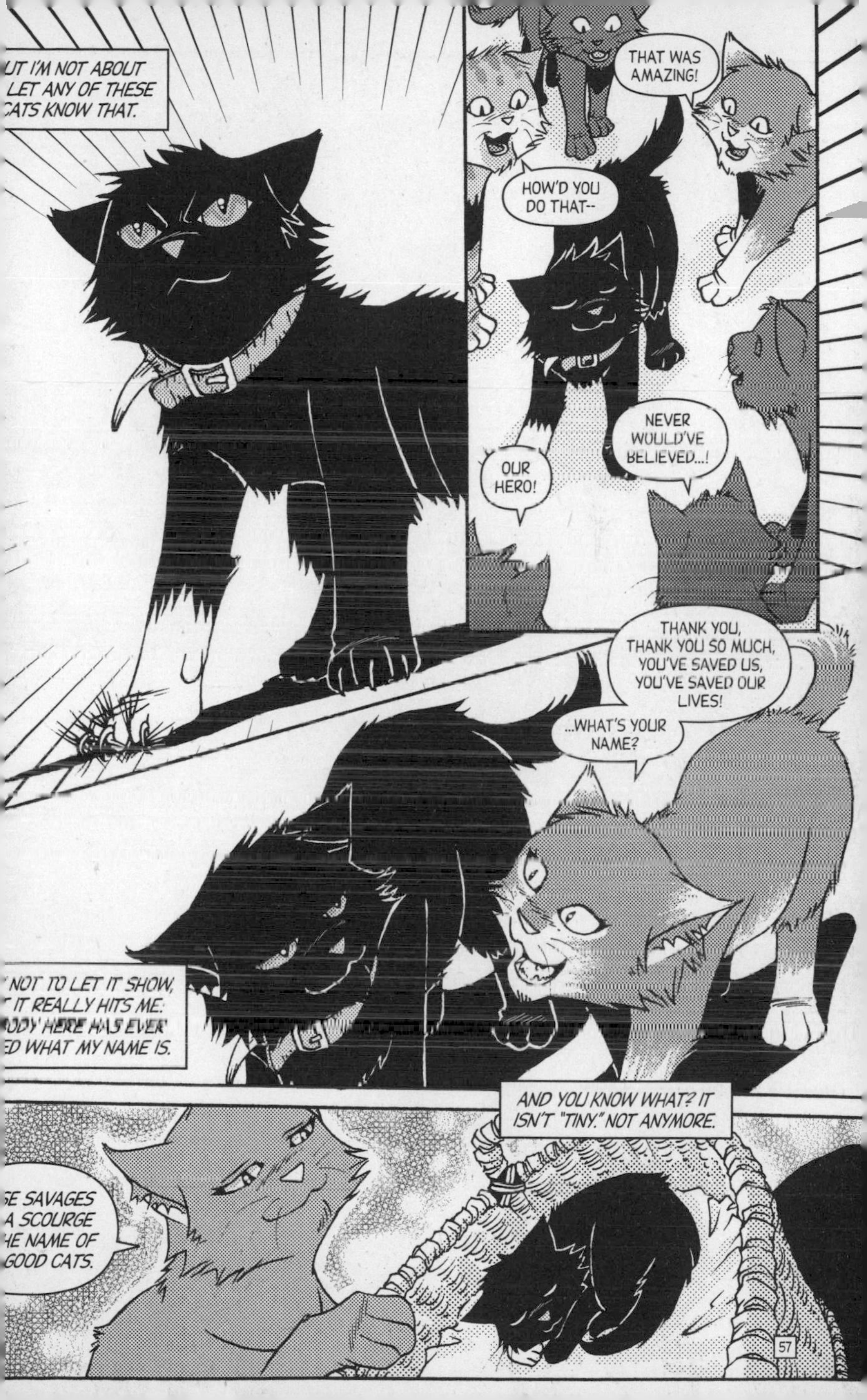
UT I'M NOT ABOUT LET ANY OF THESE CATS KNOW THAT.
THAT WAS AMAZING!
HOW'D YOU DO THAT--
NEVER WOULD'VE BELIEVED...!
OUR HERO!
THANK YOU, THANK YOU SO MUCH, YOU'VE SAVED US, YOU'VE SAVED OUR LIVES!
...WHAT'S YOUR NAME?
NOT TO LET IT SHOW, IT REALLY HITS ME: ODY HERE HAS EVER ED WHAT MY NAME IS.
AND YOU KNOW WHAT? IT ISN'T "TINY." NOT ANYMORE.
SE SAVAGES A SCOURGE HE NAME OF GOOD CATS.

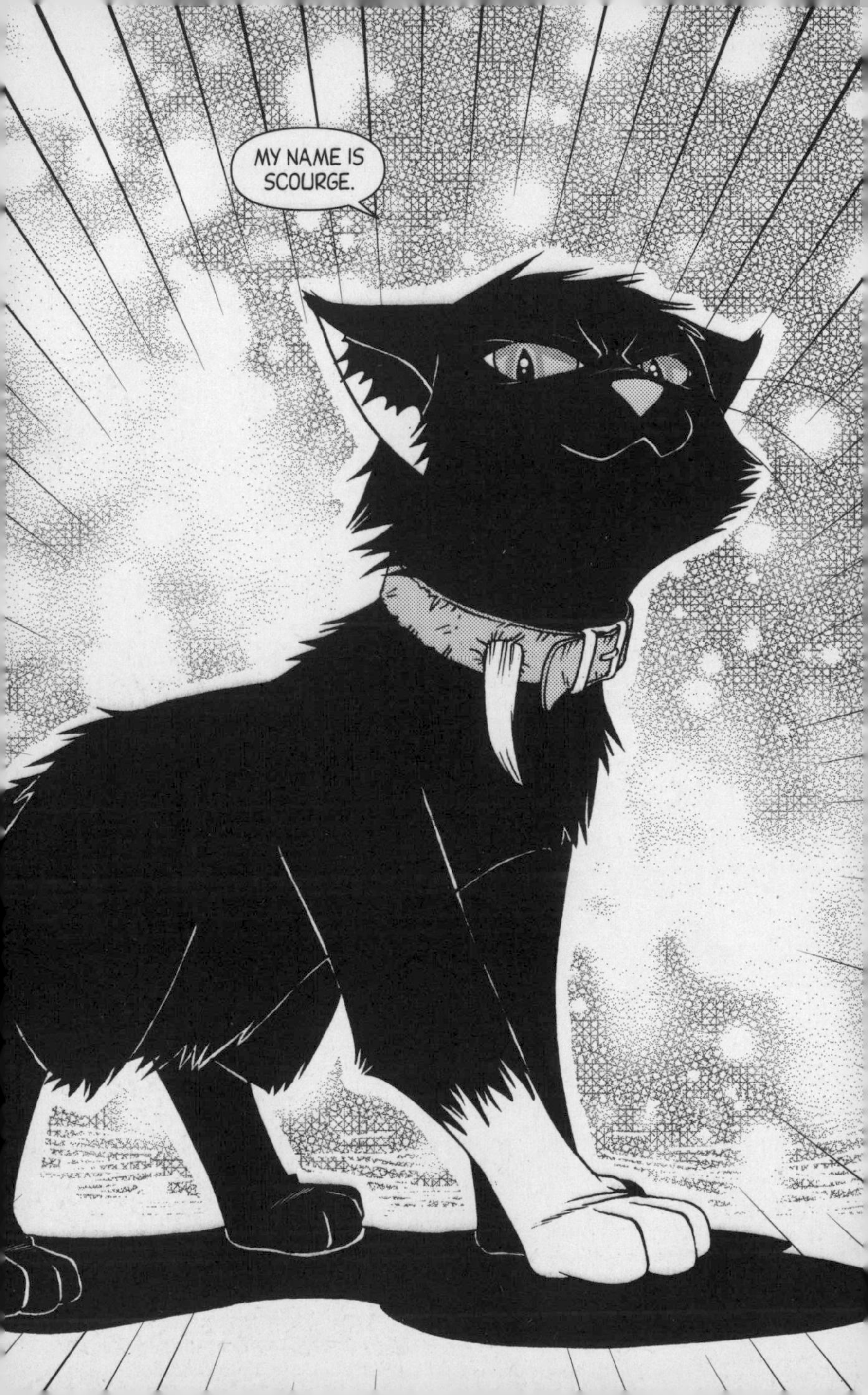
MY NAME IS SCOURGE.

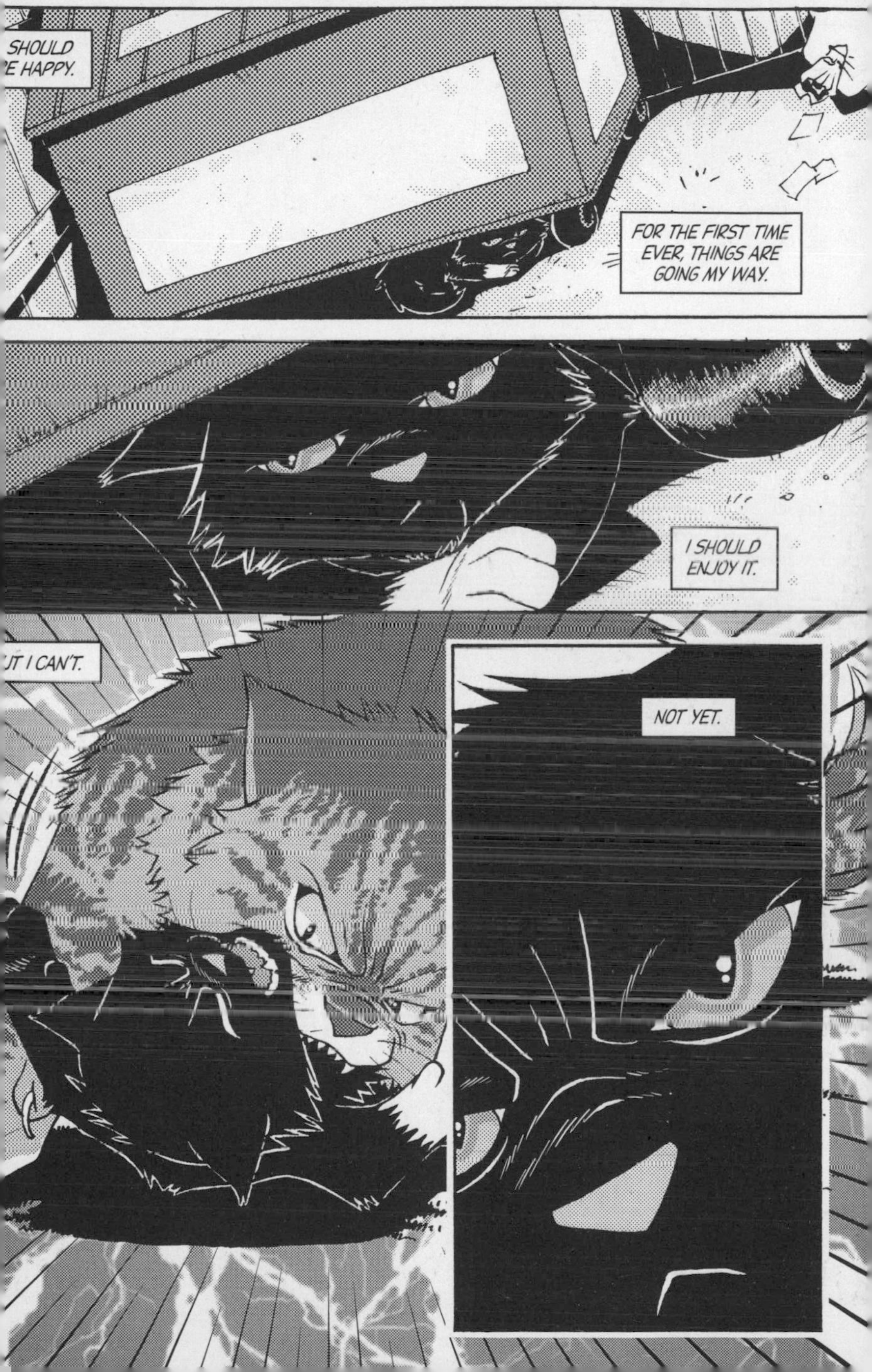
SHOULD
E HAPPY.
FOR THE FIRST TIME EVER, THINGS ARE GOING MY WAY.
I SHOULD ENJOY IT.
UT I CAN'T.
NOT YET.

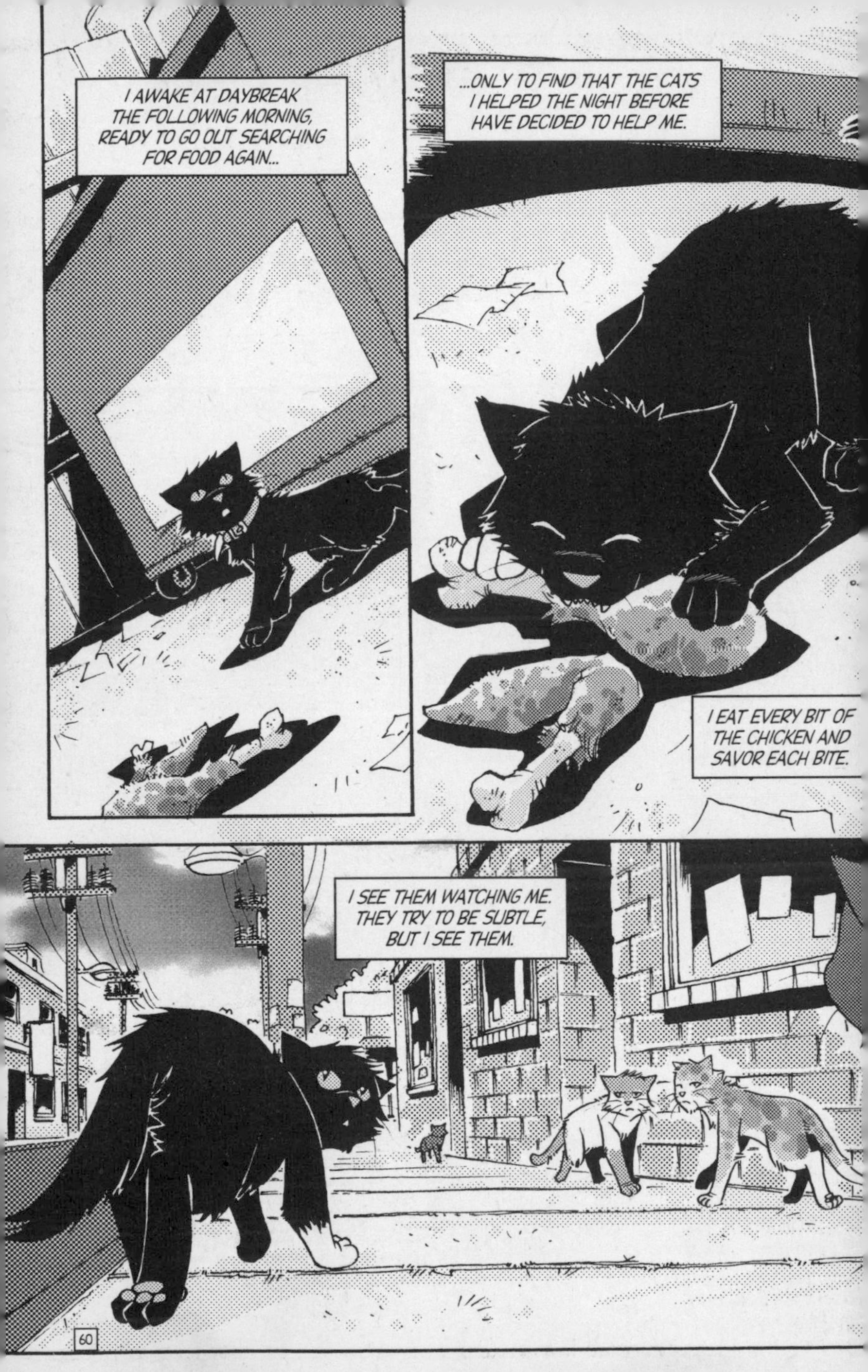
I AWAKE AT DAYBREAK THE FOLLOWING MORNING, READY TO GO OUT SEARCHING FOR FOOD AGAIN...
...ONLY TO FIND THAT THE CATS I HELPED THE NIGHT BEFORE HAVE DECIDED TO HELP ME.
I EAT EVERY BIT OF THE CHICKEN AND SAVOR EACH BITE.
I SEE THEM WATCHING ME. THEY TRY TO BE SUBTLE, BUT I SEE THEM.

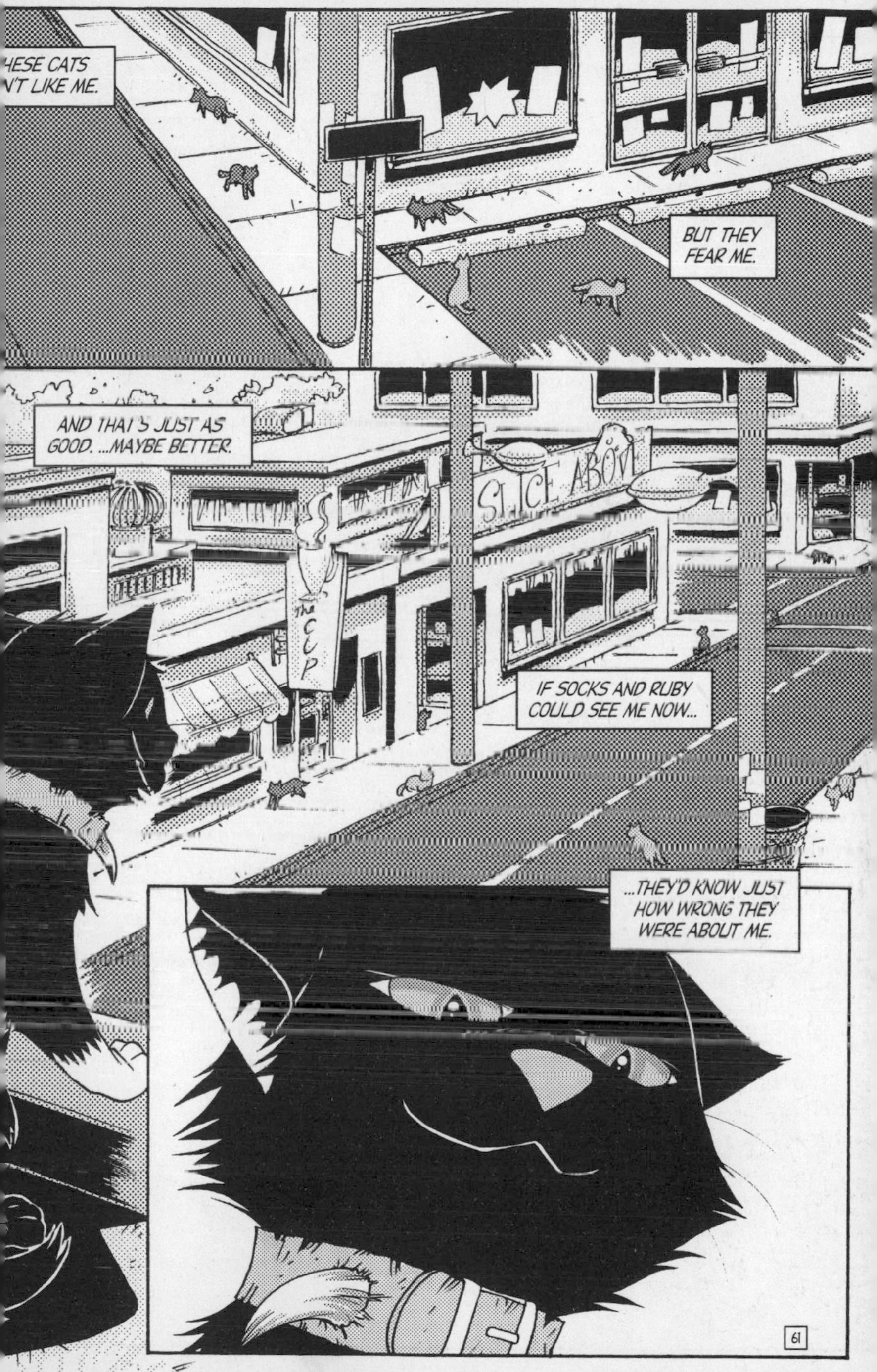
HESE CATS
N'T LIKE ME.
BUT THEY FEAR ME.
AND THAT'S JUST AS GOOD. ...MAYBE BETTER.
SLICE ABOVE
The CUP
IF SOCKS AND RUBY COULD SEE ME NOW...
...THEY'D KNOW JUST HOW WRONG THEY WERE ABOUT ME.
61

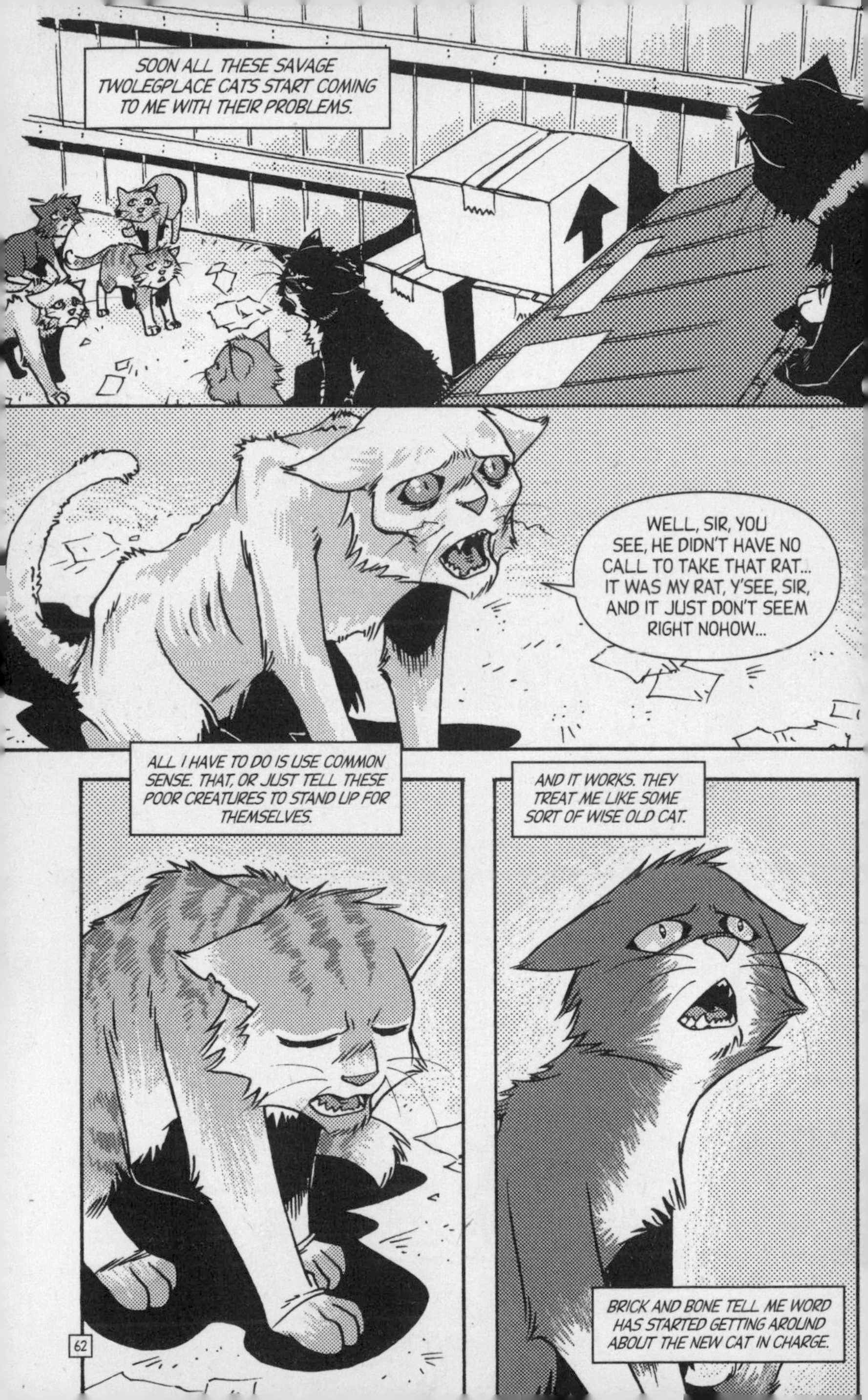
SOON ALL THESE SAVAGE TWOLEGPLACE CATS START COMING TO ME WITH THEIR PROBLEMS.
WELL, SIR, YOU SEE, HE DIDN'T HAVE NO CALL TO TAKE THAT RAT... IT WAS MY RAT, Y'SEE, SIR, AND IT JUST DON'T SEEM RIGHT NOHOW...
ALL I HAVE TO DO IS USE COMMON SENSE. THAT, OR JUST TELL THESE POOR CREATURES TO STAND UP FOR THEMSELVES.
AND IT WORKS. THEY TREAT ME LIKE SOME SORT OF WISE OLD CAT.
BRICK AND BONE TELL ME WORD HAS STARTED GETTING AROUND ABOUT THE NEW CAT IN CHARGE.

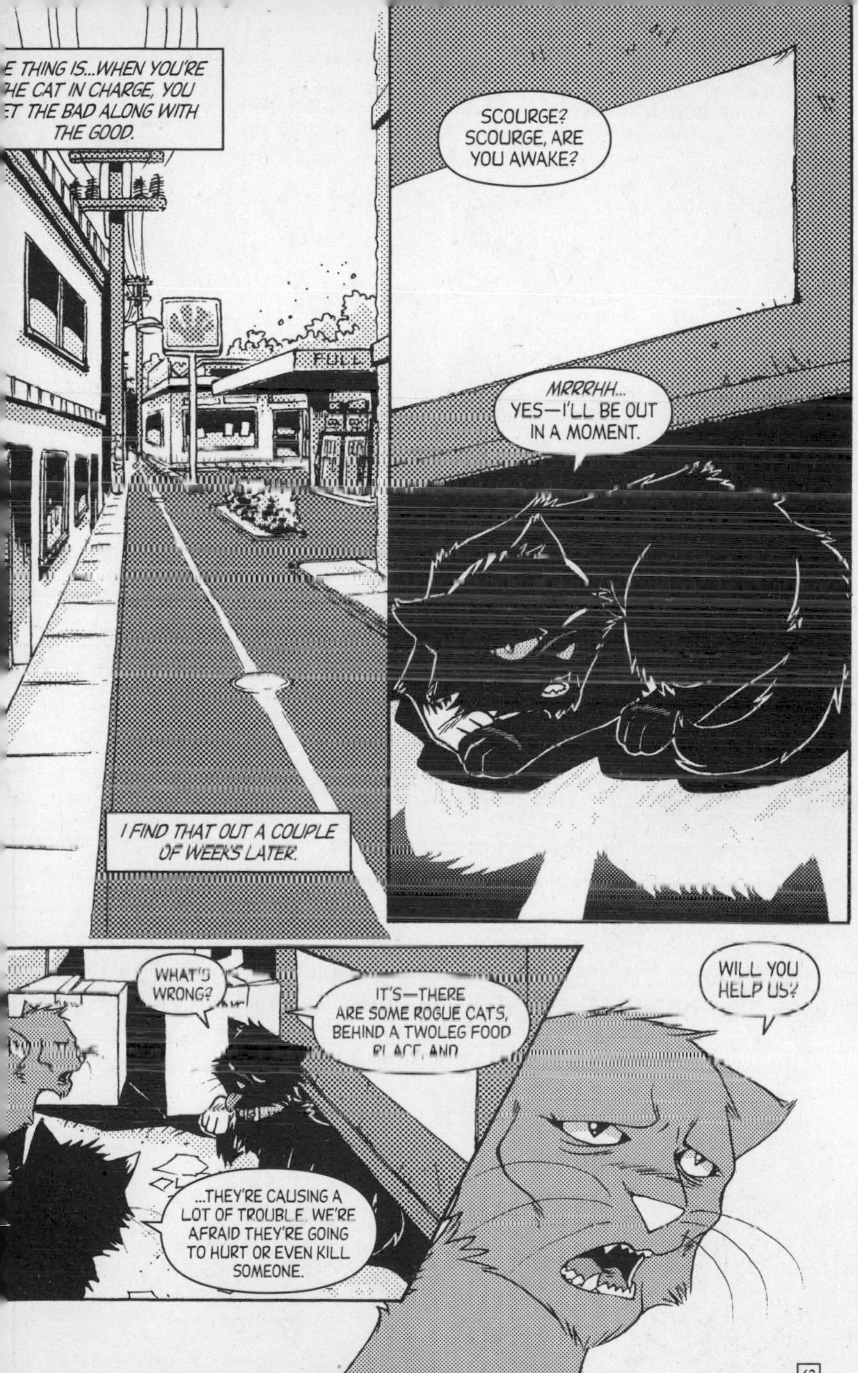
E THING IS...WHEN YOU'RE HE CAT IN CHARGE, YOU ET THE BAD ALONG WITH THE GOOD.
I FIND THAT OUT A COUPLE OF WEEKS LATER.
SCOURGE? SCOURGE, ARE YOU AWAKE?
MRRRHH... YES—I'LL BE OUT IN A MOMENT.
FULL
WHAT'S WRONG?
IT'S—THERE ARE SOME ROGUE CATS, BEHIND A TWOLEG FOOD PLACE, AND
...THEY'RE CAUSING A LOT OF TROUBLE. WE'RE AFRAID THEY'RE GOING TO HURT OR EVEN KILL SOMEONE.
WILL YOU HELP US?

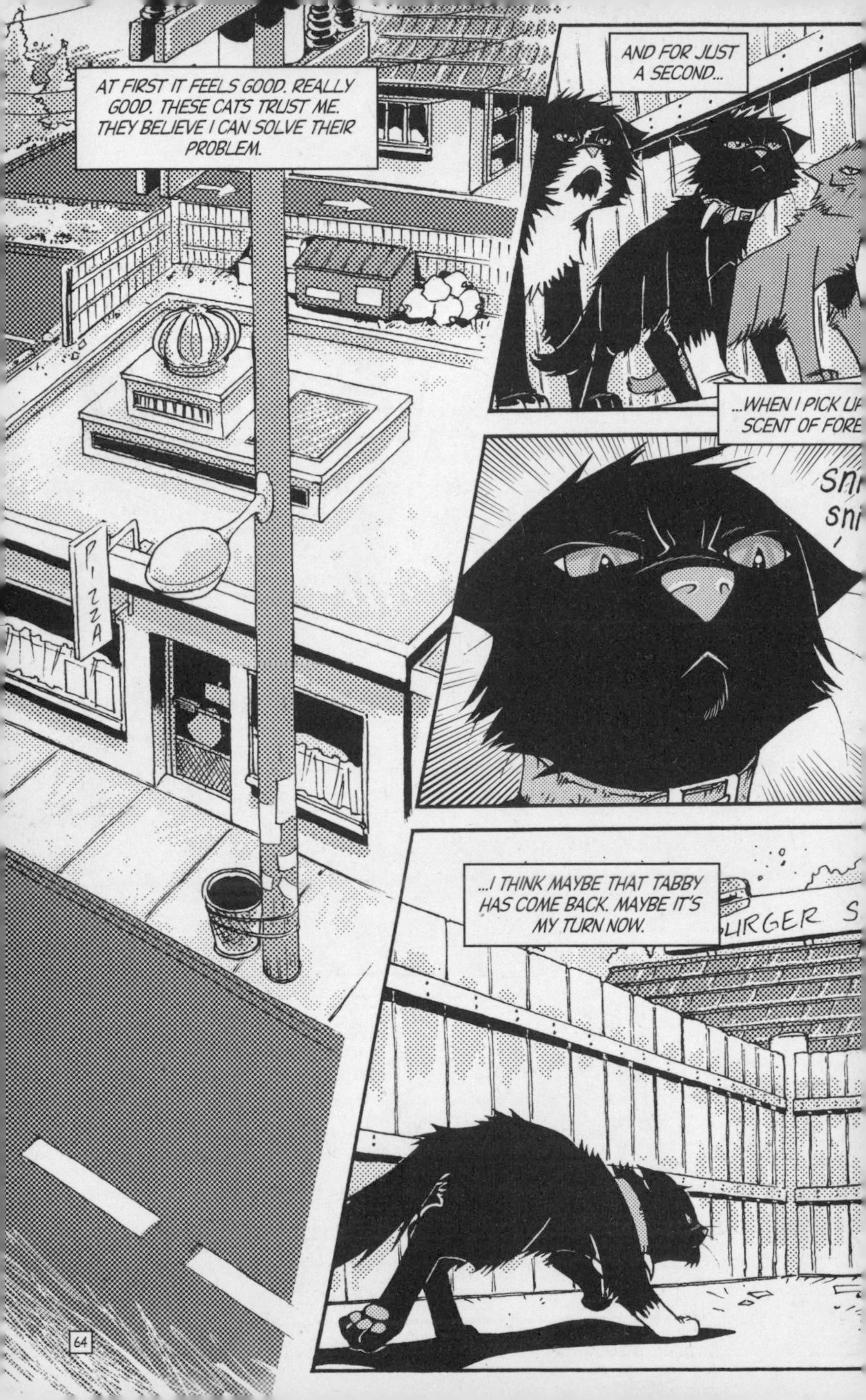
AT FIRST IT FEELS GOOD. REALLY GOOD. THESE CATS TRUST ME. THEY BELIEVE I CAN SOLVE THEIR PROBLEM.
PIZZA
AND FOR JUST A SECOND...
...WHEN I PICK UP SCENT OF FORE
SNI
SNI
...I THINK MAYBE THAT TABBY HAS COME BACK. MAYBE IT'S MY TURN NOW.
URGER S

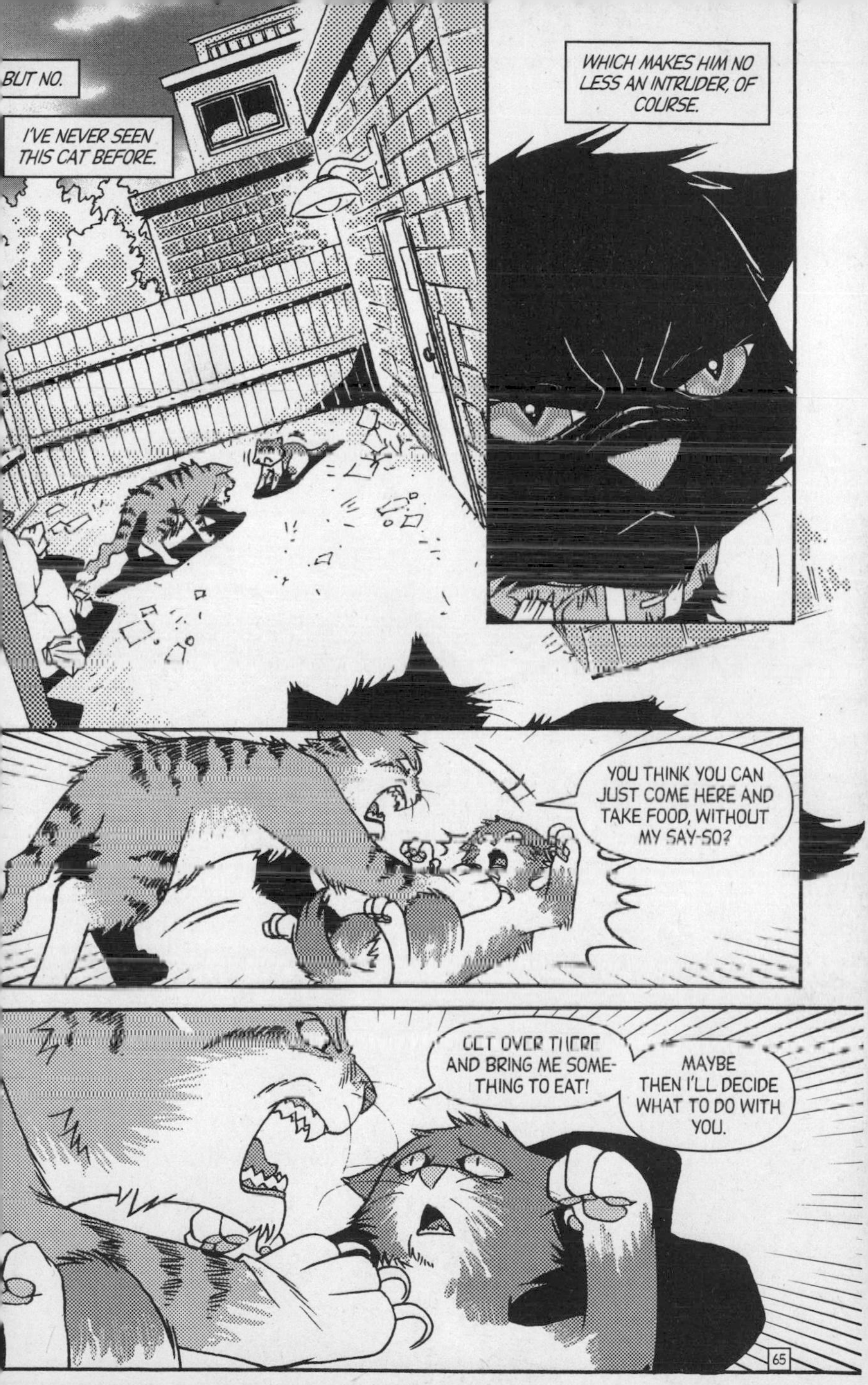
BUT NO.
I'VE NEVER SEEN THIS CAT BEFORE.
WHICH MAKES HIM NO LESS AN INTRUDER, OF COURSE.
YOU THINK YOU CAN JUST COME HERE AND TAKE FOOD, WITHOUT MY SAY-SO?
GET OVER THERE AND BRING ME SOME-THING TO EAT!
MAYBE THEN I'LL DECIDE WHAT TO DO WITH YOU.

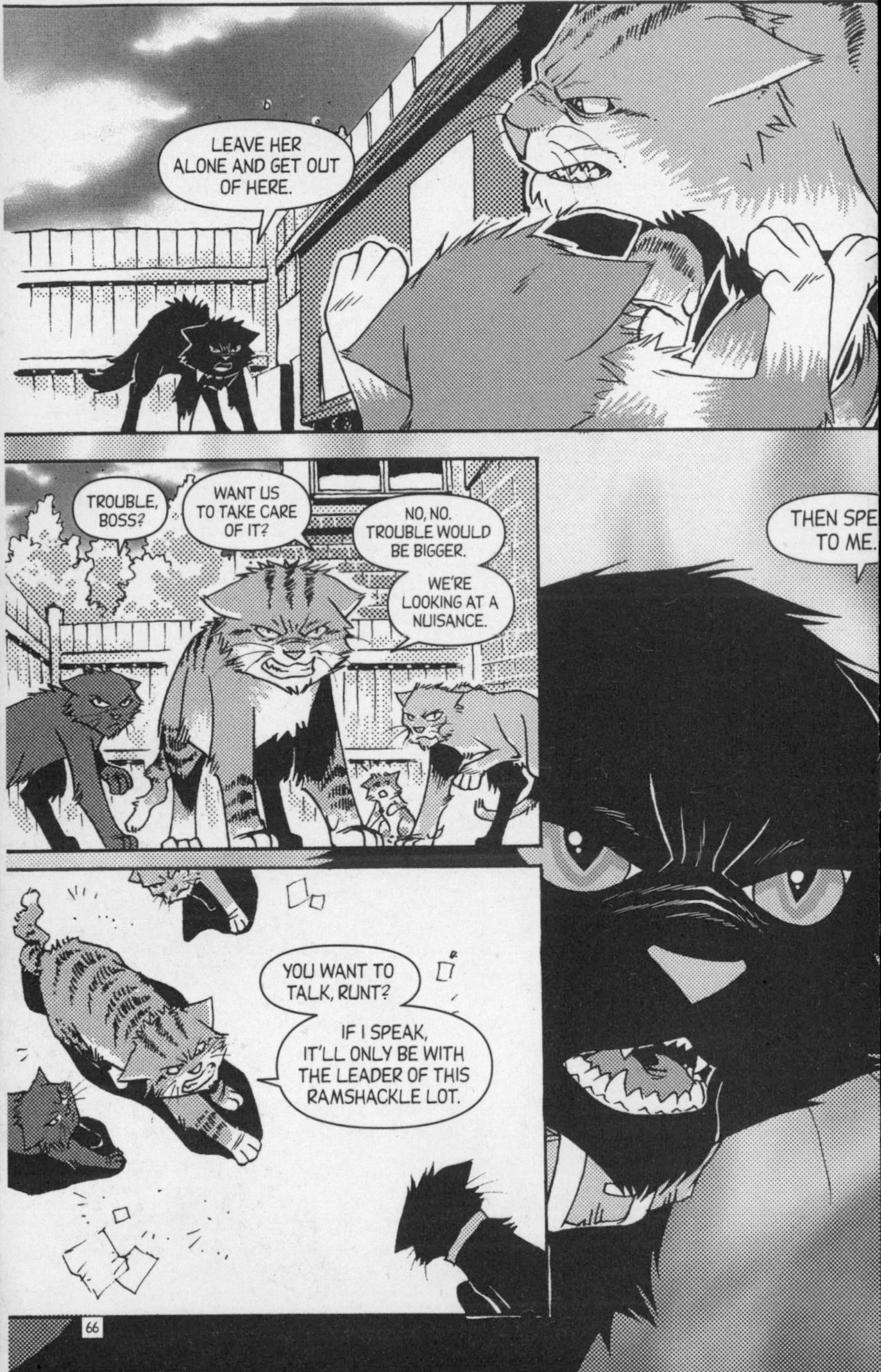
LEAVE HER ALONE AND GET OUT OF HERE.
TROUBLE, BOSS?
WANT US TO TAKE CARE OF IT?
NO, NO. TROUBLE WOULD BE BIGGER.
WE'RE LOOKING AT A NUISANCE.
YOU WANT TO TALK, RUNT?
IF I SPEAK, IT'LL ONLY BE WITH THE LEADER OF THIS RAMSHACKLE LOT.
THEN SPE
TO ME.

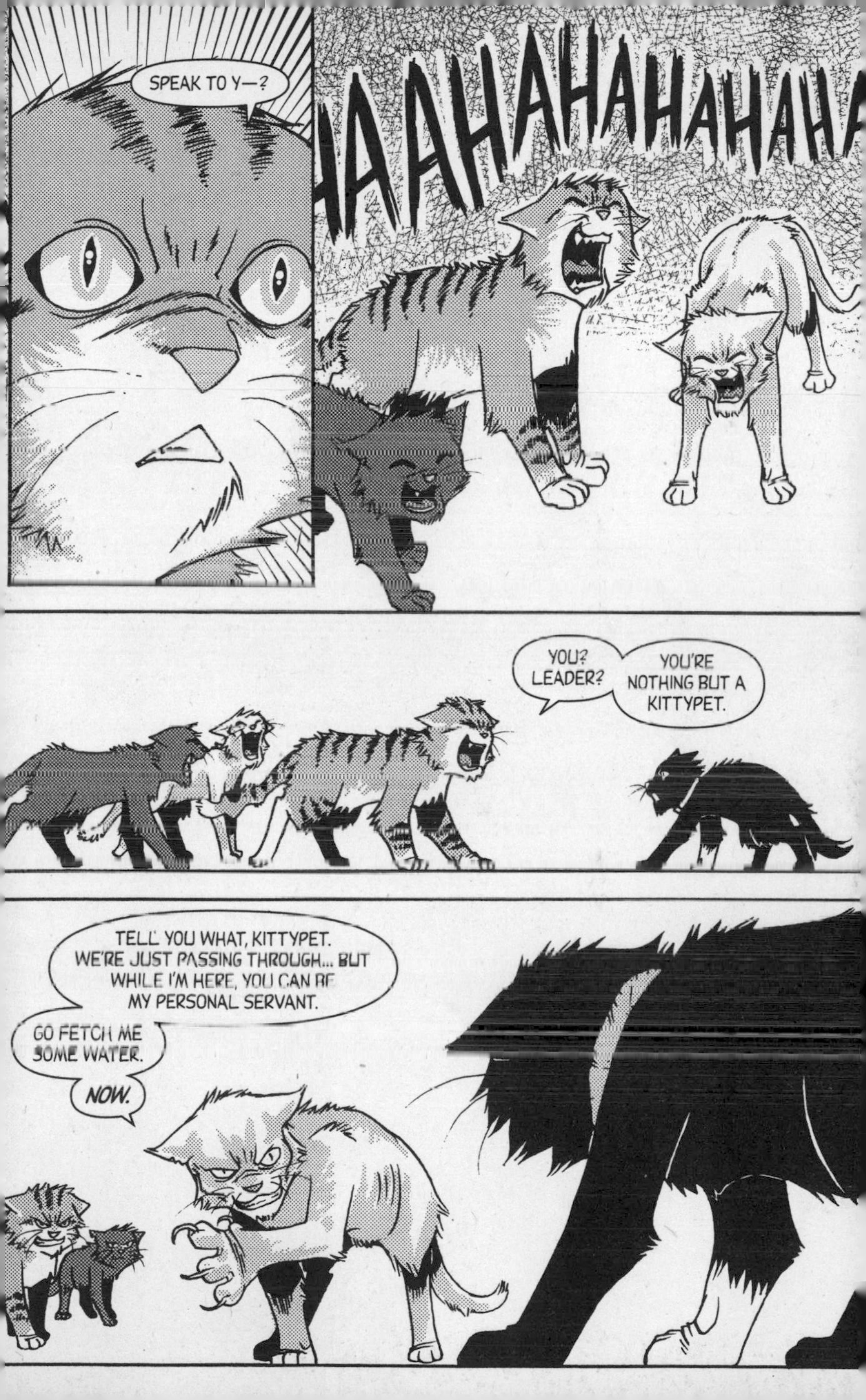
SPEAK TO Y—?
HAHAHAHAHAHAHAHA
YOU? LEADER?
YOU'RE NOTHING BUT A KITTYPET.
TELL YOU WHAT, KITTYPET. WE'RE JUST PASSING THROUGH... BUT WHILE I'M HERE, YOU CAN BE MY PERSONAL SERVANT.
GO FETCH ME SOME WATER.
NOW.

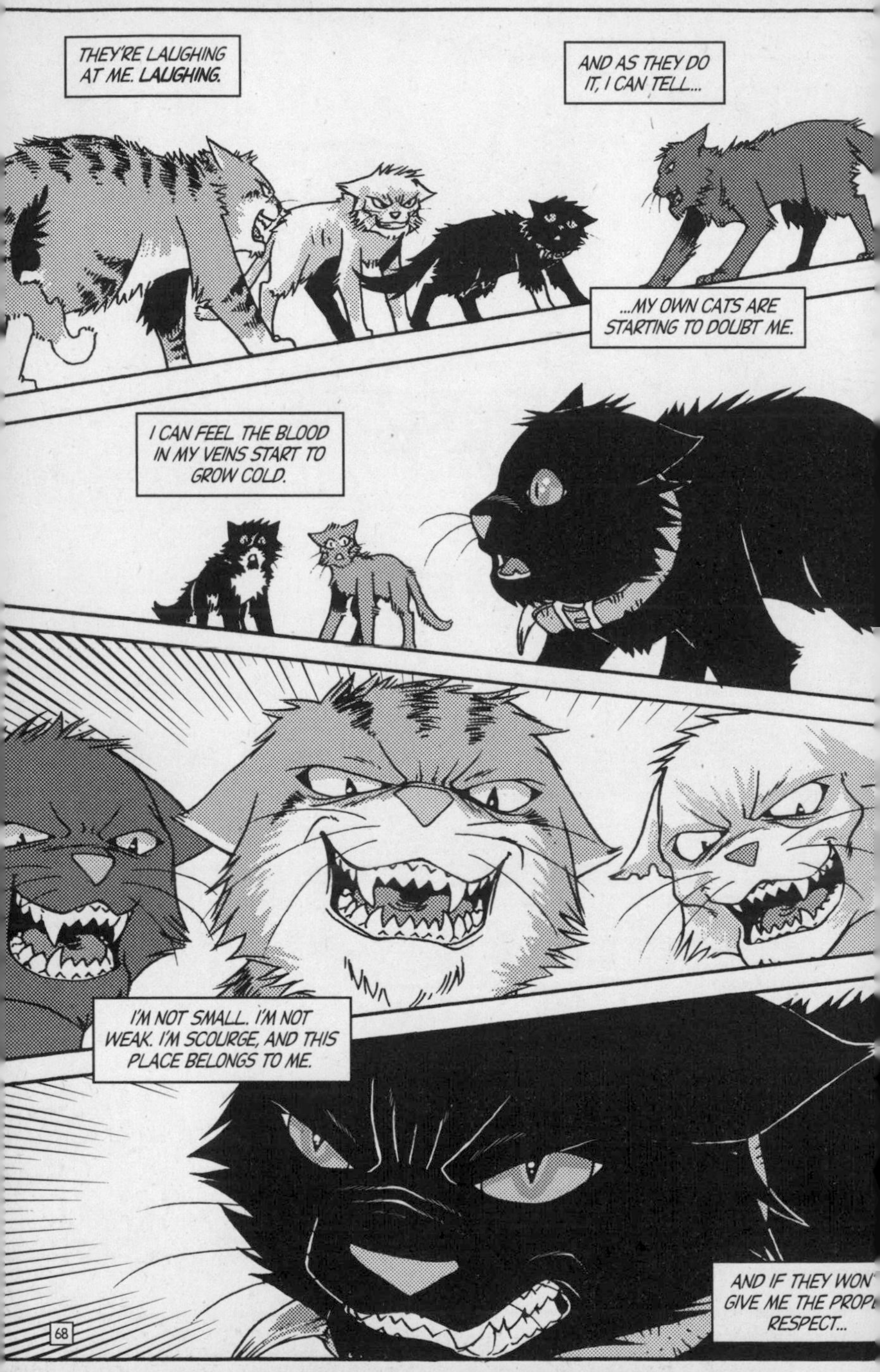
THEY'RE LAUGHING AT ME. LAUGHING.
AND AS THEY DO IT, I CAN TELL...
...MY OWN CATS ARE STARTING TO DOUBT ME.
I CAN FEEL THE BLOOD IN MY VEINS START TO GROW COLD.
I'M NOT SMALL. I'M NOT WEAK. I'M SCOURGE, AND THIS PLACE BELONGS TO ME.
AND IF THEY WON GIVE ME THE PROP RESPECT...

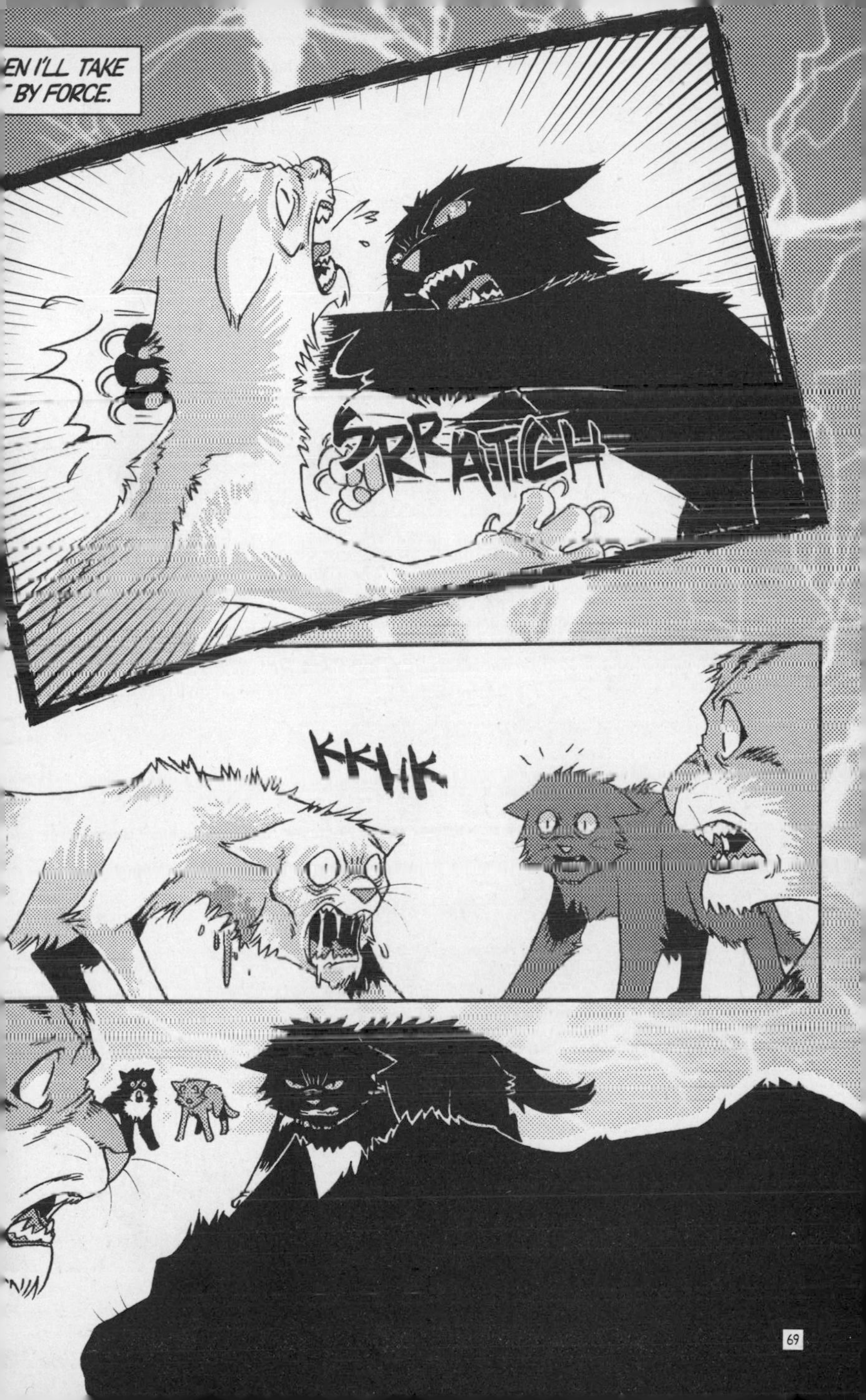

EN I'LL TAKE
BY FORCE.
SRRATCH
KKHK

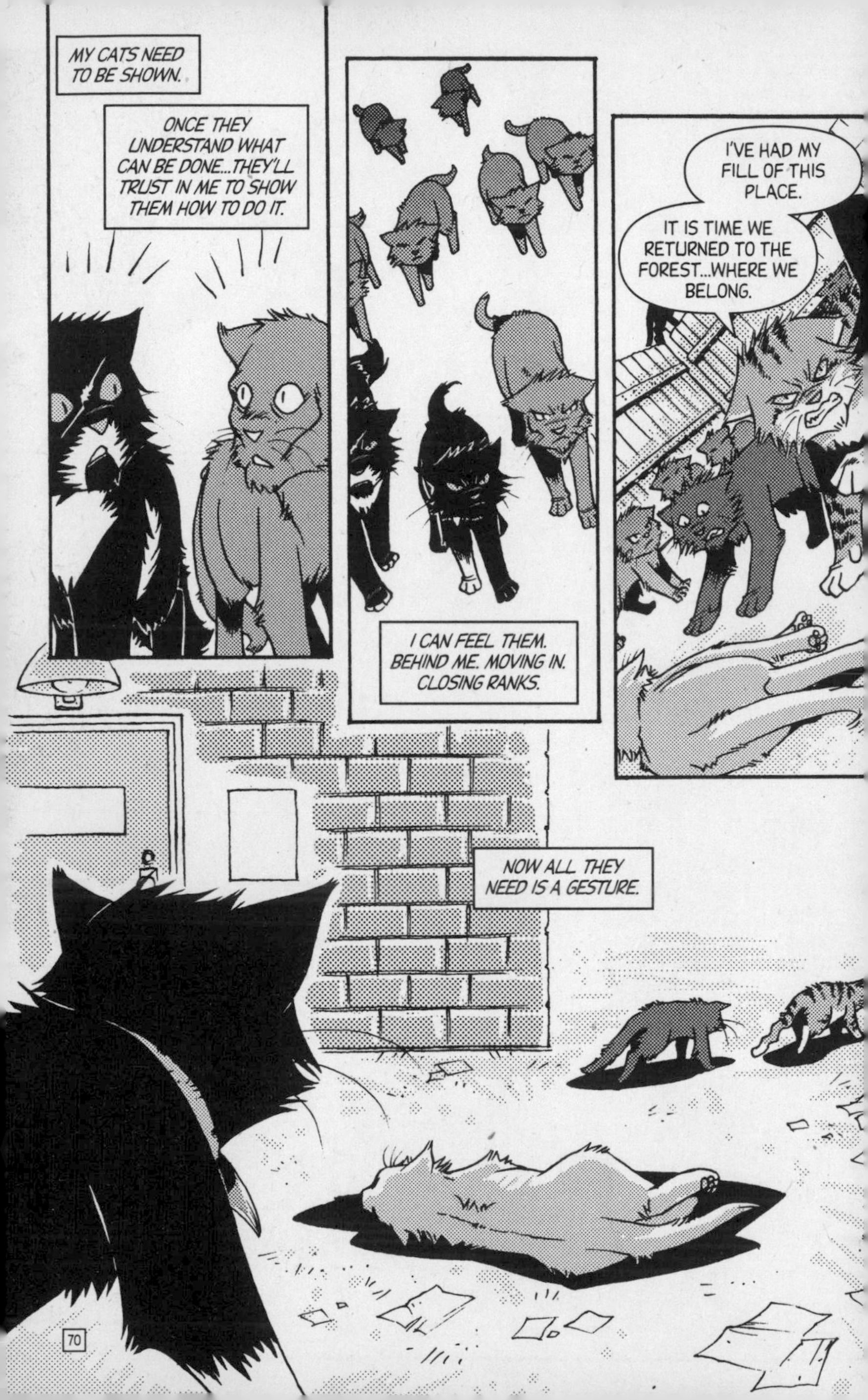
MY CATS NEED TO BE SHOWN.
ONCE THEY UNDERSTAND WHAT CAN BE DONE...THEY'LL TRUST IN ME TO SHOW THEM HOW TO DO IT.
I CAN FEEL THEM. BEHIND ME. MOVING IN. CLOSING RANKS.
I'VE HAD MY FILL OF THIS PLACE.
IT IS TIME WE RETURNED TO THE FOREST...WHERE WE BELONG.
NOW ALL THEY NEED IS A GESTURE.

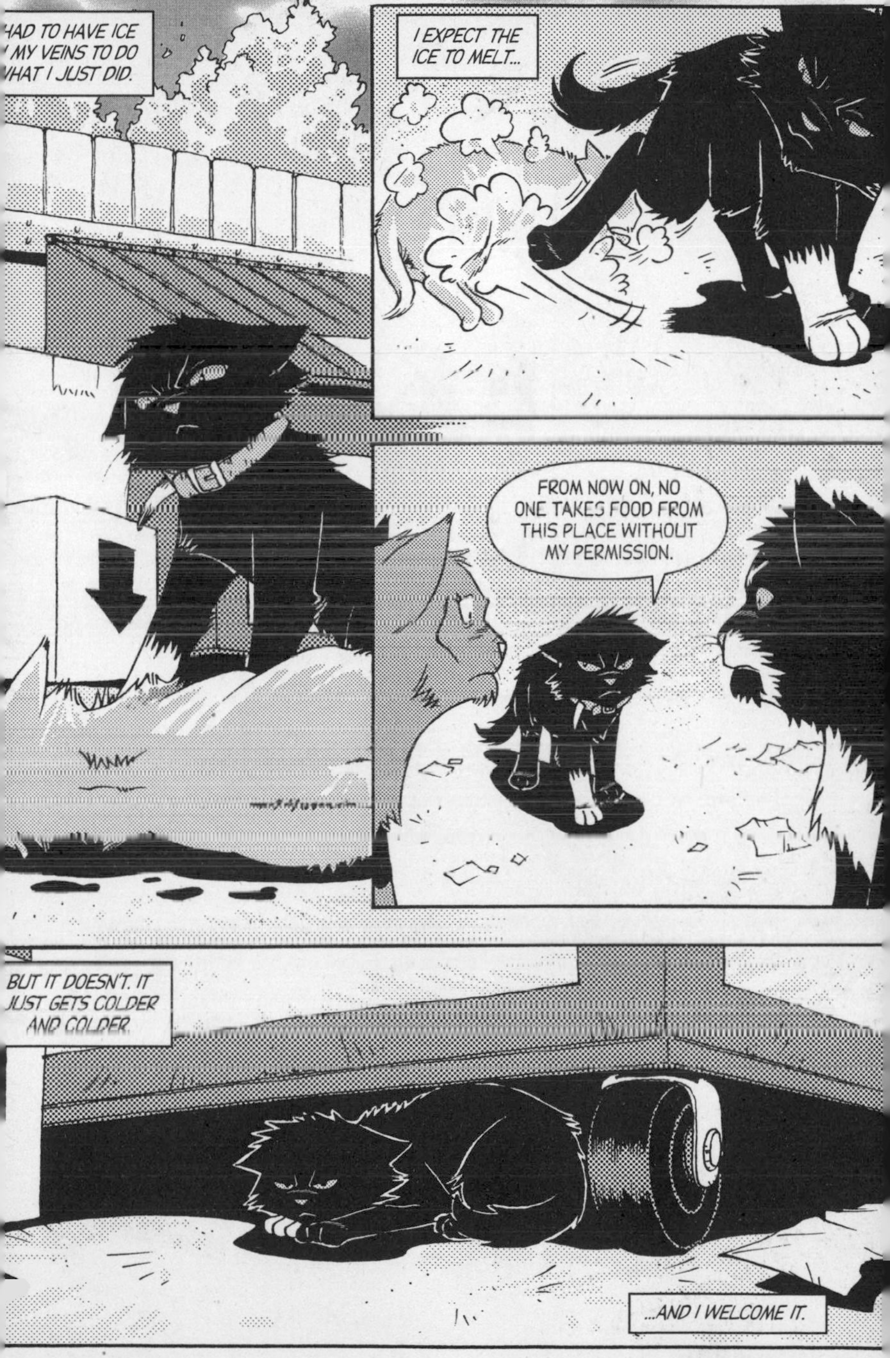
HAD TO HAVE ICE
MY VEINS TO DO
WHAT I JUST DID.
I EXPECT THE ICE TO MELT...
FROM NOW ON, NO ONE TAKES FOOD FROM THIS PLACE WITHOUT MY PERMISSION.
BUT IT DOESN'T. IT JUST GETS COLDER AND COLDER
...AND I WELCOME IT.

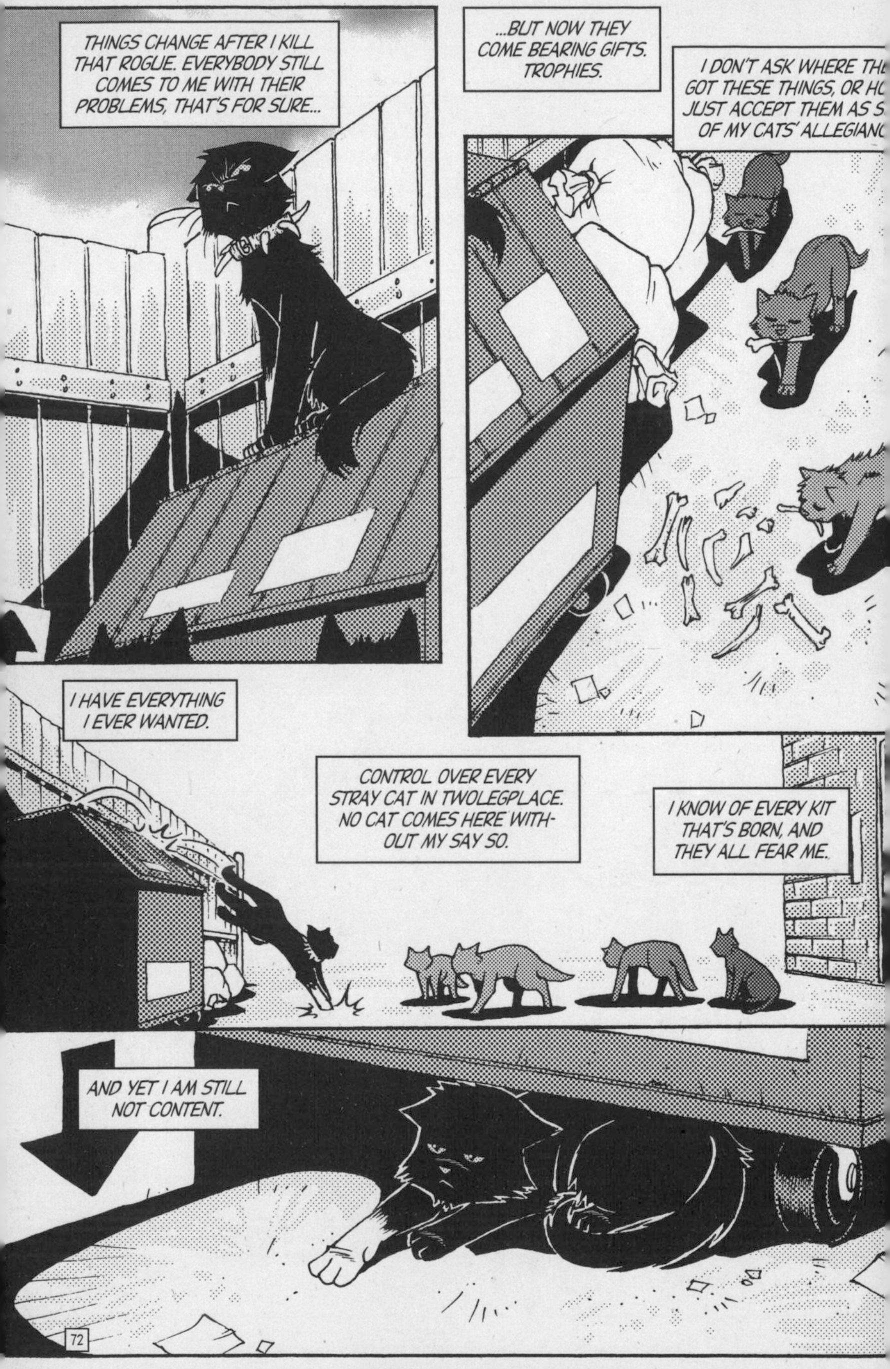
THINGS CHANGE AFTER I KILL THAT ROGUE. EVERYBODY STILL COMES TO ME WITH THEIR PROBLEMS, THAT'S FOR SURE...
...BUT NOW THEY COME BEARING GIFTS. TROPHIES.
I DON'T ASK WHERE TH
GOT THESE THINGS, OR H
JUST ACCEPT THEM AS S
OF MY CATS' ALLEGIAN
I HAVE EVERYTHING I EVER WANTED.
CONTROL OVER EVERY STRAY CAT IN TWOLEGPLACE. NO CAT COMES HERE WITH-OUT MY SAY SO.
I KNOW OF EVERY KIT THAT'S BORN, AND THEY ALL FEAR ME.
AND YET I AM STILL NOT CONTENT.

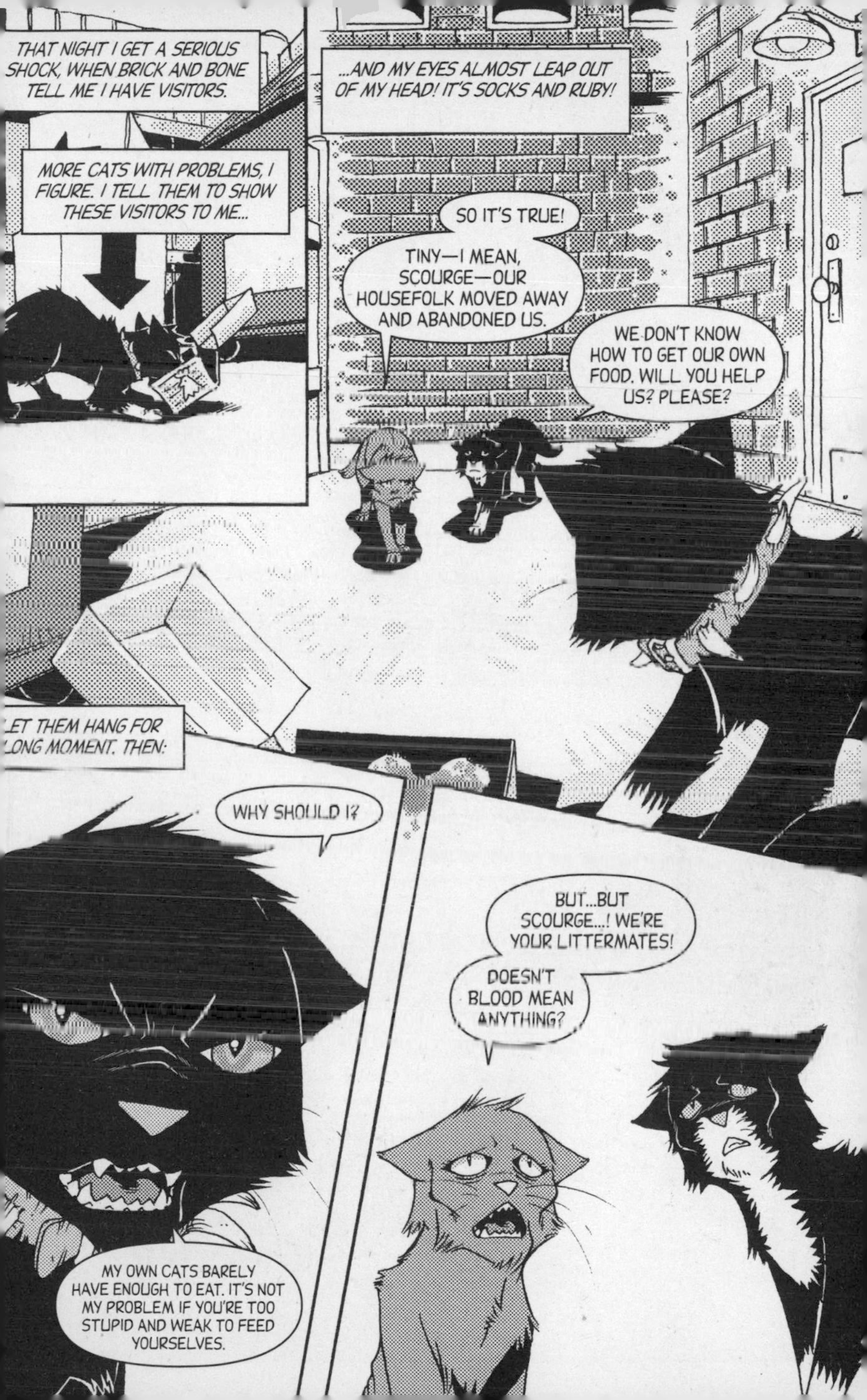
THAT NIGHT I GET A SERIOUS SHOCK, WHEN BRICK AND BONE TELL ME I HAVE VISITORS.
MORE CATS WITH PROBLEMS, I FIGURE. I TELL THEM TO SHOW THESE VISITORS TO ME...
...AND MY EYES ALMOST LEAP OUT OF MY HEAD! IT'S SOCKS AND RUBY!
SO IT'S TRUE!
TINY—I MEAN, SCOURGE—OUR HOUSEFOLK MOVED AWAY AND ABANDONED US.
WE DON'T KNOW HOW TO GET OUR OWN FOOD. WILL YOU HELP US? PLEASE?
LET THEM HANG FOR LONG MOMENT. THEN:
WHY SHOULD I?
MY OWN CATS BARELY HAVE ENOUGH TO EAT. IT'S NOT MY PROBLEM IF YOU'RE TOO STUPID AND WEAK TO FEED YOURSELVES.
BUT...BUT SCOURGE...! WE'RE YOUR LITTERMATES!
DOESN'T BLOOD MEAN ANYTHING?

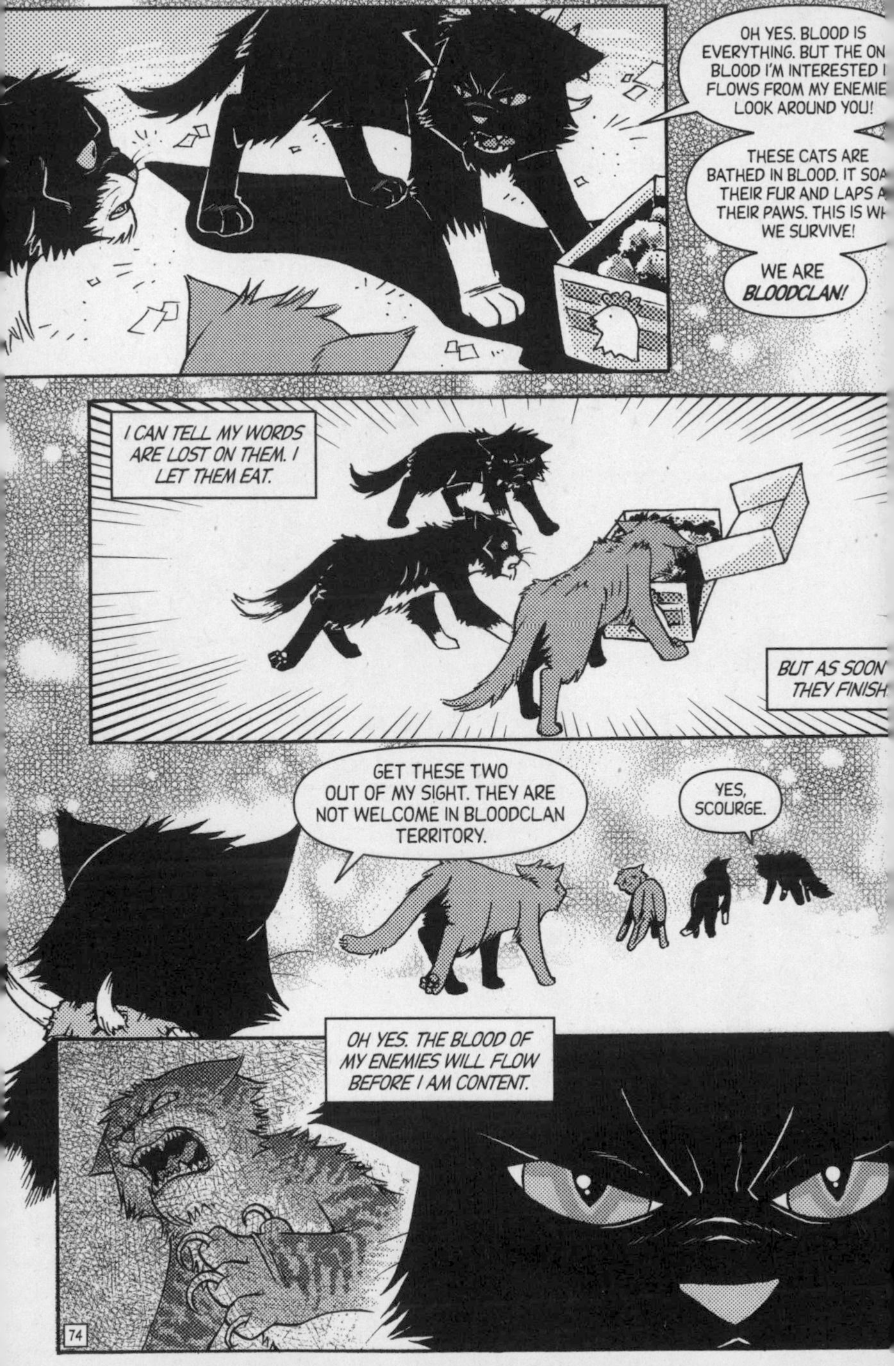
OH YES. BLOOD IS EVERYTHING. BUT THE ON BLOOD I'M INTERESTED I FLOWS FROM MY ENEMIE LOOK AROUND YOU!
THESE CATS ARE BATHED IN BLOOD. IT SOA THEIR FUR AND LAPS A THEIR PAWS. THIS IS WH WE SURVIVE!
WE ARE *BLOODCLAN!*
I CAN TELL MY WORDS ARE LOST ON THEM. I LET THEM EAT.
BUT AS SOON THEY FINISH
GET THESE TWO OUT OF MY SIGHT. THEY ARE NOT WELCOME IN BLOODCLAN TERRITORY.
YES, SCOURGE.
OH YES. THE BLOOD OF MY ENEMIES WILL FLOW BEFORE I AM CONTENT.

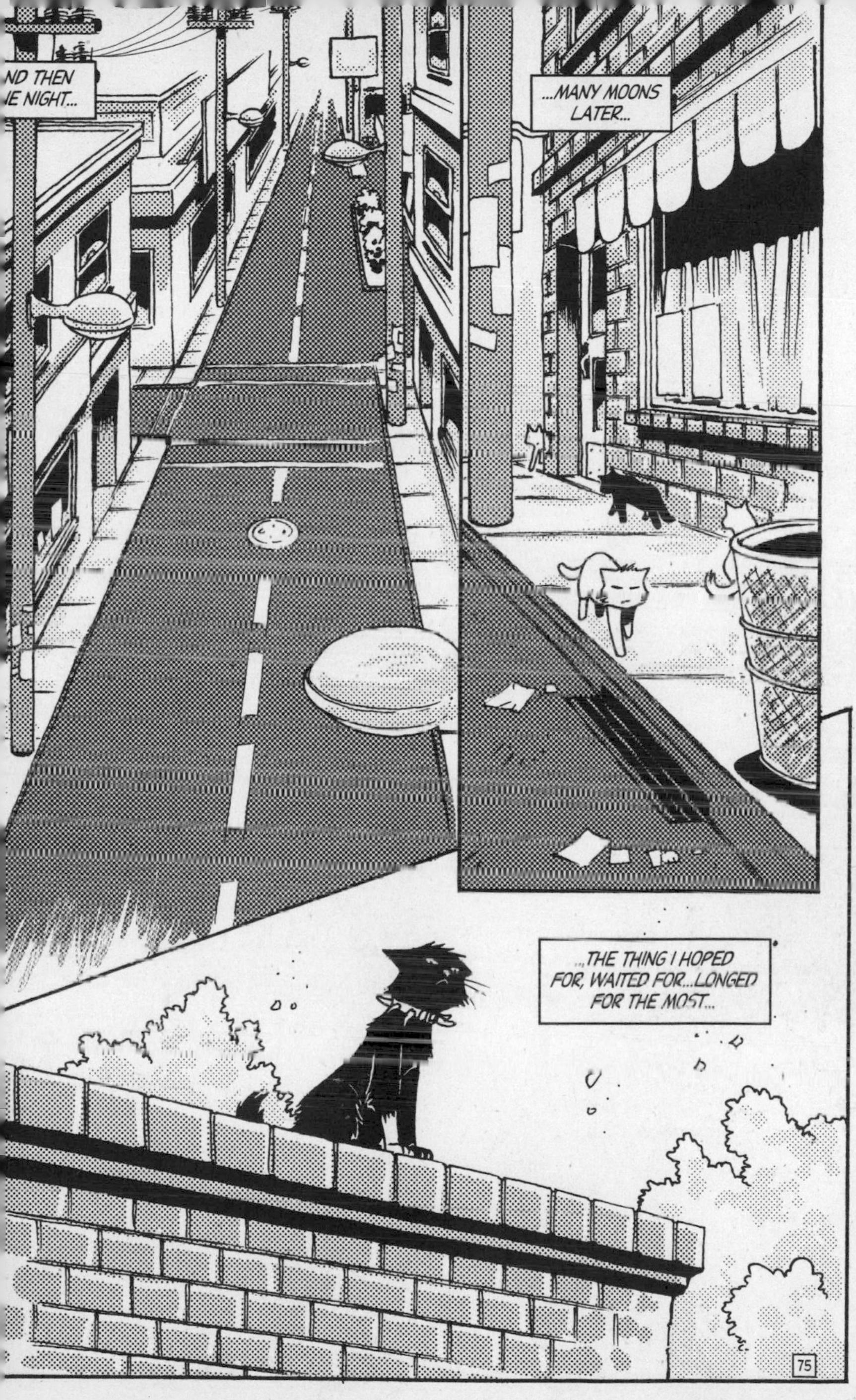
ND THEN
IE NIGHT...
...MANY MOONS
LATER...
...THE THING I HOPED
FOR, WAITED FOR...LONGED
FOR THE MOST...

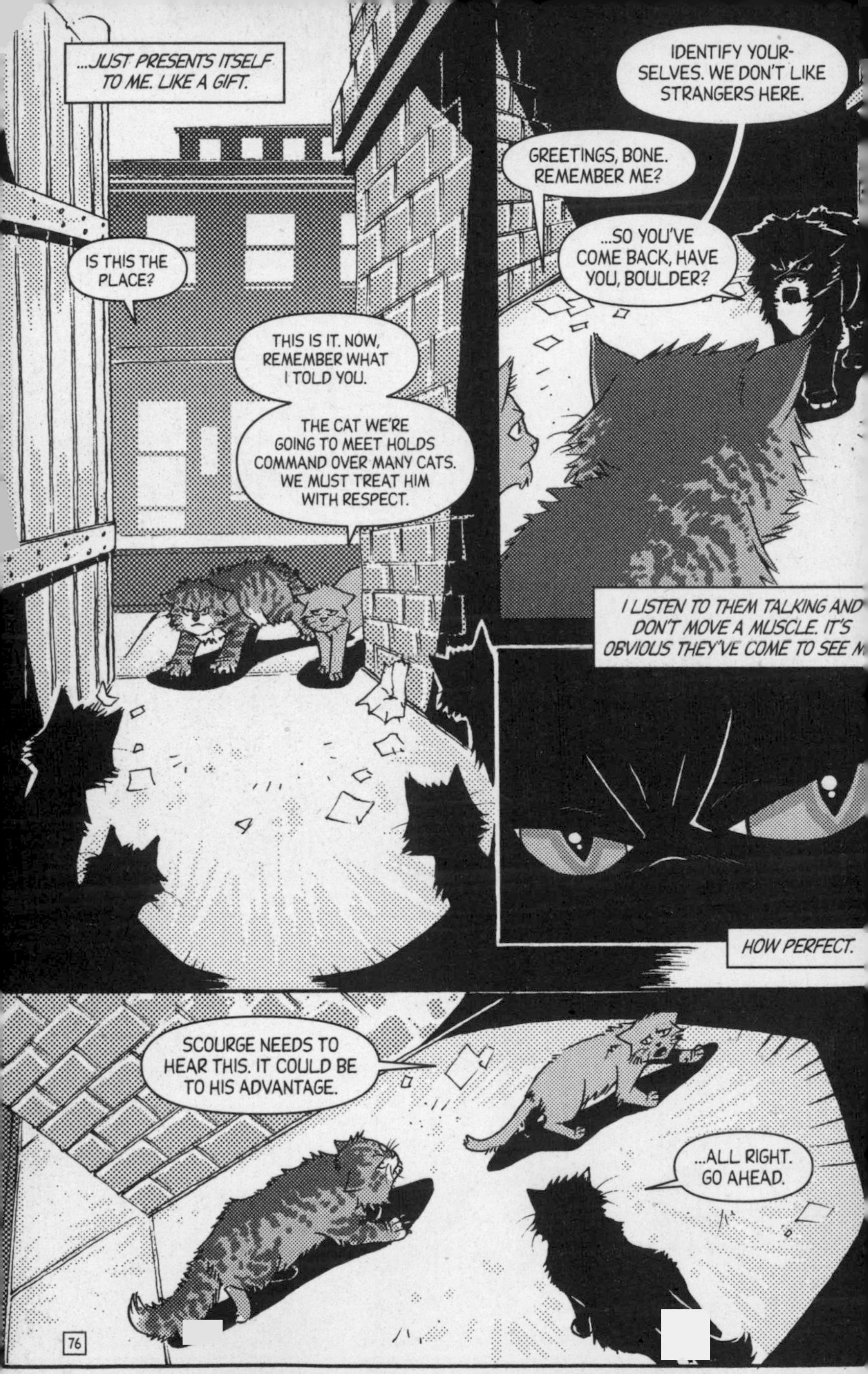

...JUST PRESENTS ITSELF TO ME. LIKE A GIFT.
IS THIS THE PLACE?
THIS IS IT. NOW, REMEMBER WHAT I TOLD YOU.
THE CAT WE'RE GOING TO MEET HOLDS COMMAND OVER MANY CATS. WE MUST TREAT HIM WITH RESPECT.
IDENTIFY YOUR-SELVES. WE DON'T LIKE STRANGERS HERE.
GREETINGS, BONE. REMEMBER ME?
...SO YOU'VE COME BACK, HAVE YOU, BOULDER?
I LISTEN TO THEM TALKING AND DON'T MOVE A MUSCLE. IT'S OBVIOUS THEY'VE COME TO SEE M
HOW PERFECT.
SCOURGE NEEDS TO HEAR THIS. IT COULD BE TO HIS ADVANTAGE.
...ALL RIGHT. GO AHEAD.

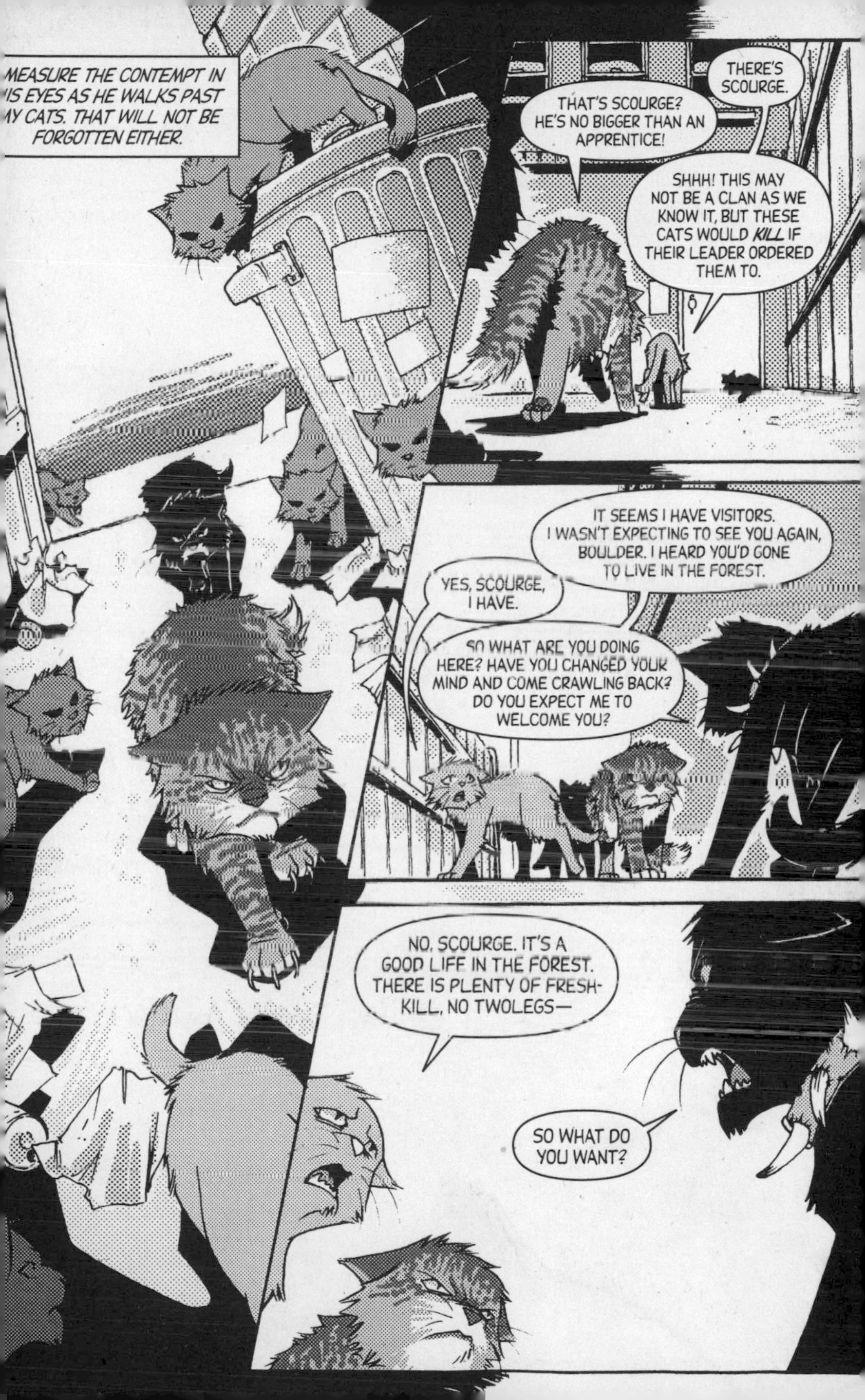
MEASURE THE CONTEMPT IN IS EYES AS HE WALKS PAST MY CATS. THAT WILL NOT BE FORGOTTEN EITHER.
THERE'S SCOURGE.
THAT'S SCOURGE? HE'S NO BIGGER THAN AN APPRENTICE!
SHHH! THIS MAY NOT BE A CLAN AS WE KNOW IT, BUT THESE CATS WOULD *KILL* IF THEIR LEADER ORDERED THEM TO.
IT SEEMS I HAVE VISITORS. I WASN'T EXPECTING TO SEE YOU AGAIN, BOULDER. I HEARD YOU'D GONE TO LIVE IN THE FOREST.
YES, SCOURGE, I HAVE.
SO WHAT ARE YOU DOING HERE? HAVE YOU CHANGED YOUR MIND AND COME CRAWLING BACK? DO YOU EXPECT ME TO WELCOME YOU?
NO, SCOURGE. IT'S A GOOD LIFE IN THE FOREST. THERE IS PLENTY OF FRESH-KILL, NO TWOLEGS—
SO WHAT DO YOU WANT?

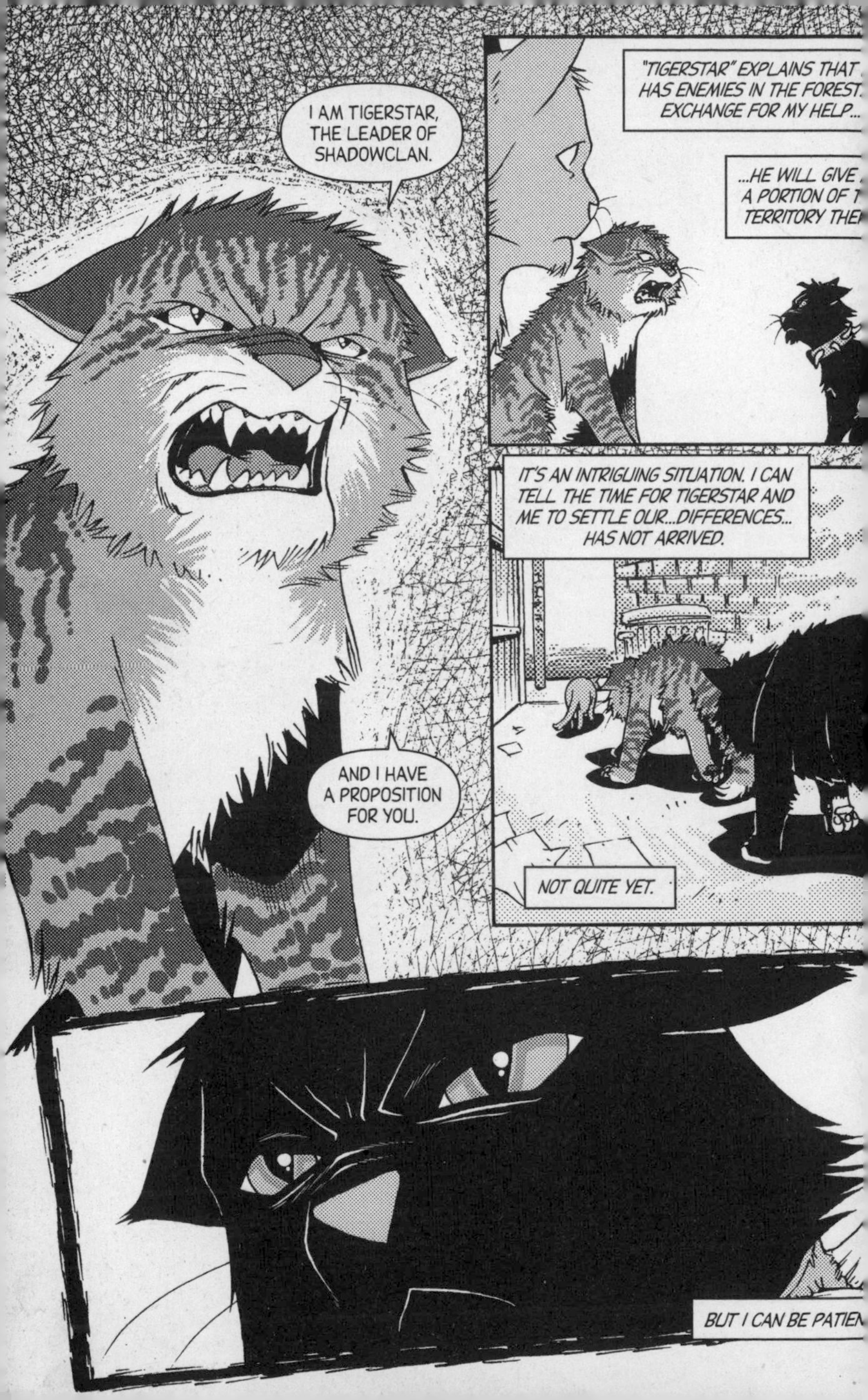
I AM TIGERSTAR, THE LEADER OF SHADOWCLAN.
AND I HAVE A PROPOSITION FOR YOU.
"TIGERSTAR" EXPLAINS THAT
HAS ENEMIES IN THE FOREST.
EXCHANGE FOR MY HELP...
...HE WILL GIVE
A PORTION OF T
TERRITORY THE
IT'S AN INTRIGUING SITUATION. I CAN TELL THE TIME FOR TIGERSTAR AND ME TO SETTLE OUR...DIFFERENCES... HAS NOT ARRIVED.
NOT QUITE YET.
BUT I CAN BE PATIEN

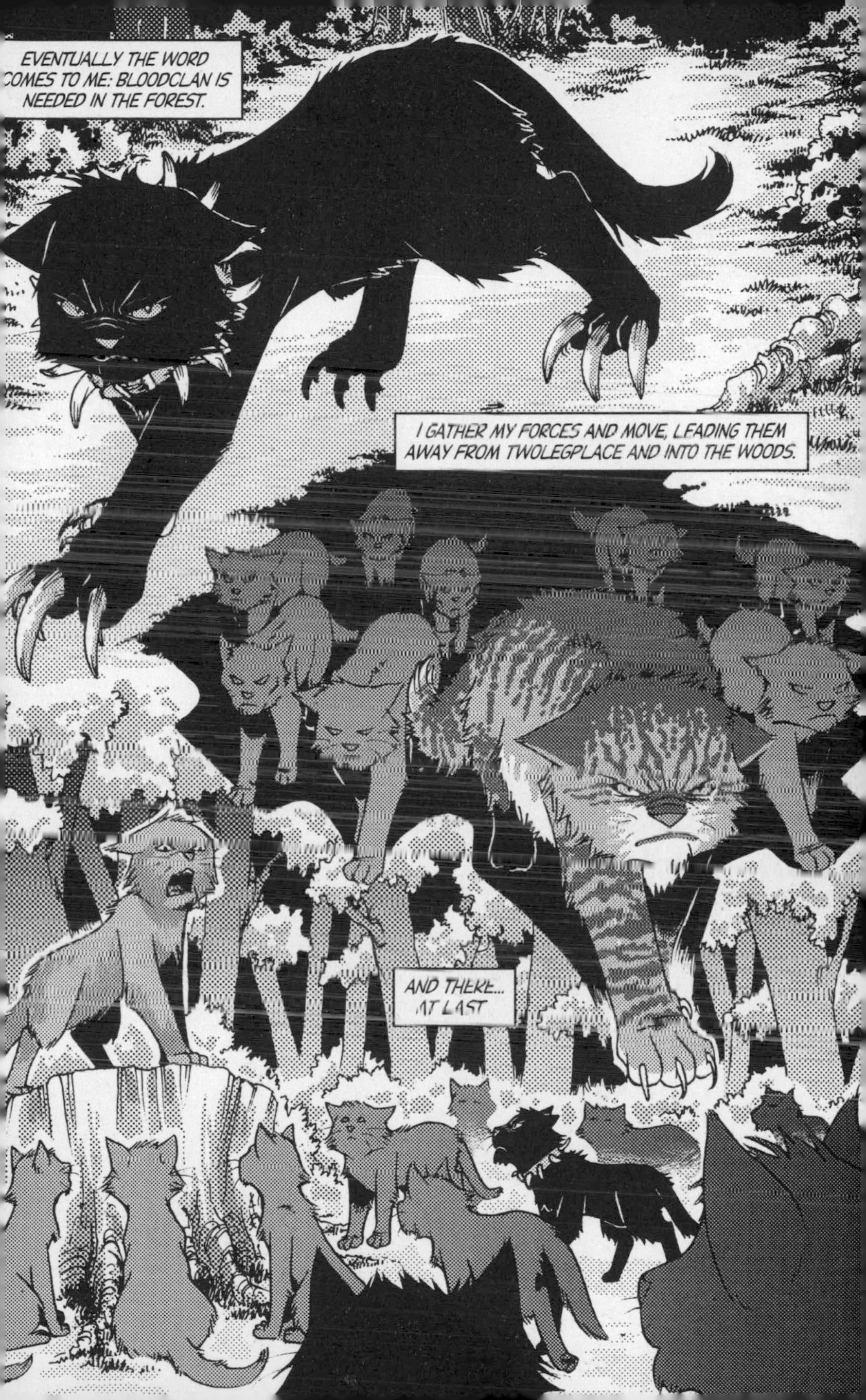
EVENTUALLY THE WORD COMES TO ME: BLOODCLAN IS NEEDED IN THE FOREST.
I GATHER MY FORCES AND MOVE, LEADING THEM AWAY FROM TWOLEGPLACE AND INTO THE WOODS.
AND THERE... AT LAST

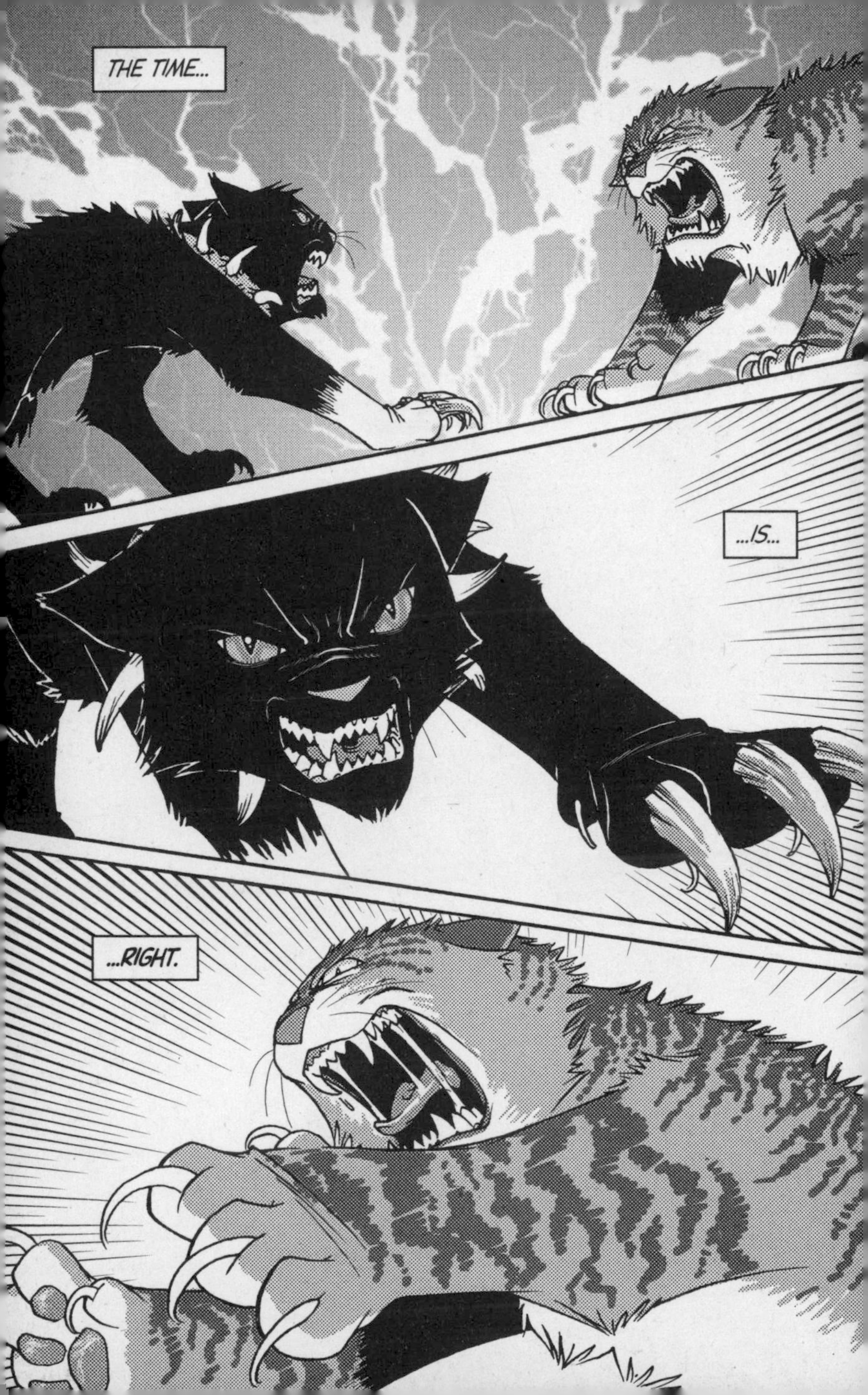
THE TIME...
...IS...
...RIGHT.

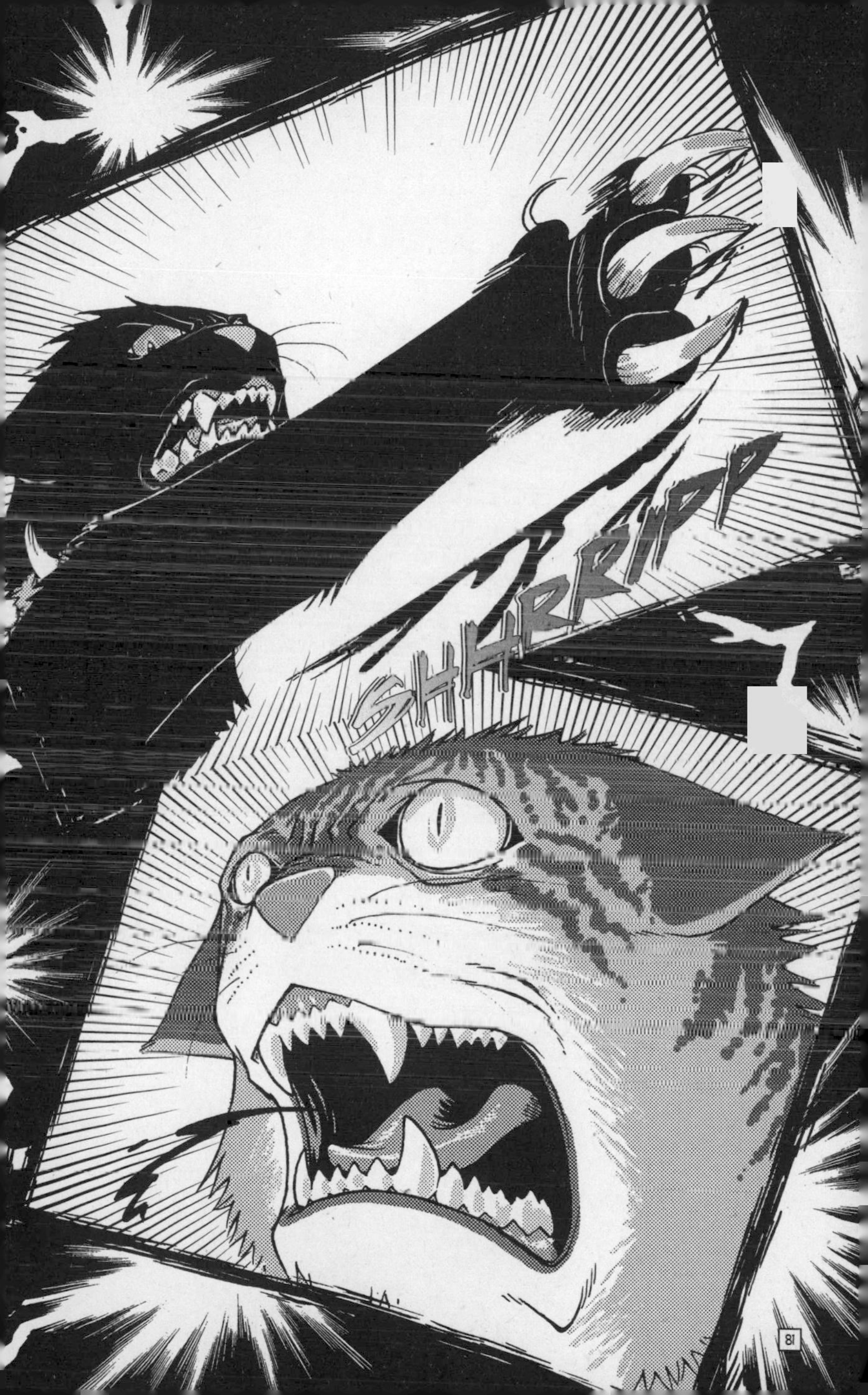
SHHRRIPP

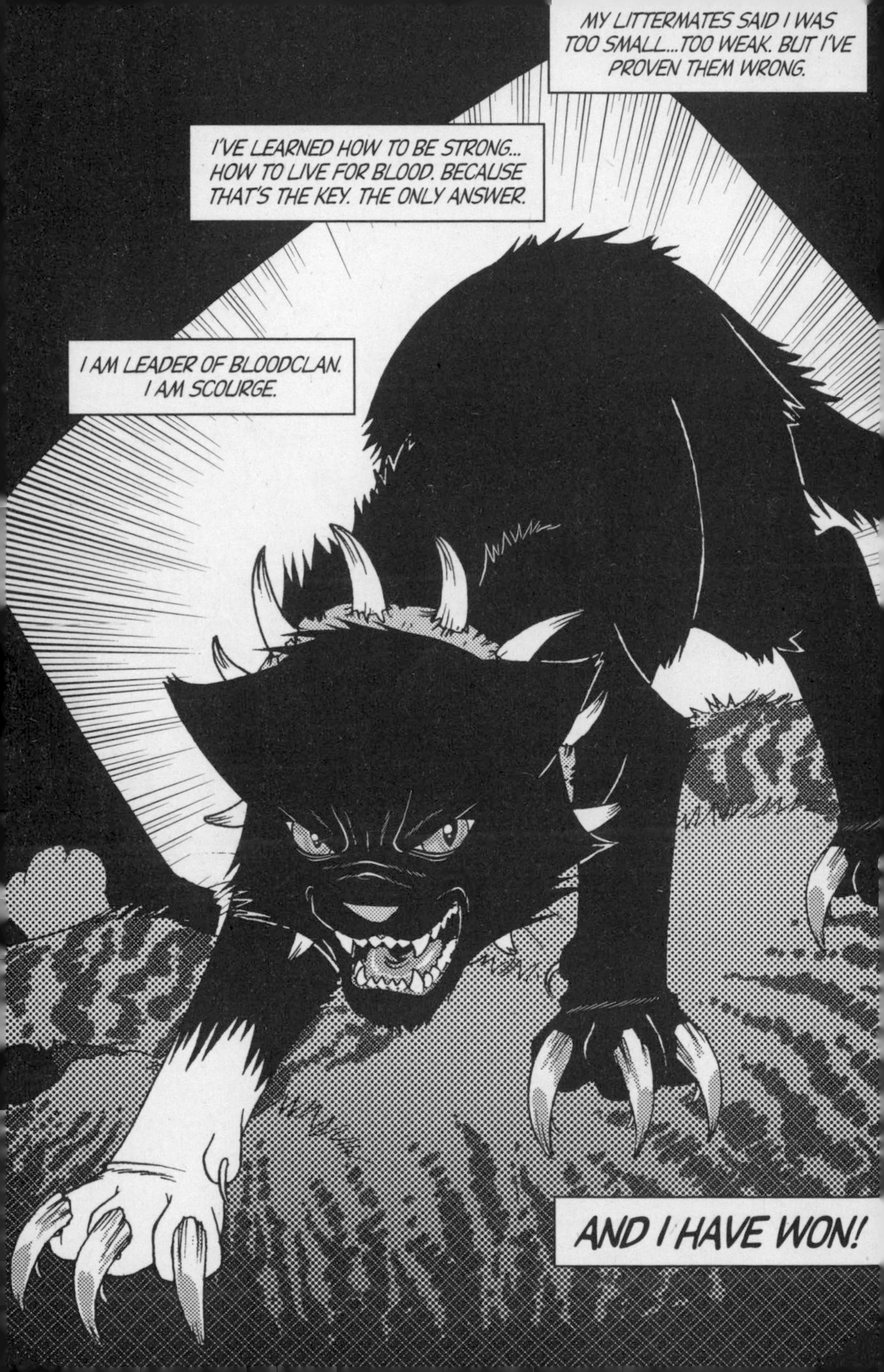
MY LITTERMATES SAID I WAS TOO SMALL...TOO WEAK. BUT I'VE PROVEN THEM WRONG.
I'VE LEARNED HOW TO BE STRONG... HOW TO LIVE FOR BLOOD. BECAUSE THAT'S THE KEY. THE ONLY ANSWER.
I AM LEADER OF BLOODCLAN. I AM SCOURGE.
AND I HAVE WON!

ERIN HUNTER

is inspired by a love of cats and a fascination with the ferocity of the natural world. As well as having great respect for nature in all its forms, Erin enjoys creating rich mythical explanations for animal behavior, shaped by her interest in astrology and standing stones. She is also the author of the Seekers series.

Visit the Clans online
and play the Warriors Quest game at
www.warriorcats.com.

For exclusive information on your
favorite authors and artists, visit
www.authortracker.com

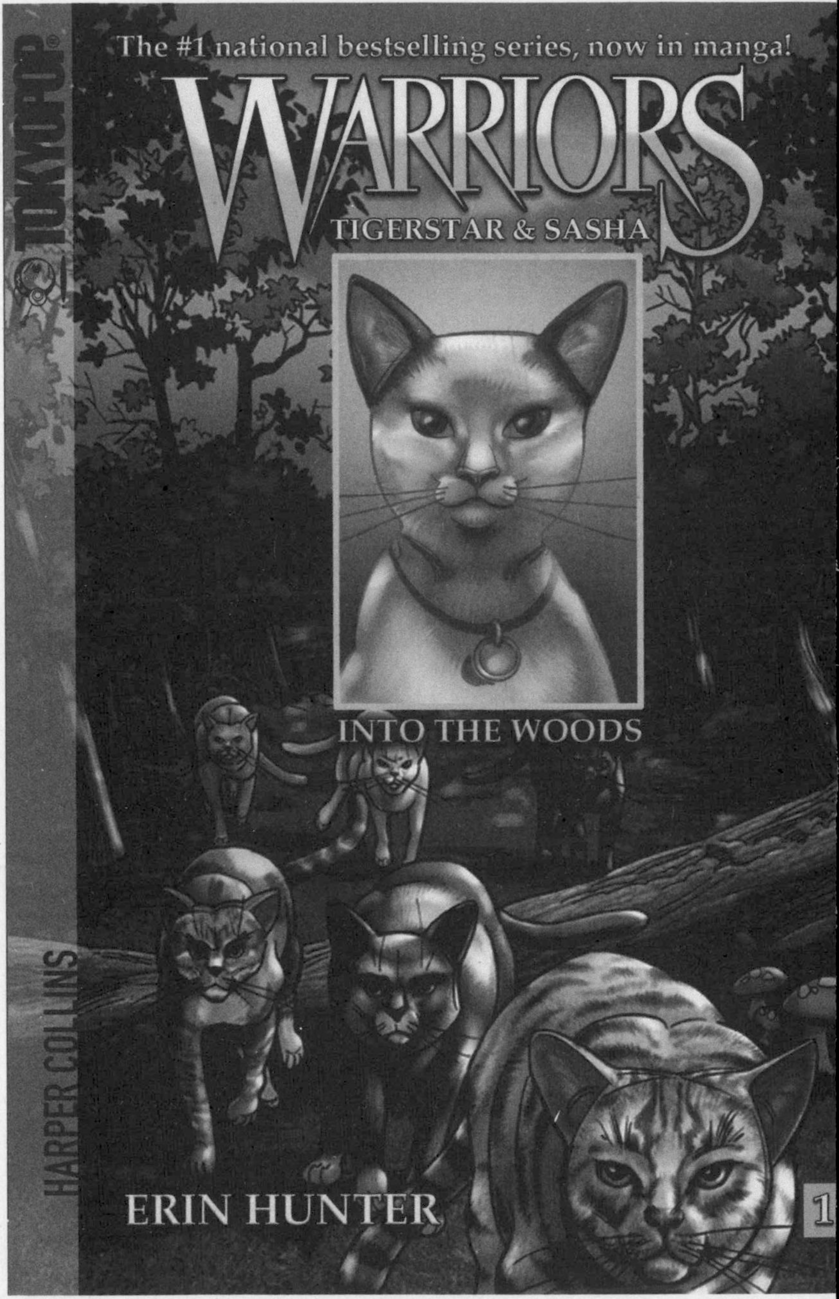
TOKYOPOP
The #1 national bestselling series, now in manga!
WARRIORS
TIGERSTAR & SASHA
INTO THE WOODS
HARPER COLLINS
ERIN HUNTER
1

KEEP WATCH FOR

WARRIORS

TIGERSTAR & SASHA
#1: INTO THE WOODS

Sasha has everything she wants: kind housefolk who take care of her during the day and the freedom to explore the woods beyond Twolegplace at night. But when Sasha is forced to leave her home, she must forge a solitary new life in the forest. Life on her own is exciting at first but quickly gets lonely. When Sasha meets Tigerstar, leader of ShadowClan, she begins to think that she may be better off joining the ranks of his forest Clan. But Tigerstar has many secrets, and Sasha must decide whether she can trust him.

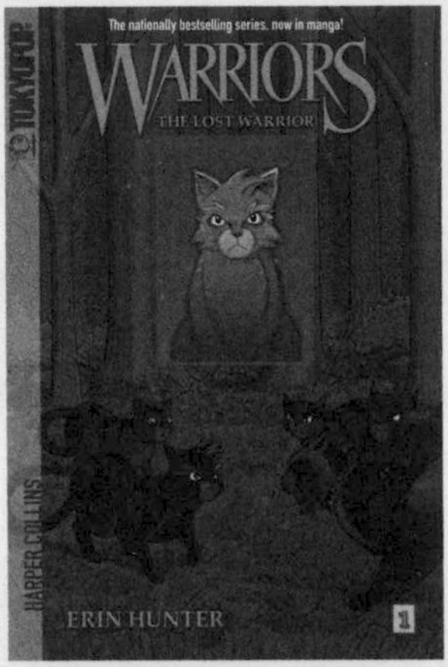
The nationally bestselling series, now in manga!
WARRIORS
THE LOST WARRIOR
TOKYOPOP
HARPER COLLINS
ERIN HUNTER
1

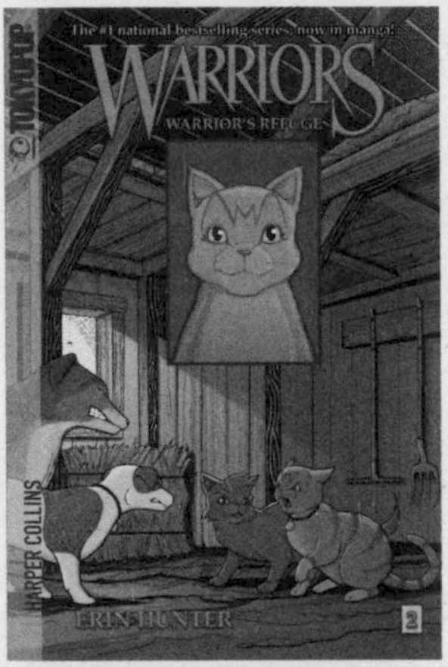
The #1 national bestselling series, now in manga!
WARRIORS
WARRIOR'S REFUGE
TOKYOPOP
HARPER COLLINS
ERIN HUNTER
2

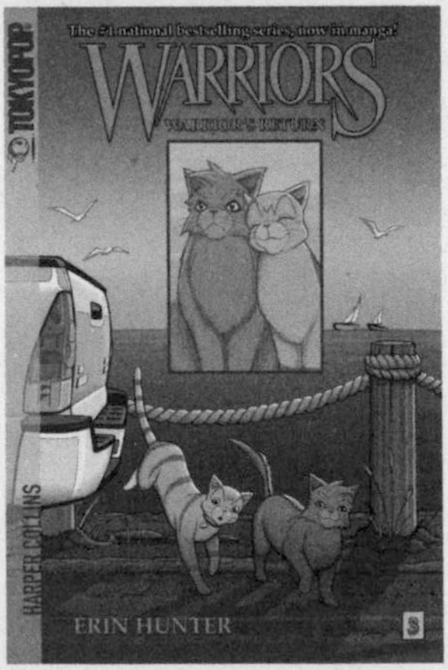
The #1 national bestselling series, now in manga!
WARRIORS
WARRIOR'S RETURN
TOKYOPOP
HARPER COLLINS
ERIN HUNTER
3

DON'T MISS THE
FIRST MANGA TRILOGY

WARRIORS

THE LOST WARRIOR

WARRIOR'S REFUGE

WARRIOR'S RETURN

Find out what really happened to Graystripe when he was captured by Twolegs, and follow him and Millie on their torturous journey through the old forest territory and Twolegplace as they search for ThunderClan.

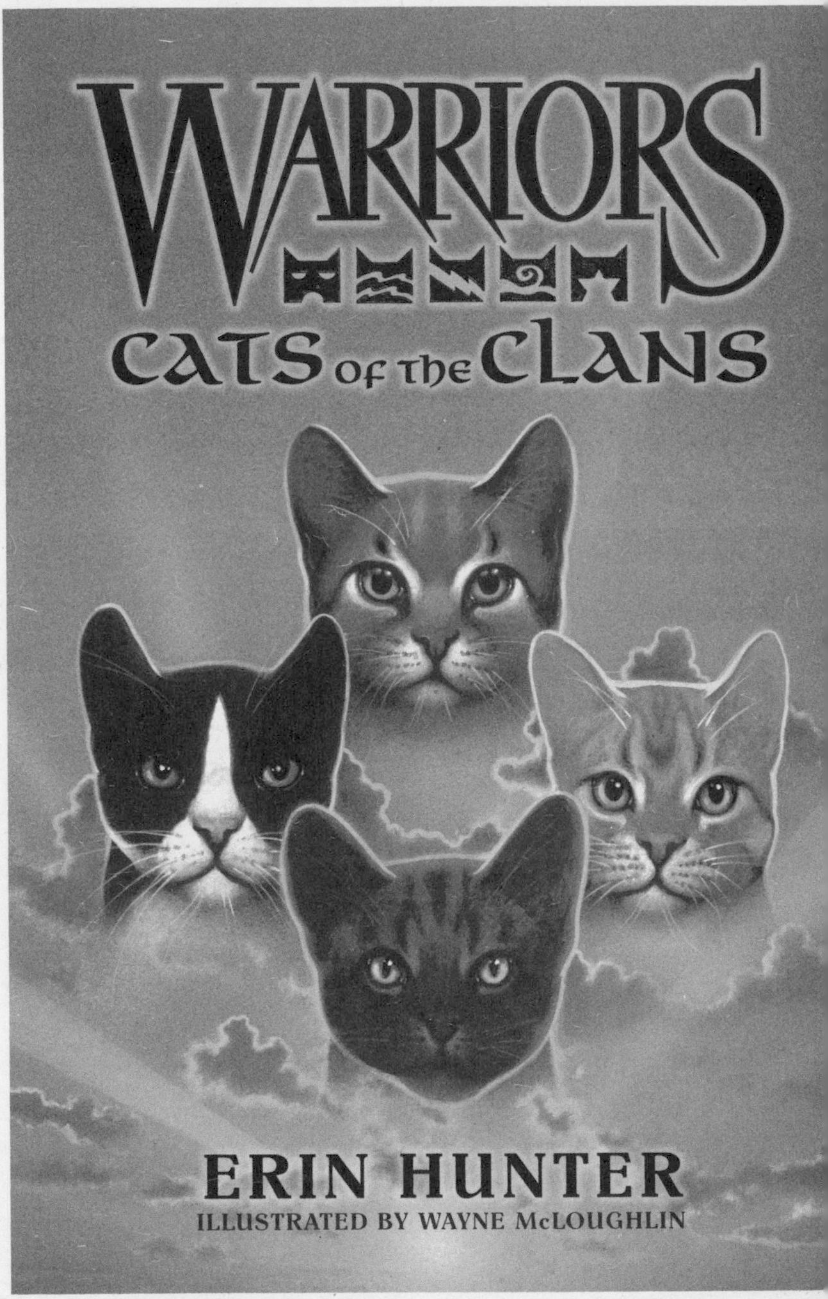
WARRIORS
CATS of the CLANS
ERIN HUNTER
ILLUSTRATED BY WAYNE McLOUGHLIN

MEET THE CLANS' HEROES IN

WARRIORS

CATS of the CLANS

Hear the stories of the great warriors as they've never
been told before! Chock-full of visual treats and cap-
tivating details, including full-color illustrations and
in-depth biographies of important cats from all four
Clans, from fierce Clan leaders to wise medicine cats
to the most mischievous kits.

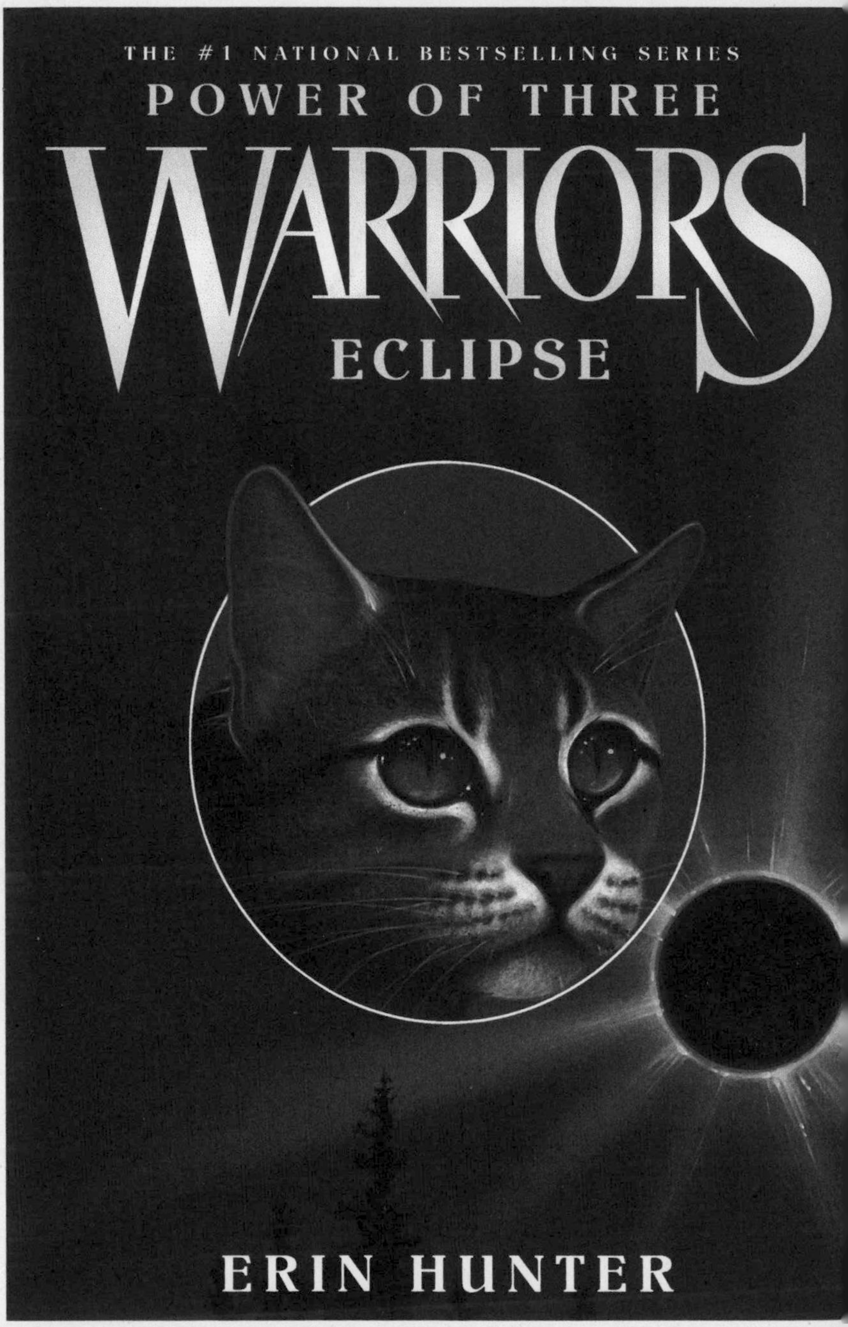
THE #1 NATIONAL BESTSELLING SERIES
POWER OF THREE
WARRIORS
ECLIPSE
ERIN HUNTER

POWER OF THREE

WARRIORS

BOOK 4:

ECLIPSE

TURN THE PAGE FOR A PEEK
AT THE NEXT WARRIORS NOVEL,
*WARRIORS: POWER OF THREE
#4: ECLIPSE.*

Firestar's grandchildren have learned of the powerful prophecy that foretells their destinies, and the responsibility of deciding the Clans' future weighs heavily on the three apprentices. Each secretly yearns for power, and their strengths are tested when ThunderClan is suddenly attacked—and all the Clans are thrown into a battle unlike any the cats have seen.

Jaypaw touched his nose to Tawnypelt's pad. It felt hot and fat. "Swollen," he pronounced. "The skin's grazed but not bleeding. But you already know that." He could hear Hollypaw's and Lionpaw's faint mews as they headed away to find prey. Were they talking about the prophecy?

Tawnypelt pulled her paw from under his muzzle. "I knew I couldn't taste blood but I wasn't sure if a stone had worked its way in." She licked it. "My pads have grown so hard from the mountains, I can't tell calluses from cuts anymore."

"No stones," Jaypaw reassured her. He nodded toward the sound of water babbling over rocks nearby. "That stream doesn't sound too deep. Go stand in it. The cold water should ease the swelling."

He padded after her and heard the splash as she leaped into the water.

"It's cold!" She gasped.

"Good," he mewed. "It'll take down the swelling quicker." He pricked his ears. Hollypaw's and Lionpaw's voices had faded into the distance. He had shared with them the secret he had carried with him for so long. Telling it had felt like walking through unknown territory, each word falling like a pawstep on uncertain ground. Lionpaw had accepted it as though something that had been confusing him had finally been explained. Hollypaw's reaction had been more frustrating: She seemed only concerned about how they could use their powers to help Thunder-Clan, and kept fretting about the warrior code. Didn't she understand that the prophecy meant more than that? They had been given a power that stretched far beyond the boundaries set by ordinary cats.

Tawnypelt's mew interrupted his thoughts. "This water's *very* cold."

"It's mountain water."

"I can tell," Tawnypelt meowed urgently. "My paws have gone numb!"

"Well, get out then."

With a sigh of relief, she landed beside him and began shaking the water from her paws, scattering icy drops on his fur.

Jaypaw shivered and moved away; mountain winds and cold water were a bad mix. "Does it still hurt?"

"I can't feel it at all," Tawnypelt replied. She paused. "Actually, I can't feel any of my paws."

Squirrelflight was padding toward them. "Any better?"

"I think so," Tawnypelt meowed uncertainly.

Jaypaw felt his mother's tongue lap his ear. "Are you okay, little one?" she asked gently.

He ducked away crossly. "Why shouldn't I be?"

"It's okay to be tired." Squirrelflight sat down. "It's been a hard journey."

"I'm fine," Jaypaw snapped. His mother's tail was twitching, scraping the gritty rock. He waited for her to make some comment about how much harder the journey must have been for him, being blind and all, and then add some mouse-brained comment about how well he had coped with the unfamiliar territory.

"All three of you have been quiet since the battle," she ventured.

She's worried about all *of us!* Jaypaw's anger melted. He wished he could put her mind at rest but there was no way he could tell her the huge secret that was occupying their thoughts. "I guess we just want to get home," he offered.

"We all do." Squirrelflight rested her chin on top of Jaypaw's head and he pressed against her, suddenly feeling like a kit again, grateful for her warmth.

"They're back!"

At Firestar's call, Squirrelflight jerked away.

Jaypaw lifted his nose and smelled Hollypaw and Lionpaw. He heard claws scrabbling over rock as Breezepaw arrived. The hunters had returned.

"Let's see what they've caught!" Tawnypelt hurried to greet the apprentices.

Jaypaw already knew what they'd caught. His belly rumbled as he padded after her, the mouthwatering smell of the squirrel, rabbit, and pigeon filling his nose. If only it wasn't going to be given to the Tribe.

Crowfeather, Firestar, and Brambleclaw were already clustered around the makeshift fresh-kill pile. Stormfur and Brook hung back as though embarrassed by the gift.

"This rabbit's so fat it'll feed all the to-bes," Squirrelflight mewed admiringly.

"Well caught, Breezepaw," Firestar purred.

Jaypaw waited for the WindClan apprentice's pelt to flash with pride, but instead he sensed anxiety claw at Breezepaw. *He's waiting for his father to praise him.*

"Nice pigeon," Crowfeather mewed to Lionpaw.

Breezepaw stiffened with anger.

"And look at the squirrel I caught!" Hollypaw chipped in. "Did you ever see such a juicy one?"

"Come see!" Tawnypelt called to Stormfur and Brook.

The two warriors padded over.

"This will be very welcome," Stormfur meowed formally.

"The Tribe thanks you." Brook's mew was taut.

Jaypaw understood their unease. By accepting fresh-kill, they were openly admitting their weakness. Hunting was poor in the mountains now that two groups of cats were sharing the territory. And yet Jaypaw could feel fierce pride pulsing from Stormfur. There was a core of strength within him, a resolve that Jaypaw had not sensed before, as though he were more rooted in the crags and ravines than he ever had been beside the lake. *He feels this is his destiny.* The Tribe were Stormfur's Clan now. *There's more than just the mountain breeze in his pelt.* He had been born RiverClan, and lived with ThunderClan, but now it seemed that he had found his true home.

Jaypaw shivered. The wind had been sharpened by a late-afternoon chill.

A howl echoed from the slopes far above.

Brook bristled. "Wolves."

"We'll get this prey home safely," Stormfur reassured her. "The wolves are too clumsy to follow our mountain paths."

"But there's a lot of open territory before you reach them," Firestar urged. "You should go."

"We should all head home," Crowfeather advised. "The smell of this fresh-kill will be attracting all the prey-eaters around here."

Alarm flashed from every pelt as Jaypaw detected a strange tang on the breeze. It was the first wolf scent he'd smelled. It reminded him of the dogs around the Twoleg farm, but there was a rawness, a scent of blood and flesh, to it that the dogs did not carry. Thankfully, it was faint. "They're a long way off," he murmured.

"But they travel fast," Brook warned. The rabbit's fur

brushed the ground as she picked it up.

"We're going to miss you," Squirrelflight meowed. Her voice was thick with sadness.

Brook laid the rabbit down again, a purr rising in her throat. Her pelt brushed Squirrelflight's. "Thank you for taking us in and showing us such kindness."

"ThunderClan is grateful for your loyalty and courage," Firestar meowed.

"We'll see you again, though, won't we?" Hollypaw mewed hopefully.

Jaypaw wondered if he would ever return to the mountains. Would he meet the Tribe of Endless Hunting again? He had followed Stoneteller into his dreams and been led by the Tribe-healer's ancestor to the hollow where ranks of starry cats encircled a shimmering pool. He shivered as he recalled their words: *You have come.* They had been expecting him and they had known about the prophecy! Yet again, Jaypaw wondered where the prophecy had come from, and how the Tribe of Endless Hunting were connected to his own ancestors.

"There's no more time for good-byes!" Crowfeather's mew was impatient.

"Take care, little one." Brook's cheek brushed Jaypaw's before she turned to say good-bye to Hollypaw. Stormfur licked his ear. "Look after your brother and sister," he murmured.

"Bye, Stormfur." Jaypaw's throat tightened. "Good-bye,

Brook." He remembered the times when Brook had comforted and encouraged him. She had always seemed to understand what it felt like to be different. And Stormfur had never patronized him, but treated him with the same warmth and strictness as he had the other apprentices. He would miss them.

Lionpaw pushed in front of him. "Good-bye, Stormfur. Show those invaders that a Clan cat is never beaten."

"Good-bye, Lionpaw," Stormfur murmured. "Remember that even though our experiences change us, we have to carry on."

A rush of warmth seemed to flood between the warrior and apprentice and Jaypaw realized with surprise that his brother shared a special bond with Stormfur, one he had not detected before. He stood wondering about it as his Clanmates began to move away down the slope while Stormfur picked up the freshly caught prey and headed uphill, after his mate.

"Stop dawdling!" Crowfeather nudged him with his nose, steering him down a smooth rocky slope onto the grassy hillside.

Jaypaw bristled. "I don't need help!"

"Suit yourself," Crowfeather snapped. "But don't blame me if you get left behind." He pounded ahead, his paws thrumming on the ground.

I'm glad I'm not Breezepaw! Imagine having such a sour-tongued warrior for a father.

"Hurry up, Jaypaw!" Lionpaw was calling.

Jaypaw sniffed the air. On this exposed slope it was easy to tell where the other cats were. Firestar led the way downhill, Breezepaw at his heels, while Crowfeather had already caught up and was flanking Tawnypelt, keeping to the outside of the group. Squirrelflight and Bramble-claw padded side by side, brushing pelts, while Hollypaw and Lionpaw trotted behind.

Jaypaw raced after them. The grass was smooth and soft beneath his paws. "It feels strange leaving them behind," he panted.

"They chose to stay," Crowfeather pointed out.

"Do you think we'll ever see them or the Tribe again?" Tawnypelt wondered.

"I hope not," Crowfeather answered. "I don't want to see those mountains again as long as I live."

"They might visit the lake," Hollypaw suggested.

A howl echoed eerily around the crags far behind them.

"They have to get home safely first," Lionpaw murmured.

"They will," Firestar assured him. "They know their territory as well as any other Tribe cat."

Padding beside his littermates, Jaypaw caught the

musty scents of forest ahead. Before long the ground beneath his paws turned from grass to crushed leaves. The wind ceased tugging at his fur as trees shielded him on every side. Hollypaw hurried ahead as though she already scented the lake beyond, but for a moment Jaypaw wished he was back on the open slopes of the foothills. At least there, scents and sounds were not muffled by the enclosing trees and there was no undergrowth to trip him up. He felt blinder here in this unfamiliar forest than he had ever before.

"Watch out!" Lionpaw's warning came too late and Jaypaw found his paws tangled in a bramble.

"Mouse dung!" He fought to free himself but the bramble seemed to twist around his legs as if it meant to ensnare him.

"Stand still!" Hollypaw was racing back to help. Jaypaw froze, swallowing his frustration, and allowed Lionpaw to drag the tendrils from around his paws while Hollypaw gently guided him away from the prickly bush.

"Dumb brambles!" Jaypaw lifted his chin and padded forward, more unsure than ever of the terrain but trying desperately not to show it.

Wordlessly, Hollypaw and Lionpaw fell into step on either side of him. With the lightest touch of her whiskers Hollypaw guided him around a clump of nettles and, when a fallen tree blocked their path, Lionpaw warned him with a flick of his tail to stop and wait while he led the way up and over the trunk.

As Jaypaw scrabbled gratefully over the crumbling bark he couldn't help wondering: *Was the prophecy really meant for a cat who couldn't see?*

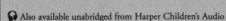

ENTER THE WORLD OF WARRIORS

Warriors: Power of Three

Join the newest generation as they begin their training as warrior cats. Prophecy foretells that they will hold more power than any cats before them.

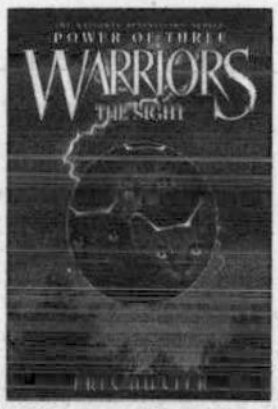
POWER OF THREE
WARRIORS
THE SIGHT

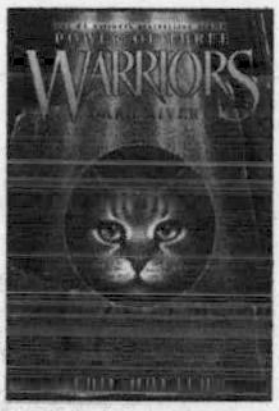
WARRIORS

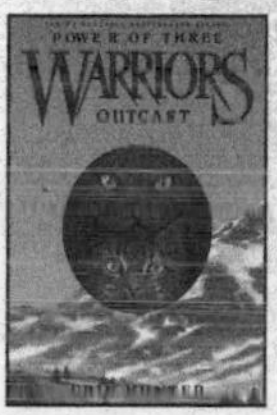
POWER OF THREE
WARRIORS
OUTCAST

Warriors Field Guide: Secrets of the Clans

Learn the secrets of the Clans, their histories, maps, battles, and more!

Warriors: Cats of the Clans

See the warriors as never before in this in-depth guide.

Warriors Super Edition: Firestar's Quest

The greatest adventure ever for ThunderClan's hero.

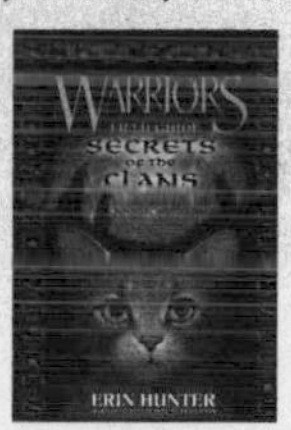
WARRIORS
SECRETS
OF THE
CLANS
ERIN HUNTER

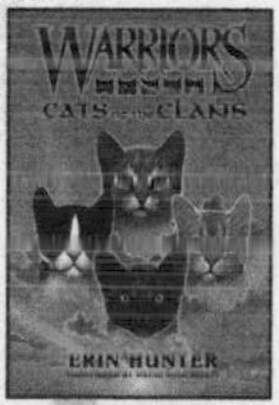
WARRIORS
CATS OF THE CLANS
ERIN HUNTER

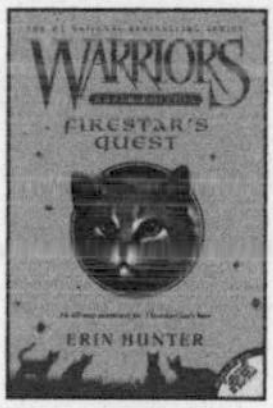
WARRIORS
FIRESTAR'S
QUEST
ERIN HUNTER

Warrior cats in manga!

Find out what really happened to Graystripe.

Warriors: The Lost Warrior

Warriors: Warrior's Refuge

Warriors: Warrior's Return

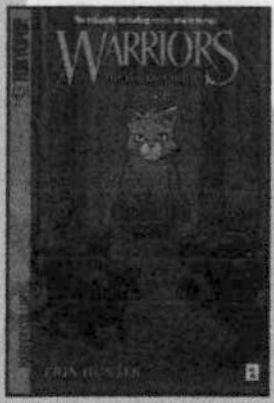
WARRIORS

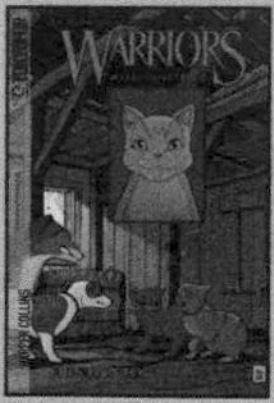
WARRIORS

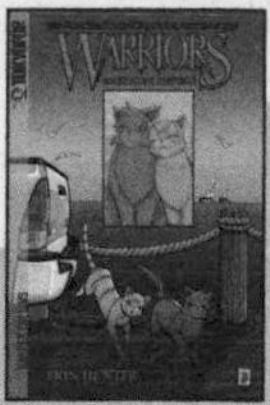
WARRIORS

Visit www.warriorcats.com for games, Clan lore, and much more!